HIDEOUS FACES, BEAUTIFUL SKULLS

ALSO BY MARK McLAUGHLIN
FROM WILDSIDE PRESS

Beach Blanket Zombie
Best Little Witch-House in Arkham

HIDEOUS FACES, BEAUTIFUL SKULLS

TALES OF HORROR AND THE BIZARRE

MARK McLAUGHLIN

WILDSIDE PRESS

To Michael Sheehan, Jr., for believing in me.

Published by Wildside Press LLC.
www.wildsidebooks.com

CONTENTS

ACKNOWLEDGEMENTS

Stories in this collection previously appeared in *Gaslight, The Bone Marrow Review, Rictus, Slime After Slime, Freezer Burn, Not at Night, GothicNet, UnReality, Something Wicked, In Delirium, Darkness Rising, Ghosts & Scholars, You Shall Have This Delicacy, Naked Came the Plowman, Roadworks, Argonaut, Dark Tome, Bending the Landscape: Fantasy, Tekeli-li!, Black October, Carnage Hall, Raising Demons for Fun and Profit, The Book of More Flesh, The Dream Zone, Talebones, Horror Garage, Not One of Us*, and *At the Foothills of Frenzy*.

INTRODUCTION: DARKNESS, THE GREAT EQUALIZER

Most of our lives are spent in the light. Sunshine and artificial illumination surround us as we eat our meals, do our work, chat with friends, surf the Internet, and watch TV. When we go to bed, we at last surrender to the darkness. We spend that time asleep, wandering the well-lit corridors of our dreams.

We may do our best to avoid the darkness, but it is still there, waiting to embrace us.

Why should we go to such great lengths to drive back the darkness? Darkness is our friend. Darkness is the great *equalizer.*

In today's appearance-conscious society, we all wonder, "Am I attractive enough? Is my appearance somehow holding me back? Should I lose some weight? Should I get some plastic surgery?"

In the dark, none of that matters. Beauty is no longer an advantage. Ugliness is no longer a shameful problem.

My Greek grandmother, a very earthy and vivacious woman, used to tell a naughty joke about a young fellow's first visit to a brothel. She told the tale in a coy fashion, euphemizing the saucy details. The fellow in the joke thinks he has procured the services of the brothel's loveliest employee—but since the transaction took place with the lights out, he doesn't realize until the end that in fact, he'd dallied with the plainest lady of the house.

When he takes his complaint to the proprietress, she replies: "You got your money's worth. All women are the same in the dark!"

See how kind, how *empowering* darkness can be? In the dark, a wallflower can blossom into a luscious rose. In a tale of dark wonder, a monster can prove to be more seductive that any beauty queen.

The darkness holds many surprises. In this collection of thirty stories of horror and the bizarre, we shall explore some of those surprises.

Even though I've been extolling the virtues of darkness, I do encourage you to read this book with the lights on. Light does have its practical applications, you know.

You have to see the words.

ADROITLY WRAPPED

"So what's in the sack?" Anthony said, eyeing the bundle that pale, leatherclad Punkin dragged along the path. A full moon brought a greenish-silver glow to the pebbles in the path and the chains on Punkin's jacket.

"'What's in the Sack?' Sounds like a game show." Punkin's nervous gait sped into a loping gallop, so that Anthony had to run to keep up with him. Odd slitherings and slappings issued from the burlap sack as it bounced in the dust. "I'll give you three guesses," the pale youth said.

"Is it…" Anthony flipped his long black bangs out of his face. "Is it a baby pterodactyl, flapping its membranous wings in the throes of death?"

"No…but you know, they taste just like chicken." Punkin swung the sack over his shoulder. Startled, a flock of crystal birds flew out of the trees lining the path.

"Is it…an oversized jungle slug? A miniature sea-squid?" Anthony listened closely to the wet whisperings inside the sack. "The lymph glands of a dead Cyclops? Munchkin roadkill from the Yellow Brick Highway?"

"Wrong and wrong and wrong and wrong again, Contestant Number One." Punkin flashed the gap-toothed Halloween smile that had earned him his nickname. "No new car, no trip to Tierra del Fuego. So sorry."

Anthony glimpsed yellow eyes glowing in a shadowed tree-top. Three…? Leaves rustled and the eyes disappeared. He stopped to peer into the shadows, searching for the dubious owner of the eyes. Then he noticed that Punkin, still running, was far ahead of him. He could hear the pale youth whistling a shrill, pointless tune. Anthony raced to catch up.

He was out of breath by the time they reached the long, low house of Athena Moth. He ran his fingers through his bangs and static crackled…no doubt his hair was standing on end. He spit onto his fingers and slicked his bangs into place.

Punkin rang the doorbell and a snippet of Verdi's *Un Bel Di* echoed through the house. Athena answered the door wearing white face, a black wig, and a geisha costume.

"Oh, why, hello." She always seemed surprised to see them, even when the visit was scheduled. "Come in, come in…but please, forgive the mess."

With every visit, Anthony pondered the same riddle. Athena was a *she*…but was she a woman? Athena had a low voice and a large-boned build. She always wore heavy make-up—even on her hands. And of course, there were the costumes… Still, there were other factors that clouded the issue. The delicacy of the mouth, the hands, the ears. The lack of both an Adam's apple and a crotch bulge. The exciting way that she gazed at him through half-closed purple eyes (men are taught to stare down their world).

This time, Anthony decided to address the issue directly. "So, Athena. What's under the kimono?"

"My body. What else—a diesel engine?" She led them to an over-stuffed couch in a parlor lined with shelves. These shelves were filled with books, jars of herbs and animal hair, lipsticks and stone statuettes.

"He's full of questions tonight," Punkin said, plopping down onto the couch. "He also wanted to know what was in the sack."

Anthony sat by the pale youth's side. His hips sank down between the soft cushions. He hated this couch, this wicked, butt-eating couch.

"We have a surprise for you, Anthony," Athena said, taking the sack from Punkin. "Did you think that we'd forget that tomorrow was your birthday?"

Anthony glanced at his cheap digital wristwatch—9:30 PM—then pressed the button that brought the date to the screen. 10-12. "God, you're right. I'd forgotten myself." He sighed. "Twenty-one and still living with my parents. Still flipping burgers at Fry-Pappy's. Still…" He didn't care to go on.

Athena nodded. "I understand." She opened a door in a shadowed corner of the parlor. With one hand, she lifted a department store mannequin out of the closet and leaned it against a table in the center of the room. Was the mannequin quite light or was Athena quite strong?

"You're lonely," she said. "Lonely in that special way." She then opened Punkin's sack and pulled out a length of pink ribbon. Soft. Thick. Moist. And really, far too pink.

She proceeded to pull yards of ribbon from the sack. "Looks a bit like human skin, doesn't it? Well, that's just what it is. But don't worry, Anthony, it doesn't belong to anyone. Isn't that right, Punkin?"

Punkin grinned and nodded. "Athena gave me the recipe. Anybody can make it."

Anthony watched as Athena began to wrap the ribbon tightly around the left foot and ankle of the mannequin. "But—is it *real* skin? As real as mine or Punkin's?"

"Of course it is," Athena said. "I can make anything out of anything. You should know that by now. Look at me...I used to be a tiny Malaysian fellow. Before that I was an old woman in a nursing home. Skin? Skin can be made from silk ribbon, soaked for three weeks in a special solution." The geisha wrapped faster and faster to the top of the thigh. "One must take great care in the winding. I allowed Punkin to prepare the skin—he wanted to help so badly—but the wrapping is my area of expertise. See how I'm folding the tissue between the legs? You'll not have cause for complaint later, birthday boy."

"What smells like vanilla?" Anthony said.

"The solution for the ribbon." The geisha touched the pink strip with the equally pink tip of her tongue. Her purple eyes flashed. "It contains vanilla. And cinnamon." The pink strip flew round and round the abdomen. "And oregano and ground quartz crystals and fish-eggs and white wine and—"

"*White* wine?" Punkin exclaimed. His eyes went wide. "You told me 'wine.' You didn't say that it had to be white."

"Oh." Athena slowed in her wrapping. "Oh. Oh." She paused, then continued to wrap at full speed. "Oh, well. Even the most precise recipes should allow for a degree of improvisation."

She covered one arm, the head, the other arm, then shot back down to the right leg. When she had finished with the wrapping, she fished through a large jar of marbles on one of the shelves.

"Pretty green eyes for a pretty dolly," she said, tucking two green marbles into the folds of the mannequin's face. She then stepped back from her creation and pointed at it with the thumb and ring-finger of her left hand.

"Be as we will. Be what we wish," she murmured. "What you should be you shall be. You shall be what we wish you to be..."

Anthony had seen Athena perform this sort of ritual before. One can actually hypnotize soulless but spiritually energized objects through the repetition of significant nonsense. Athena did not have wiring in her house, but all of her appliances worked.

"Now you must say a few words, Anthony," she said. She grabbed him by the hands and pulled him from the soft jaws of the couch.

He stood before the dolly. The wrapped figure was an inch or two shorter than himself. "What should I say?"

"Tell it how long you wish it to live." The geisha tapped him on the wrist. "And make the hand."

Anthony thought for a long moment. Then he pointed the appropriate fingers at the mannequin and said, "Live until you've done what you've got to do."

Slowly, the wrappings melded together, forming a smooth sheath of flesh. Openings appeared in the flesh—ears, nostrils, mouth and more. The sheen of life glowed in its eyes of solid green. The mannequin had no hair, nipples, or fingernails. The navel was shaped like a shallow clockwise swirl.

The mannequin had a sweet, small-featured face. It took Anthony by the hand and led him out of the house as Punkin and Athena sang "Happy Birthday."

The mannequin tried to lead him into the very heart of the woods, but Anthony held back, keeping to the more familiar paths. He didn't want to stray too far from the house. Athena was the eye of a magickal hurricane... Perhaps the dolly would cease to function if allowed to walk beyond the boundaries of Athena's influence.

"Can you speak?" Anthony asked.

The mannequin opened its mouth and moved its lips, but the only sound that came forth was a faint hiss. Just as well, Anthony thought. The dolly had been alive for less than fifteen minutes. What was there for it to talk about?

Soon they found a small open space where the ground was covered with moss. The mannequin settled down on this soft green bed.

Anthony was about to join his companion when he heard a shrill, distant whistling. Was Punkin going home without him? He stared into the shadows of the woods. The sound was fading. He turned and looked down at the dolly. It was lovely and petite—and utterly boring. He suddenly wished that the dolly could be clever, like Athena. And exotic, like Athena. And stylish and sexy and wise. Like Athena.

Rows of thin black lines began to slice across the dolly's face and body, and Anthony leaned closer. Was this a trick of the moonlight? The effect resembled the shadow of venetian blinds. Slowly he realized that the widening bands of blackness were not shadows at all.

The wrappings were coming loose.

Anthony backed away. The mannequin stared curiously at him. A hard look crept into its eyes.

He turned and began to walk in the direction of the whistling. He heard a hiss—a hiss that grew steadily louder, angrier. Leaves crackled behind him and he began to run.

"Punkin!" he cried. "Help me, Punkin!"

Through the trees, Anthony saw the path. He broke through a tangle of weeds and landed in the dust. He scrambled to his feet and looked about. Which way to run? Surely Punkin couldn't be too far away.

Suddenly, Anthony was grabbed fiercely by the shoulder. He glimpsed a loosely-fleshed hand out of the corner of his eye. Grabbing the dolly's wrist, he fell to his knees and pulled the creature to the ground.

The mannequin's hiss rose to an enraged squeal. Pale ribbons of its flesh hung down, revealing a pinkish-brown musculature that resembled wood grain.

"Where are you?" Punkin voice drifted out of the shadows. "What's that noise? Is it a pig?"

One of the dolly's eyes had fallen out—the other stared lividly at him. The creature tried to grab Anthony by the forearm, but he moved away just in time. He noticed a long loop of flesh trailing from the dolly's knee. He seized the loop and pulled, ripping free a yard of skin. He dug the heel of a boot into the joint and the entire lower leg flew off.

Shrieking with pain, the mannequin pushed Anthony onto his back and climbed on top of him. Pink ribbons flailed through the air as it pounded madly at his chest. The creature's other eye popped out. One of its hands broke off as it pummeled him. A pinkish froth dribbled from its writhing lips. Anthony stared into the black sockets of the mannequin's face. These sockets were not empty…they were filled with a horrible, insatiable hunger.

He was still staring when a hollow thump sounded and the face— disappeared.

Punkin was standing by his side. "I kicked its head off," the pale youth said. "Was that okay?"

Anthony crawled out from under the mannequin. "Yes. That was fine, thank you," he said tiredly. Punkin helped him to his feet.

They looked down at the dolly's still-writhing body. Then Punkin searched the weeds along the path until he found the head. He held it at arm's length by ribbons of its skin. "It's going to keep living 'til it does what it's got to do," he said.

Anthony picked up the mannequin's twitching hand. "Oh, how sad," he said. "I weep big tears." He threw the hand deep into the woods. Then he picked up the broken piece of leg and flung it into the woods as well. He nodded to his friend.

Punkin swung the ragged head by its ribbons to gather momentum. Finally he let go, and it flew through the night like a fleshy comet.

* * * *

Anthony entered Athena's long, low house without knocking. He found her in the parlor.

"Oh. Why, why…hello," she stammered.

Anthony regarded her with what he hoped was a smouldering stare. "I want you."

"Oh. Oh." Athena looked to the shelves—to the books, the jars, the statuettes. "Is Punkin with you?"

"No. I asked him to go on home without me. Didn't you hear what I said? I want you, Athena."

"I heard you." Her eyes settled at last on a brown bottle nestled in a pile of yellow rags. "Do you realize what you are asking?"

Anthony shrugged. "I don't care if you're a guy or a lady or what."

"'Or what' can cover quite a bit of ground." She opened the bottle and poured a thin amber fluid onto one of the rags. "I've been many people over the years, Anthony. I've been old, young, large, small, male, female…" She rubbed the wet cloth over her face and hands. "It takes quite a while to prepare an acceptable—*facade,* I think, is a good word. Still, it takes only a moment to undo the illusion. Only a moment to reveal the real me."

Athena's thick makeup hid more than blemishes, more than even mere gender; this magickal concoction hid the very contours of the flesh. Unleashed, her purple eyes crawled slowly over the surface of her opalescent face. A delicate lacework of gills fluttered at her jawline. Her shining claws fumbled at square black buttons, and the kimono dropped to the floor.

"So," she whispered through the uppermost of her mouths. "Do you still want me?"

Anthony studied Athena Moth for a full minute. Then he took a step forward.

Then another.

LARGESSE

Mr. Pash, Mr. Pash. Could anyone be more wonderful than Mr. Pash? He was the best employer I ever had—a wise, thrilling person. And so generous.

Bosses are usually such atrocious beings. You have to nod and grin and act as though you are not afraid of them. You must appear to condone their boorish, money-hungry wickedness. You must pretend to be other than yourself. Such was not the case with Mr. Pash.

My work at his store, *Movie Mania*, was quite simple. I waited on customers, kept the display boxes in neat rows, vacuumed a bit... Nothing too strenuous. Every now and then Mr. Pash stopped in to check on the store. To peek into the cash register. To offer a word of encouragement.

His eyes were deep, brown, and utterly unfocused. His nose was long and curved like the beak of a bird that eats meat. Thick brown hair, pale skin, a mildly spicy body odor, black stubble no matter what the time of day...and fat. Mr. Pash was fat, yet obliquely so in his bulky sweaters and baggy pants. It was hard to tell where Mr. Pash ended and the sag of his loose outfits began. But make no mistake: his clothes were clean and fashionable.

When he placed his long white fingers on your shoulder, you knew instantly that he cared. If your mother took sick, or if your pet lost a limb in a freakish accident, he would give you the day off without question. If he had candies in his huge pockets, and he usually did, he would give you several nice plastic-wrapped mints. Large and fresh, with red and white swirls. No lint on these pocket treats.

The customers at *Movie Mania* often spent a great deal of money. The store offered, for rental or purchase, a wide selection of strange and obscure films. Most were DVDs, but Mr. Pash also offered vintage videotapes, too, and the rental of VHS players. Mr. Pash had a fine retro fondness for the videotape format. "There's something utterly wonderful about all that black tape," he once said. "Black tape, loaded with black magic!" Our gentlemen usually rented six or seven movies at a time. I say "gentlemen" because our female clientele never exceeded a handful of poorly dressed, foreign-looking women of indeterminate age.

There was always plenty of time for me to watch movies during working hours. Mr. Pash did not mind. In fact, he insisted that I watch the movies so I would be able to tell our gentlemen about them. A salesperson should be thoroughly familiar with his products. The bulk of the inventory was esoteric. To this day, I have no idea where Mr. Pash had acquired such oddities. New movies were never delivered to the store; Mr. Pash brought them in personally.

The Green Claw was very popular, as were a number of other releases—*Spine-Eaters, Flytrap Hell* and *Liquifier III: The Bubbling Death.* There were many more, of course, but those four were our top renters. The store's computer inventory did not list any prequels to *Liquifier III,* and I have not been able to find this series online or in any catalog.

Mr. Pash brought several copies of *Liquifier III* to the store on a rainy July afternoon. It was a very hot day, and the rain made the air steamy. I remember worrying that so much moisture in the air had to be bad for the tapes.

"This title should rent well," Mr. Pash said; his voice was low and purring. "I watched it last night. Very exciting—I think you will agree. Let me know how it does." He wandered the store for a minute or so, biting his nails (not out of nervousness, I'm sure: perhaps out of hunger or mild ennui). Then he left, smiling so warmly that I thought for a moment of my father, who also had a large nose.

I watched the movie on the store monitor. The Liquifier of the title was a giant demon from outer space—a spiderish humanoid over sixty feet tall, with three-fingered hands and milky eyes. The Liquifier spun its victims into cocoons and injected them with acid venom, turning them into large bubbling bags of dinner. I did not feel uncomfortable about running such a graphic feature; children rarely visited the store.

I was not Mr. Pash's only employee. A frail old man named Bernard was also on duty. Bernard had unusually tight skin—so tight that it gleamed. I doubt if facelifts had been performed; he didn't make that sort of money. "How can you watch that garbage?" he said, pointing at the screen with his cigarette. "All that death and screaming and whatnot. A movie didn't used to have blood spilling all over the place to be scary. It's not right. Don't tell me it is."

"Variety is very important these days," I said. "What's life without variety? Even sex would get pretty boring if that was all you ever did."

"That's for damn sure." Bernard blew a cloud of smoke in my face. "You never met my Mrs. Spoon..." Bernard prefaced every anecdote about his deceased wife with this remark. "The woman was an animal. Whittled me down to a pencil, she did. Sometimes I'd catch her giving that look of hers to some man on the street. A nice-looking guy like you—she'd have sized you up. How did I ever get mixed up with a woman like that? She knew her way around a kitchen, though—I'll give her that."

A customer came in and Bernard went to wait on him. Bernard's stories about his dead wife always included some reference to her voracious sexual appetites. The week before, he had showed me a yellowed photograph of Mrs. Spoon, taken on their honeymoon. The woman had been quite pretty in a cruel sort of way, with short blond hair, sharp features, and snarling, oddly inviting lips.

The next day, I asked Mr. Pash if he had ever met Mrs. Spoon.

"The sex monster? She passed away just before he came to work for me. Has Bernard told you about the farm incident yet?" He didn't wait for my answer. Instead, he moved to the Staff Favorites shelf. "Is *Spine-Eaters* in? I haven't seen that for a while."

Whenever Mr. Pash rented a movie, he paid the usual fee like any customer. Bernard and I were allowed to view movies at home for free. Mr. Pash was a wonderfully generous man.

Bernard popped his head around the corner of a large display. "I heard you two badmouthing my Mrs. Spoon. The woman may have had her faults, but I won't have you slandering my dear departed wife. If I want to talk about her, that's my business." He came closer, scowling. "You two. I don't know about you two. Why do I even stay here?" He shook his head. "You two. My Mrs. Spoon had a salmon casserole recipe fit for royalty. I mix a drop of Holy Water with her ashes every Sunday so she won't have to stay in hell too long. As for you two—I just don't know."

Mr. Pash raised an eyebrow as Bernard shuffled off. "*Spine-Eaters* please, Roger. And *The Green Claw.* I never tire of the scenes in the temple of Uranus."

* * * *

Business improved as the summer temperatures rose. Obviously, our gentlemen were spending more time indoors. For my birthday, Mr. Pash gave me a box of monogrammed handkerchiefs. He also brought a box of pastries to the store. Bernard ate most of them.

I had never especially favored *The Green Claw,* not being a fan of fantasy epics, but at Mr. Pash's gentle insistence I watched it again with a critical eye.

The story, set in ancient Atlantis, concerned an ample-breasted, sexually active princess who needed to find a way to protect her people from a swarm of giant winged goats. *The Green Claw* was a rather avant garde production. The princess often spoke directly to the audience, and her breastplates were made of fluorescent plastic.

Upon my initial viewing, I had considered the film to be nothing more than a frothy morsel of soft porn. During one of his visits, Mr. Pash assured me that this work was fraught with inner meaning. "Think of the attack on the city," he said. "Was not Aleister Crowley incessantly mocked by horned beasts?"

"I'm not entirely familiar with Crowley's career," I said. I knew that the man was some sort of grim mystic, but that was all, really. "No doubt the sexual aspects overshadowed the symbolism."

"Yes and no, Roger. All activity is sexual, as are all symbols. Sex is all that is left after one dispenses with the extraneous. What were your impressions of the Atlantean temple to Uranus?"

"Wasn't Uranus a Greek god? Still, the Atlanteans could have worshipped him, too." I was talking like a fool, but words continued to issue from my mouth. "Needless to say, the ancient world didn't have fluorescent plastic. It was a very confusing movie."

"Uranus and Gaea were the first parents. Uranus was the Heaven and Gaea was the Earth; their children were Titans." Mr. Pash's eyes glowed with pleasure. "Think on this, Roger. The world's first act of love spawned giants."

When Mr. Pash left, Bernard took it upon himself to inform me of Mr. Pash's shortcomings. "That Mr. Pash has his nasty side. I once spilled some coffee on a cassette and he threw a fit. The coffee landed on the label and I wiped it right off. The tape was perfectly fine."

"What was the movie?" I had never seen Mr. Pash is a foul mood and I found this news most distressing.

"One of his top favorites—*Spine-Eaters*. New copies haven't been available for years. It was never released on DVD. He doesn't have his own copy—he rents the store tape along with everyone else."

"If he likes it that much, why does he even rent it out?"

Bernard shrugged. "Who knows? Funny thing is, that tape's still in great shape! You'd think it would be a tattered mess by now."

In *Spine-Eaters*, a family of cannibals was exposed to nuclear radiation in a bizarre military operation. They became as tall as trees and all the more hungry for their favorite delicacy—human spinal cords.

The summer grew even hotter and steamier. Our air-conditioning system did little to ease the swelter. The heat reminded me of the infernal jungle dimension of *Flytrap Hell,* where oversized meat-eating plants reigned supreme. Bernard developed a rasping cough. Mr. Pash and I suggested that he stop smoking, but like many older people set in their ways, he refused to take advice.

Mr. Pash, ever concerned, set up a cot in the back room so that Bernard could rest if the heat made his day too taxing.

"You never met my Mrs. Spoon," Bernard said to me one afternoon, "but that woman couldn't pass a flat surface without looking around for a man. A devil and a half, she was. Still, she fried up chicken to die for. Did I ever show you the cocktail ring I gave her? It's dangling on a string in my bedroom window. It catches the light."

The gentlemen rented their movies in even greater quantities. Many asked why we stocked so few copies of some of our most in-demand selections. In turn, I asked Mr. Pash.

His reply was rather confusing. "Those movies are special, Roger. There is a concentrated energy in that specialness which should not be diluted."

I wondered what Mr. Pash would do if someone stole one of our "special" movies, or lost it. My curiosity was satisfied by the matter of one Mr. Trisk, who would not respond to our correspondence regarding his failure to return a copy of *Liquifier III.*

The news shows made much of the explosion in Mr. Trisk's home; there was even talk of spontaneous combustion. A few days after Mr. Trisk's interment, a lean, silent gentleman bundled in an enormous overcoat entered the store and set the tape on the counter. His face was lost under the brim of his hat. His gloved hand creaked as he clutched a display to steady himself on the way out.

For the rest of the day, Bernard complained of bits of ash on the carpet. I insisted that he had probably dropped them from his cigarette. Nevertheless, I vacuumed.

The Mr. Trisk episode left me disconcerted. Mr. Pash was a wonderful employer and an exciting individual; even so, the suspicions that swam and roiled in my mind gave me constant headaches. The heat didn't help, and Bernard's coughing was beginning to get on my nerves. The gentlemen were always very nice, but there were so many of them now.

I decided to have a talk with Mr. Pash.

* * * *

As I have mentioned, Mr. Pash was an extraordinarily generous man. When I mentioned that I was having difficulties with my work, he immediately suggested that we have dinner that evening at his home to discuss the problems at hand. Mr. Pash asked if a late dinner would be agreeable, since he had a number of errands to attend to early in the evening. I told him that would be fine.

I arrived at his house at eight-thirty with a bottle of wine (a truly thoughtful guest never shows up empty-handed). Mr. Pash lived in an artistic sector of the city. His brick house was narrow and very old. The bricks were dark and exceptionally large; many were broken and askew. I felt sure that my hand would come away bleeding if I ran it over a wall. The yard was completely overrun with weeds. Tongue in cheek, I wondered if Mr. Pash had allowed the the yard to go wild in homage to the jungle villages of *Flytrap Hell.*

Mr. Pash welcomed me in and led me down a dim hall to the dining room. Our meals were already served up on our plates. The room was poorly lit and smelled spicy—like Mr. Pash, only stronger. I guessed that Mr. Pash probably did not entertain often.

As I detailed my concerns, Mr. Pash listened closely, chewing at his stringy cut of meat. Mr. Pash was a fine employer, but a poor chef. The meat was tough and flavorless and the vegetables were overcooked. I was nervous, so I drank my wine rather quickly.

"I am so glad you decided to share your thoughts with me, Roger," he said. "I see that it is time to tell you more about myself. I hope you will not mind, Roger. You are a very special person in my life. Am I special to you?"

"You are the best boss I ever had," I said. With a sigh, I downed a second glass of wine.

"The store satisfies more than just my financial needs, Roger." Mr. Pash leaned closer. "Do you believe in magic, Roger? Not the kind with rabbits in tophats. Not the kind with pentagrams and candles. Do you know what I'm talking about?"

I thought for a moment, but nothing came to mind. "You'll have to spell this matter out for me, Mr. Pash. Certainly I've had too much wine."

"Too much? You haven't had enough." Mr. Pash refreshed my drink. I suddenly noticed that he wore a lavish ring on his pinky. A woman's cocktail ring.

Mr. Pash followed my stare. "Do you like my ring? I took it from Bernard earlier this evening."

"You took it from him?" I blinked like a fish as I drained my third glass. "Why did you take it from him?"

"He no longer needed it. I think I can use these stones…" Mr. Pash shrugged. "But we were discussing the different kinds of magic. Crowley came close to the truth, but he relied too heavily on ritual. The best sort of magic—the most potent—is the kind you make up as you go along."

I found that I couldn't stop blinking. "Could we return to the topic of Bernard? Is he all right?"

"No, he is not all right." Mr. Pash shook a blizzard of salt over his filet. "In fact, he tastes perfectly awful."

I rose very slowly from my seat and walked around the room, looking for the door. It was not to be found.

Mr. Pash watched me with his head cocked to one side. "I want you to be my disciple, Roger. I hope I haven't alarmed you. Would you like some more wine?" He rubbed his new pinky ring against his stubbly chin. "Join the new Order of Uranus. Consider it a promotion, if you like. That may make it seem less threatening. Less like a religious endeavor and more like a business proposition. What do you say, Roger?"

* * * *

In the basement of the narrow house, Mr. Pash showed me the four magic VHS players, the four magic DVD players, and the eight magic televisions. By this time I was halfway through my fourth bottle of wine. Mr. Pash had several excellent vintages in his larder.

He explained to me that special copies of the store's top-renting movies had been instilled, through a series of complex rituals, with his own living essence. These mad dollops of his soul absorbed mental energy from our renting gentlemen. Mr. Pash would then take the movies and transfer the accumulated energy from the cassettes and DVDs into the magic televisions. The power built up so far was truly incredible: the merest spark had been used to persuade Mr. Trisk, with remarkable results.

Of course, Mr. Pash was correct—about magic, that is. You have to make it up as you go along. My employer handed me an urn. Her name had been Spoon, so I used a spoon to insert her ashes into the magic players. We then plucked the diamonds from the cocktail ring and tossed those into the players as well.

"Are you sure this won't hurt the machines?" I said. I picked up a cassette, looking vainly into its little windows for some sign of Mr. Pash's magic essence. "Mr. Spoon used to mix Holy Water with the ashes."

"You needn't worry. Our purpose is holy, Roger," Mr. Pash said, removing his shoes and socks. He started to unbutton his shirt. "Are we not preparing for a wedding?"

I pushed the cassette into its slot. Soon all of the tapes and DVDs were in place.

I looked into Mr. Pash's eyes. It had been his generosity, his royal largesse, that had convinced me to follow his path. I knew that once the new way was in order, I would be rewarded handsomely.

"Mrs. Spoon, Wanton and Licentious One," I intoned, making up the words, "rejoice: from this moment on, you shall be known as Gaea, the Earth Mother. Prepare to receive the seed of Uranus, the Sky Father." Mr. Pash removed the last of his clothes. His flabby body was a miracle of the grotesque; shallow, ribbonlike grooves covered every inch of his abdomen and legs.

"From this union shall spring Titans," I cried, taking a swig of wine. "With their Father, they shall reign supreme throughout the universe. O Gaea, take from the magic televisions the mind-power of our gentlemen, our unknowing congregation…"

Mr. Pash stood amidst the magic players, arms outstretched. The tops of the VHS players bulged into round pods which soon opened, spewing forth yard after yard of tape. The tapes coiled and writhed around Mr. Pash's body, sliding through the fleshy grooves. Curling metal vines grew from the tops of the DVD players—vines dotted with spinning silver blossoms. The vines also slid through the grooves, side by side with the tapes.

I continued to drink wine and rant. In retrospect, I believe I should have set the bottle aside. "Noble Earth Mother! Arise from death! It is at last time to meet you. What shall you be cooking for us, sweet Gaea? We have already eaten Mr. Spoon. Arise: your new husband awaits."

A cloud of ash rose from the players and formed itself into a translucent grey succubus. Sparks danced through the apparition as it lavished its affections on Mr. Pash.

On the screens of the magic televisions, scenes from the movies played—but with a difference. The prodigious creatures now wandered from movie to movie. Hulking cannibals stormed the Atlantean city. Immense carnivorous plants tried to steal a cocooned victim from the Liquifier. Outsized winged goats trampled helpless villagers in the jungle dimension.

Mr. Pash shuddered and groaned with ecstasy. Wires snaked up from the players and plunged into my employer's heaving gut as he consummated the marriage ritual.

The expression of rapture on Mr. Pash's face was simply too ridiculous—or at least, so I thought at the time. Drink can turn the kindest man into an unfeeling Judas. "I've had a wonderful time," I said, "but I'm afraid that I have overstayed my welcome. Where was my mind? What must you think of me, Mr. Pash? But then, what must I think of you? It's dreadfully impolite to rut in front of guests." So saying, I laughed and laughed and laughed like a mad boy.

Poor Mr. Pash—scoffed by his own disciple! The rapture on his face was replaced by a look of terrified doubt. With a cry of triumph, the ash-temptress fled through a crack in the basement floor. Undone by his own momentary uncertainty, Mr. Pash was at the mercy of reality. I watched helplessly as the wires in his belly fried him alive. A horrid, oily steam rose from his body. I ran up the stairs and out of the house.

Bottle in hand, I wandered the streets of a changed world.

Mr. Pash had perished, yes; but not before he had consummated the union, passing the magic on to Mrs. Spoon. I'm sure that his sacrifice had only served to strengthen her.

A winged goat larger than any ocean liner soared across the moon, bleating thunderously. A monstrous Venus flytrap shot up from the turf of a children's playground and snuffled ravenously at the swings and slide.

Screams of pain and horror echoed through the city. The earth thundered as impossible monstrosities lumbered through the night. From the shadows, I watched giant cannibals tear the heads from policemen at a doughnut shop. With great slurping noises they sucked the spinal cords from their victims. A few blocks down the road, a Liquifier slathered its web into a parked car and trapped a pair of lovemaking teenagers. Another Liquifier draw near to watch its sibling feast.

* * * *

The Titans are everywhere. Spider-demons, cannibals, winged goats, vile plant-things. They see me, but leave me be. In fact, they regard me with trepidation. And why not? I am the usurper of their father's throne. In their eyes, I am capable of unspeakable devastation.

I am writing this in a luxurious penthouse apartment. I had to walk up sixty floors. Mr. Pash, Mr. Pash—all of this should have been yours. I am sorry that I laughed. So terribly sorry. I had planned to throw myself off the balcony, but in the end, I could not.

Just as I was about to jump, an enormous pair of snarling, oddly inviting lips opened up in the pavement below.

BUCKTOOTHED BOY, BELOVED BY MILLIONS

"Little Perky! Come home this minute!"

Mommy's calling for you, Little Perky, little bucktoothed, black-haired boy. Mommy found a firecracker in your room. Firecrackers are so very naughty! You could lose a finger if you're not careful.

Brush those heavy bangs out of your eyes and look around. Look around with those large round eyes, those shiny black eyes, those sweet mischievous eyes (beloved by millions!).

There's Mr. Finkle's house. Mr. Finkle is so funny when he's mad. The veins stand out on his face and neck like big icky worms.

Way down the block—that's where the Widow Prim lives. That noisy old crow! Her long nose is just like a beak. She always yells at you whenever you walk on her grass. "Get those big clodhopper feet off my grass, Little Perky, or I'll tell your Daddy!"—that's just what she yells.

Finkle, Prim, Finkle, Prim… Yes, visit Mr. Finkle today. A good long visit. You should wait a while before going home. Daddy teaches school to big kids, and he's got some pretty old-fashioned ideas about discipline. That firecracker might have made him mad enough to get out the Board of Education (yee-ow!).

Mr. Finkle is working in his garden this afternoon. Oh, it's a nasty garden, all weed-choked and silly. The tomatoes are tiny and hard! The cucumbers look like green bite-sized snack sausages! The lettuce is wormy and wilted (just like his face!). His garden was a lot better last year. Remember? You used his watermelons for slingshot practice.

"Well, if it isn't Little Perky." Mr. Finkle harrumphs at you as he hoes at the soggy clay. "In trouble again, I'll wager. Didn't I hear your mother calling?"

"Gee, Mr. Finkle—I don't think so!" Your big eyes roll with glee. "That was Mrs. Finkle calling for *you!*"

"Oh, dear! Coming, Bitsy!" Mr. Finkle drops the hoe and trots off toward his tidy little pink-with-blue-trim house.

Dig deep in your pockets, Little Perky. You've got lots of firecrackers—might as well put them to good use. Wouldn't the Finkles like a nice tossed salad...?

Run, Little Perky! Outrun the flying dirtclods and chunks of tomato!

Time for a commercial break, Little Perky. Koala Kough Drops are eucalypti-licious! Australian nights can get mighty cold, and when Kippy Kangaroo gets a scratchy throat, he turns to Koala Kough Drops for oh-so-fast relief.

Oh, what a day! What a sunny, wonderful day! You skip down the sidewalk, happy as a big, goofy dog. Your bangs bounce up and down as you skip. Time to peek in on Widow Prim...

Up to her little yellow house you creep. Peek through every green-trimmed window, Little Perky. Now where's that Widow? She has to be home—she never goes anywhere.

Oh, goody! The back door is unlocked. You creep into the Widow's kitchen and—what's this? Pots and pans are scattered everywhere. She's making pudding! The greedy old thing! Whipping up a big batch of butterscotch pudding all for herself!

On the windowsill you spy a vial of pills. The Widow's heart medicine! Quick as a bunny, you pop the pills into your hanky, grind them under your heel, and pour all the white powder into the sugar bowl.

Suddenly you hear the flush of a toilet. It's funny to think that Widow Prim actually goes to the bathroom. You mix the powder into the sugar with your finger. Then you slink out of the kitchen, easing the back door shut behind you.

You pick up a sturdy twig and rattle it against a picket fence as you stroll down the street. What to do now? Suddenly, someone steps in front of you. Mr. Finkle! His face is as red as a beet. The veins look just like thick, pulsy nightcrawlers! Now you're in for it, Little Perky!

"You awful child! You've ruined my garden!" Mr. Finkle's hands clench and clench. "I'm going to spank your bottom, you little vandal!"

Mr. Finkle reaches out for you, then stops as a scream erupts from Widow Prim's house. The back door flies open and out shoots Widow Prim, clutching at her chest. Her face sure looks funny. All pale and twisty. Mr. Finkle pushes you aside and runs to help the Widow.

Now the sky's all full of words. That's weird, ain't it? They're all backwards, but you can figure some of them out. Ronald something, Ingrid Pretty... The words are getting smaller. What's a producer? Does he sell produce to Mr. Furgeson's grocery store? Those words sure go by fast!

"Little Perky! Little Perky, come home this minute!"

Uh-oh, the show's starting again and you're in trouble deep. Why did you leave your roller skates on the stairs? Poor, poor Daddy. How come he's not getting up? You skip out of the house and down the street—

Suddenly you stop. There's Mr. Finkle, walking down the sidewalk. He's turned from you, but you can tell it's him 'cause his head is so big. The back of his head reminds you of a ripe melon! You check your back pocket—yep, you've got your slingshot handy. You find a big old rock, load up and let fly.

Gee. The inside of his head looks like a melon, too!

You'd better run, Little Perky! Run as fast as you can! Down the street, past Mr. Finkle's house, past the school, the fire station (wouldn't it be nice to slide down the pole?), Mr. Furgeson's grocery store, the hardware store, the pet shop (too bad Daddy wouldn't let you buy that talking bird…still, Daddy knows best!), the barber shop, oh, your feet barely touch the ground, you're running so fast!

Oh no, Little Perky! You ran too far! You've actually left Smartville behind. And now—why, this won't do! You're wandering in a big smelly city (smells just like doggy doo) and is that *your* reflection in that pawn-shop window?

No, no, no—that's some greasy-haired baggy-pants, some no-good drifter, some boozy old has-been with a saggy booze face. The kind Daddy used to warn you about.

Better run back, Perky! Back to Smartville and all its wacky citizens. Back to Smartville, where every housewife wears her hair in a flip and every husband does important work in a big office. No one is homeless in Smartville. No one ever goes hungry. Oh, it's good to be back.

Time to play in the treehouse!

You shimmy up the old oak behind the house and scoot into your little plywood hidey-hole. You love all your little treehouse treasures. Baseball cards, bugs stuck on pins, neat candy wrappers, an old squirrel skull, and—a bottle of whiskey? What's that doing here? For a second the treehouse seems—Yucky. Cold. Like the inside of one of those metal boxes behind fancy restaurants. No, surely that's not booze! That's a bottle of Koala Kough Syrup! Kippy Kangaroo takes a swig whenever his throat gets a tricky tickle! Koala Kough Syrup—ask for it by name!

Oh, but what's happening? The top of the treehouse is being lifted up! A Nice Officer looks down on you and smiles.

This must be a dream.

Yes, you must have fallen asleep in the treehouse. What an exciting dream! The Nice Officer takes you to the station and starts talking about The Show. He says he used to watch The Show back when he was a kid.

He also says your old costars are dying off and thats pretty weird 'cause they're scattered all over the country. Gee whiz!

Martha Fine (who's that?) died of an overdose of heart medicine. Some people are so careless. Ronald Bain (that name rings a little bell) somehow broke his back while he was sleeping! Imagine that. Conrad Elmore (who's *that?*) got his skull bashed in today while he was taking a shower. Well, most accidents do happen in the bathroom. They've left a message on Nancy Verrick's answering machine—the Nice Officer reminds you that she's the one who played Mrs. Finkle.

The Nice Officer tells you that Ingrid Pretty (that name rings a BIG bell) was the lucky one. She died peacefully in some nursing home just before this whole mess began.

The Nice Officer says, do you know anything? Sure, you know that vinegar and baking soda and modeling clay make a neat volcano!

He says he's going to let you Sleep It Off. What does that mean? You're already asleep! He leads you to a shadowy room with a nice soft cot.

"Little Perky! Come home this minute!"

You find yourself hiding in the attic, eating yummy, gooey chocolate chip cookies (snatched from the cookie jar!). Oh, they're so good, so good. You like the attic—Mommy has all her old clothes up here and they smell like perfume.

Suddenly you remember—you're in trouble on the double! Why did you get Mrs. Finkle all wet? Sure, she smokes an awful lot, but if you wanted to put out her cigarette, you should have filled that balloon with water—not gasoline! You'd better stay in the attic for a good long time, Little Perky!

You look out the window. From here you can see the Smartville Cemetery. Some of those graves look mighty fresh…

Listen!

What was that? A creaking door? Is it the boogeyman, Little Perky?

Listen to that soft padding on the stairs…

Listen to this soft voice in your head…

A shadow looms before you, but it's not the boogeyman. It's—it's—

Why, it's me! Your loving Mommy!

I've brought you a glass of milk, Little Perky. Nice and cold—just the thing to wash down those cookies. A little later, we'll go down to the pet shop and buy that talking bird. Oh, I know Daddy said it would cause a lot of commotion, but Daddy can't hear it from underground!

It's so good to be with you again, Little Perky. I was alone for so long! Forgotten by my friends, my family (my *out there* family), even my fans. Just another sicky in that terrible nursing home. Trapped in a cancerous old body, wasting away.

I wrote to all my old co-stars but none of them wanted to visit. I couldn't get in touch with you…Conrad was the one who called to tell me that—well, that your career was going poorly. The bastard (Oopsy! Pardon my French!)—he sounded so *pleased.*

Oh, I despised the whole slimy lot of them. They wouldn't visit me and they wouldn't help you. What's a mother to do?

When I died and none of them came to the funeral…that was the last straw. Not all ghosts wear sheets, Little Perky. Some wear lovely lacy aprons that say KISS THE COOK. You've made a nice little world for yourself, Little Perky. I let you decide what to do about Daddy and Widow Prim and Mr. and Mrs. Finkle. Whatever you did to them in here, I did to them *out there* (my poor apron—some of these stains will never come out).

You have no idea how much I've missed you. We'll have so much fun! I'll dress you and feed you and comb your lovely black hair (a ribbon will keep it out of your eyes). I'll give you nice hot baths and make sure you wash behind your ears and everywhere else (little boys can get so dirty in all their little secret crannies), which reminds me, I'd better buy some cotton swabs. I'll give you hugs and kisses morning, noon, and night. We'll be so close. I'll never let you out of my sight. You won't know where you end and I begin. You and me, Little Perky, together in your mind for the rest of your days.

You look ill…have a Koala Kough Drop. They're eucalypti-licious! Kippy Kangaroo loves them because they pack a punch of Vitamin K to knock out those awful germs!

Home is the loveliest word I know, Little Perky. It really is. Home. Home. Home. Home. Home.

I'm home.

THE FINAL BROADCAST OF SUGARVILLE'S CHANNEL 7 ACTION NEWS

With a sweeping rush of majestic orchestra music, bright lights came up on the set of Sugarville's CHANNEL 7 ACTION NEWS, 10 p.m. broadcast. The name of the program was emblazoned on the back wall of the set in bold italic, sans serif, purple letters edged with gold. Under the letters was a large monitor showing random scenes from the Sugarville metro area.

The two anchorpeople chatted at the sky-blue news desk, their tanned faces set in expressions of cheery attentiveness. As the music faded, they turned simultaneously toward the camera.

"Good evening, and welcome to Channel 7 Action News at ten! I'm Brett Bellamy!" The anchorman had green eyes, a square jaw and dark-brown hair with golden highlights.

"And I'm Jessica Michaels!" The anchorwoman had bright blue eyes, an almond-shaped face and shoulder-length, moussed black hair with a long, ash-blonde forelock. "Tonight's top story—Sugarville find itself locked in the icy grip of a cold snap!"

The expressions of the anchorpeople turned deadly serious as the theme music blared, while on the monitor, a navy-blue and icy cyan logo sprang up that read, COLD SNAP! SUGARVILLE IN PERIL.

"So far, we've been enjoying a fairly mild October," Brett said, "with a daytime high of sixty-eight degrees, and a nighttime low of forty-seven. But this evening at 9 p.m., Sugarville citizens trembled as the mercury dropped to forty-four degrees! But that wasn't the worst. Brisk winds combined with that frigid temperature to create a wind-chill factor of forty-one degrees. And since that time, the temperature has dropped even further—to an arctic thirty-nine degrees!"

"Bone-chilling!" said Jessica, brushing her forelock, which was drooping a bit, away from her cheek. "We now have a live report from Chad Yamata, who is out in the community in our Channel 7 Action News Van, experiencing this sudden change in the weather firsthand."

On the monitor, a handsome Asian man in a suede jacket appeared. He wore blue contact lenses and his black hair was frosted golden-brown at the temples. At his side was a middle-aged, heavyset woman in an orange parka. "Thanks, Jessica!" Chad said. Curls of mist lightly billowed from his lips. "I'm on Lincoln Street, talking with Emily Randolph, who tells us her puppy, Mindy, ran out of the house when one of her children left the door open after coming home from a friend's house. The puppy is now lost—*outside*—in these icy temperatures."

"Outside!" Jessica repeated with dread.

"Mrs. Randolph," Chad said, "what is going through your mind right now, knowing that little Mindy is somewhere out in the cold, alone and helpless?"

"It's not *that* cold," Emily Randolph said. "I mean, it's no big deal. Why are you even here? Geez, this must really be a slow news day! You're stirring up a big panic over nothing."

"Have you printed up posters of the missing puppy?" Chad asked earnestly, his face a study in polite concern. "How much are you willing to offer as a reward?"

Emily rolled her eyes. "Give me a break! It's not even cold enough to freeze an ice cube out here. Mindy will be okay."

"Maybe so," Chad said. "But what if it suddenly gets even colder? In blustery conditions, every second counts!"

The housewife shrugged. "I suppose I could run some posters off on my laser printer, and put them around the neighborhood first thing in the morning. It's a black-and-white printer, though. The posters don't have to be color, do they?"

Chad raised an eyebrow. "A color printout would be much more helpful in ensuring positive identification of the missing family member."

"Wha—? It's not like one of my kids is lost. It's just a puppy." The woman sighed. "Well, my boy Skip has a scanner on his computer. I suppose I could scan in a color picture, take it down to Kinko's on a disk and—"

Suddenly a boy's voice rang out off-camera. "Hey, Mom! I found Mindy! She was in the garage."

"And there you have it!" Chad said. "Crisis averted here on Lincoln Street. A beloved puppy has been reunited with her human family!"

Jessica breathed a sigh of relief. "That was a close call."

Chad nodded. "Maybe a little too close. Back to you, Brett and Jessica!"

"Thanks, Chad." Brett smiled for the camera. "We'll be right back. When we return—more on Cold Snap! Sugarville in Peril!"

It was time for a commercial break.

A potbellied man shoveled snow from the sidewalk in front of his house. He waved to his wife, watching him from the living room window. Suddenly he clutched his chest and collapsed.

"Don't let this happen to you!" boomed a deep male voice. "Clearing the walk can be a breeze with a Winter-Pro Sno-Blower, on sale now at Munsen Hardware."

The image of Munsen Hardware filled the screen. By the door stood the owner, Harold Munsen, who said, with a cheery nasal twang, "Serving Sugarville for twenty-seven years! We're at the intersection of Lombard Street and Culpepper Avenue, with plenty of free parking. And as always, free balloons for the kids!"

The screen returned to the sidewalk, where the wife was proudly pushing a Winter-Pro Sno-Blower as the paramedics took away her dead husband.

In the next commercial, a thin, pale man in a black suit blew his icy breath over an old woman's hands as she tried to unlock her ice-encrusted front door on a winter's day. The man's face glittered like a fresh snowball. The woman winced with pain.

"When winter's numbing gusts make your arthritis flare up, take action!" purred a throaty but still very feminine voice. "*Soooothe* the pain with deep penetrating Campho-Supreme."

The old woman pulled an orange tube out of her purse and rubbed some pink cream onto her hands.

Three chorus girls in orange sequined gowns then danced into view. The old woman finally opened the door of the house and the three dancers led the pale man inside. Suddenly the girls and the man, minus their eveningwear, are seen soaking in a large hot tub. Behind them, the old woman happily opened pickle jars and broke walnuts with a nutcracker, delighted by her newfound manual dexterity.

The pale man sighed with pleasure as he slowly melted into the tub. Apparently his flesh and bones were made of packed snow.

"Campho-Supreme!" purred the voice. "Available at all HealthPal Drugstores!"

With a blare of dramatic music, the news returned.

"We've just learned," Brett said, "that the temperature has dropped another two degrees."

On the monitor, the logo popped up again—COLD SNAP! SUGARVILLE IN PERIL.

A crew member moussed Jessica's hair a bit higher during the commercial. "Let's look in on Channel 7 Action News meteorologist Jason Kincaid," the anchorwoman said. "Jason, are these temperatures just going to keep dropping and dropping until Sugarville reaches absolute zero?"

"Ummm…" Jason sported red hair, a golden moustache and a black goatee. The weather set was actually located less than forty feet to the right of the news desk. "That sort of thing very rarely happens, Jessica. In fact, it never happens."

He then turned to the huge map of the metro area and outlying communities behind him. Sugarville was represented by red outlines around various districts of the city. Jason glanced at an off-camera monitor to check the wall behind him, since from his perspective, it was only a flat blue-screen surface.

Turbulent white and gray swirls appeared to be closing in on the city. Within one of the larger swirls, a bizarre, multi-limbed figure writhed fitfully. "We have an—unusual—atmospheric condition on our hands tonight, Jessica."

"Is this the start of a new Ice Age?" she suggested.

"Ordinarily," Jason said, "I would tell you…no. That's really unlikely. But—" He gestured toward the writhing figure. "With this squirmy, spidery thing here, which seems to be some kind of living creature—I'm not sure what to tell you."

"So Jason," Brett said, "this spidery-looking thingamajig we're looking at… That's not normal?"

The weatherman cocked his head to one side. "Earth to Brett! No, it is *not* normal. Calling it *unusual* would even be a gigantic understatement. This is way beyond weird. This is like some kind of alien freakshow from space-Hell. It's horrible. Frightening. And it's happening to us."

"Did you say 'alien'?" Jessica said, her eyes bright with the promise of a sensational story.

Brett nodded. "He did indeed say 'alien'. And I think the question on everybody's mind right now is: What does this alien being want, and why is it trying to freeze Sugarville?"

Suddenly a new logo appeared on the monitor—a picture of the multi-limbed shape, surrounded by the blood-red, dripping words ALIEN MENACE! SUGARVILLE IN TERROR.

Brett's forehead furrowed with concern. "Jason, do you think there's any connection between this alien and the Martians in the classic science-fiction movie, *War of the Worlds*?"

On the weather map, the writhing figure began to grow and swirl, swirl and grow, until it was three times bigger than before. Jason saw this on the off-camera monitor. Alarmed, he studied yet another monitor to check the latest weather readings. "Oh my God!" he shouted. "The temperature has just dropped *thirty degrees!* I can't believe you people.

Some kind of freaky space-spider is freezing Sugarville and you're all just as flaky as ever, acting like this is some kind of movie, logos and all! Well, I quit! I'm leaving before this stupid town turns into one big idiot iceberg!"

So saying, he snatched off his chip-on microphone, threw it to the floor and ran out of the studio.

Jessica and Brett gazed at the weather map, enthralled by the unearthly image that stirred there. The grotesque silhouette had at least a dozen twitching, multi-jointed legs, as well as numerous clusters of groping tentacles.

"We have another report from Chad Yamata and the Channel 7 Action News Van," Brett said at last. "Chad, what's happening on the streets of Sugarville?"

On the monitor, Chad had his coat wrapped tightly around him. The wind had whipped his moussed hair into a frenzied bird's-nest. Behind him, the sky had the same color scheme as a three-day-old bruise—mostly deep purple, but lightly tinted with pus-yellow and a nauseating shade of green.

"This cold snap has really taken a sudden turn for the worse," Chad said. "It's as cold as a deep-freeze out here. The wind has gone wild—and then there's that thing up there..." He pointed up, and the cameraman diligently aimed above their heads.

And there it was.

The creature from the weather screen.

Except here it wasn't a mere silhouette.

Here it was a loathsome abnormality with flesh like ice-blue alligator hide. Crystalline fibers grew in bristly tufts all over its body. Muscular tentacles sprouted from the joints of its flexing legs. The monster stared down at Sugarville with six clusters of blood-red eyes, like enormous cocktail rings loaded with rubies as big as watermelons.

But the creature's most horrific feature by far was its mouth. Its gnashing, vertical maw was loaded with saber-like teeth, with two prominent tusks in the center of each sideways jaw. The mouth was surrounded by longer groupings of the crystalline bristles, and judging from the direction in which they moved in the wind, it looked like the creature was sucking in air rapidly as it descended upon the city.

On the roof of the Sugarville Bank Building, a man in a trench coat took pictures of the monster. Suddenly he was caught up in the wind that rushed into that insatiable mouth. He was carried aloft, and the grinding sabers slashed him into thin red ribbons in mere seconds.

"Good night, Sugarville," Chad said. "We're getting the hell out of here! Terry, let's roll!"

"You bet your ass," a gruff voice said as the camera was clicked off.

Brett gnawed his lower lip lightly, fretfully. A minute passed. Then at last he turned toward the studio camera. "And so an unspeakable alien menace threatens Sugarville." He then moved to face Jessica—

But Jessica wasn't there.

He reached over to her chair and picked up a piece of paper. "Jessica left a note. It says, 'Brett, I'm going to get my kid and then we're heading south. You and the crew had better take off, too. Save yourself. Love, Jess.'"

Brett stood up and looked out past the cameras.

"Well," he said, resuming his seat, "I see the crew has already left. Looks like it's just me, this camera and whoever happens to be watching. Wow."

He stared straight ahead, thinking.

"My wife left me two years ago," he said. "We never had any kids. I don't have any pets. All my relatives hate me—personal matter, no need to get into *that*. So I guess I'll…stay. I don't have anywhere else to go.

"Besides, this TV station is probably a pretty safe place to be. It's on the outskirts of town, so maybe that spider-thing won't notice it.

"It looked like that creature was sucking in air… Maybe it's somehow sucking in all the heat. But then, I'm no scientist, so what do I know? The thing seemed to be made of some kind of icy stuff, so that could also be part of the whole temperature deal.

"If there's anybody watching, I just want you to know I've had a lot of fun being your news guy. When I was little, my family always called me stupid—my wife used to call me 'the talking head' and I know she didn't mean that in any kind of nice way. But being a news guy, that has always made me feel smart. Really, I had mostly good grades in high school and college. I'm not an idiot."

He pulled a small earphone out of his left ear. "I mean, sure, I have this little whatchamacallit so they can tell me what to say if there's a problem. I guess Ashley must've left, too. That's the copywriter at the other end of this thing. She was the one who came up with that *War of the Worlds* line. That *was* pretty stupid. I mean, that movie was all made-up stuff, right? That Ashley! She could have at least said goodbye."

He threw the earphone across the studio. Then he simply sat and listened.

Outside the building, the wind—and perhaps something else—roared like thunder. Then the ground began to shake.

"Listen to that!" Brett cried. "That big space-monster must be coming this way! It's so fucking huge—maybe it's already destroyed Sugarville. Something that big, it wouldn't take long!

"You know what? I'm just going to stay right here. If it gets me—it gets me. As simple as that. I'm no technical wizard, but the power is still on, so this place must have some kind of back-up generator. And Camera One's little red light is still on! I bet somewhere in the building, this broadcast is being recorded. Maybe my death can be a big contribution to the news world, and science, and humanity in general. Folks can watch that thing eat me close-up, and then maybe in the process, they'll learn something really important about the monster…something that will help Earth to defeat it."

A tear rolled down his cheek. "I really do care what happens to people. I'm not just a talking head. And by the way, my name's not Brett Bellamy. It's Harry Peters. Yeah, go ahead, make fun of my name. I don't care. Make fun of some poor guy who's probably going to be dead in about two minutes."

At that moment, an enormous ice-blue cylinder—a single leg of the creature—burst through the wall and then jerked quickly upward, flinging off the entire roof.

Harry Peters looked up in utter horror at a mouth filled with hundreds of enormous teeth, streaked with bright blood and dark gore. The larger tusks gnashed hungrily.

Harry turned with a crazed smile toward the camera.

"Are you watching? Are you? Watch, you fuckers! Watch this! Watch! *Watch!*"

The nightmare mouth began to descend.

Then the creature stepped inside the building to steady itself.

An enormous, razor-clawed foot landed right on Camera One, smashing it to bits.

I AM NOT PAINSETTIA PLONT

Painsettia Plont eats
teddy bears and dollies,
rubber ducks and robots,
rocking horse surprise!
—from "Painsettia's Theme,"
Santa's Elves Meet Painsettia Plont

Arla stepped up to the cosmetics counter and examined the lipsticks. Spring Strawberry? Caribbean Coral? Jungle Pink? Anything would be better than—

"Sorry, Miss Plont, but we're all out of green," said the clerk, a plump, fortyish woman with frosted hair and a toothy smile. "I bought your show on video for my youngest, Debbie. She just loves it. She goes around the house singing that song, 'Painsettia Plont eats teddy bears and dollies...'" She thought for a moment. "'Rubber ducky pies'? Is that how it goes?"

"Well, no," Arla sighed. "I'll take the Spring Strawberry. I'm in a bit of a hurry."

"Certainly, Ms. Plont." The clerk began to ring up the sale. "Or can I call you Painsettia?"

"My real name is Arla. Arla Merrick."

On her way out of the department store, Arla noticed a sales display for the video of her old Christmas special, *Santa's Elves Meet Painsettia Plont.* The cover of the box depicted her in full Painsettia array: green lipstick, white face powder, red fright-wig, sequined ornament earrings, white fur robe and silver curly-toed boots. The special, first aired in 1977, was broadcast each year during the holiday season. It had been released on video a few weeks ago, in time for Christmas shopping.

Above the display, the video played on a monitor. On the screen, Painsettia Plont was menacing her kindhearted younger sister, Mrs. Claus, in the Secret Christmas Cave.

"Ashamed of me?" hissed Painsettia, raising a bright red eyebrow. "You silly, mindless fool! I am very much a part of your life, and you cannot silence me! Now I have you, my sweet—and soon, you shall know the terror and the chill of my wintery vengeance!"

Arla crossed the mall corridor to a toy store. She needed to buy gifts for a niece and two nephews. She saw a few Painsettia dolls on a shelf next to some plush elves.

A red-haired girl in a quilted jacket pointed at Arla. "Look, Mommy! It's the mean toy-eater lady!"

The girl's mother looked up. "Oh my God!" She hurried to Arla's side. "You're Poin—*Pain*settia, yeah, Painsettia Plont! The kids watch your show every year. I love the scene where the elves roll you into that big snowball—"

Arla cleared her throat. "That was a part I played fifteen years ago. My real name is Arla."

The girl moved closer, but remained half-hidden by an enormous stuffed panda. "You're not gonna eat all these toys, are you?" she said. Her mother laughed.

"You'll have to excuse me," Arla said. "I have shopping to do."

As she browsed the shop, children gaped and pointed. She used to be proud of her patrician good looks: high brow, full lips, noble curved nose. Now she hated her face—or more to the point, she hated having to share it with Painsettia Plont.

"Wanna eat this?" shouted a stout blond boy, holding out a baby doll.

"Leave her alone," another boy whispered, "or she'll eat *all* the toys." The chubby boy looked from Arla to the doll to the shelves and shelves of toys. Then he started to cry.

An elderly woman poked her in the ribs with a bony finger. "Just look what you did. You've got a lot of nerve, scaring kids in a toy store."

A thin housewife with horn-rimmed glasses stared at Arla. "The next time your show is on, I'm going to cheer when you go down the bottomless pit in that snowball." She looked the actress from head to toe. *"Bitch."*

"I'm just trying to buy some gifts," Arla said.

A girl in an oversized pink sweatshirt hurried up to her and kicked her in the shin. Arla cried out as she fell into a display of toy fire engines. The pain brought tears to her eyes.

"She's gonna eat all the fire engines!" screamed the girl in the sweatshirt. "She's gonna eat everything!"

Arla pulled herself out of the pile. "I'm an *actress,* for Christ's sake!" she moaned. She wiped the tears from her eyes and her hands came away streaked with mascara. She glared at the elderly woman. "Because of idiots like you, I can hardly even get a job in dinner theatre! Directors won't take me seriously because people think I'm that damned

Christmas witch! Painsettia Plont is a character from a TV program. I am not Painsettia Plont!"

Several children backed away from Arla. Many of them were crying.

Arla shouldered her way past the thin housewife and rushed out of the store. Out in the mall, she realized that she had dropped the small sack containing her lipstick. The hell with it. There was no way she was going to return to that damned toy store.

She found a restroom and cleaned the mascara from her face. She then left the mall, searched out her car in the packed parking lot, and drove until she found a restaurant. She parked and checked her reflection in the rearview mirror. Her eyes were red and she looked pale. She decided to visit a tanning salon soon. A pale complexion only emphasized her resemblance to bone-white Painsettia.

The walls of the restaurant were lined with bookshelves and mirrors. The hostess showed her to a table in the no-smoking section.

"You look familiar," the hostess said. "Oh, you look like my old landlady, Mrs. Prescott. Any relation?"

Arla shook her head tiredly.

"My roommate and I used to call her the Snow Queen," the hostess continued, handing her a menu. "She looked like that weirdo lady on that Christmas show. You know—what's her name?"

Arla stared at her reflection in a mirror near her table. "Painsettia Plont. Painsettia Plont. Tell the waitress to bring me a Manhattan."

Soon the drink arrived, and Arla downed it in three swallows. For dinner she ordered the Surf & Turf Special. She felt that she needed to pamper herself after the day's ordeal.

A slim, black-haired woman waved to her from a booth at the far side of the room. She looked vaguely familiar. The woman left her seat and approached Arla.

"Well if it isn't Painsettia Plont!" the woman said. "I'm Maggie Carlson."

With the name, Arla now recognized the face. Maggie Carlson was the host of *DayBreak,* a local morning program.

"I never miss your Christmas show," Maggie said, taking a seat across from Arla. "Do you live in town or are you just visiting?"

"I've lived here in Detroit for about ten years. And I watch *Day-Break*. I'm a morning person." Arla wondered if her breath smelled too boozy. Then she decided that she really didn't care.

"I bet my viewers would just love to see what Painsettia Plont is up to these days," Maggie said.

"She's up to her knees in monkey-doo." Arla found the statement wonderfully liberating. "It's hell trying to find work when everyone still thinks of me as Painsettia. My last job was as an extra in some penny-ante production of *Oklahoma*. Before that, I played a burn victim on a cop show. They covered my face with bandages."

Maggie tapped a scarlet fingernail against Arla's glass. "Let me buy you another. Your real name is…?"

"Arla Merrick. And thank you for asking. Most people don't."

Maggie pulled a small notebook from her purse. "Can I have your phone number, Arla? I'd like you to be on my show next week. Who'd have thought a cherished Christmas special could have a downside?" She winked. "I don't mind tipping the occasional sacred cow."

* * * *

On the morning of Christmas Eve, Arla wrapped gifts for her niece, nephews, and sister Mavis. She had bought them all gloves and scarves. She was determined never again to set foot in a toy store.

Her guest spot on Maggie's show the day before had gone quite well. Arla felt good, even optimistic. Perhaps a sympathetic director had seen the show. God, but she longed to play a real role. Lady MacBeth. Titania from *A Midsummer Night's Dream*. Even old Mrs. Paroo from *The Music Man* would be better than nothing.

Mavis had said that she and the kids would be stopping by around noon. Arla glanced at her digital wristwatch. 7:42 AM. She still had plenty of time to finish a few chores around the house. She wondered if it had snowed the night before. Perhaps she needed to shovel the walk. She looked to the window, but of course, the drapes were drawn to help keep out the cold.

She crossed to the front door and opened it a crack. A little more. Then all the way.

Her neighborhood was—gone. Before her stretched an endless expanse of snowy hillocks and ice boulders. A blast of sub-zero wind blew snow into her eyes and momentarily stole her breath away.

She slammed the door shut and leaned against it. Something was wrong, incredibly wrong. It was as though her house had been picked up and dropped in an Arctic wasteland. Had some sort of freak blizzard covered everything in the neighborhood except her house? The lights were on; blizzard or not, she still had electricity.

She looked for the remote control but as usual, couldn't find it. She clicked on the power button of the television. Perhaps she could find a news show that would tell her something.

When the screen lit up, the first thing Arla saw was the face of Painsettia Plont. She was looking at a close-up of the video box for *Santa's Elves Meet Painsettia Plont*.

A sandy-haired man with a dark moustache appeared on the screen—Chip Carlyle, co-host of a national morning show, *Breakfast with Chip & Sandra.*

"Painsettia Plont has never been a happy camper," he said, "and it seems that the same can be said for actress Arla Merrick. Yesterday on Detroit's *DayBreak,* she claimed that the role has ruined her career."

His blond co-host, Sandra Dupree, rolled her eyes. "It's funny. I never really thought of Painsettia Plont as just an actress in a costume. She was like Scrooge, or a Christmas version of the Wicked Witch of the West—half legend, half real. At least, she was to me. I do feel sorry for Arla Merrick, but it's a pity she had to spoil the illusion. Know what I mean, Chip?"

"Sure do, Sandra," Chip said. "I'll never be able to watch that show again without thinking of old Arla sitting by the phone, year in and year out, waiting for Hollywood to call."

The show cut to a clip. Painsettia Plont was standing on a moonlit mountaintop. Her white fur robe billowed and flapped in the wind. In the distance, lightning streaked across a steel-grey sky.

What was this? Arla didn't remember this scene. Painsettia was smiling her crooked smile straight into the camera. Yes, Arla was sure of it; there were no such shots in the special.

"Ashamed of me?" The voice of Painsettia Plont roared thunderously. *"You silly, mindless fool! I am very much a part of your life, and you cannot silence me!"* The voice grew louder, and Arla clapped her hands over her ears. *"Now I have you, my sweet—and soon, you shall know the terror and the chill of my wintery vengeance!"*

Painsettia sneered and began to laugh. The volume continued to rise, until the cups and plates in Arla's living room cabinet rattled on their shelves. Arla tried to turn down the volume, but the knob was colder than ice—so cold that it turned the flesh of her fingertips dark grey. The knob would not move; she tried the power button, but it too was frozen.

The roar of Painsettia's laugh rose so high that it shattered the glass in the windows. Icy gusts of wind tore the drapes from the walls and blew snow into the room. Arla felt twin bursts of pain in her head. She realized with horror that her eardrums had ruptured.

Arla stumbled away from the television, down the hall to her bedroom. She would lock herself in and wrap herself in quilts to keep out the cold—

The bedroom was a complete shambles. The windows had shattered here too, and snow covered her bed and nightstand. Arla cried out as the wrinkled face of a little man peered in through a broken window.

The little man leaped into the room. He wore a green suit and a red wool cap. Santa's elves wore the same sort of outfit in the Christmas special.

More elves slipped into the room—Arla lost count after eight. Several of the elves grabbed her and proceeded to manhandle her through the broken window.

"What are you doing?" Arla shouted. "Let go! Let go of me!" She tried to shake free of them, but they were too strong. They dragged her through the windswept wasteland, over jagged shards of ice that tore at her clothes and flesh.

Eventually the elves stopped and scooped up handfuls of snow. They grinned wickedly as they packed the snow against her body.

Arla gasped with shock when she saw that they were situated on a edge of a huge chasm. She now knew that the elves were reenacting the finale of the Christmas special, in which they packed Painsettia Plont in the center of an enormous snowball and dropped her down into a bottomless pit.

"I'm not her! I'm not!" she cried. "For Christ's sake! Stop it! You're killing me!"

The elves packed the snow tighter, tighter, adding more and more. She tried to catch the gaze of even one of the elves. If only they would look at her—really *look,* and see that she was not their true enemy. But they were all so intent upon building the giant snowball. In a moment, only her head extended from the icy sphere. "You've got to stop," she pleaded. "I am not Painsettia Plont!"

The elves pushed at the snowball. At first it wouldn't budge, so they pushed harder. In a moment it rolled forward, teetered on the edge of the pit, and fell.

Arla screamed as she hurled into the chasm. Long after exhaustion forced her into numb silence, she continued to fall, down and down into an endless nightmare abyss of utter cold.

HUNGRY FOR FACES

It was horrible, watching Mr. Linfield move through his life like a maggot through shit. Michael saw him at least twice a week—in the streets, outside the supermarket, even at the mall. Young boys shouted at Mr. Linfield; sometimes they threw rocks or pop bottles at him. Everyone else walked past him, ignoring his outstretched hand.

That was what hurt the most: seeing Mr. Linfield beg. But then, what else could he do? He was a streetperson. A statistic with a ravaged face.

Something was wrong with the old guy's mind. Whenever Michael handed him a few bucks, Mr. Linfield would nod and mumble incoherently. It was horrible, and it had to end.

* * * *

The potbellied mechanic pointed to a gray, two-story house. On the upper floor, a single window gave forth a faint blue glow. "He lives there. See that light? Now gimme my fifty bucks."

As Michael handed him the money, he took a good look at the older man's face: red nose, shiny cheeks, eyes all but buried in flesh. A too-ripe face. The mechanic counted the bills twice, then shoved them in a pocket and ran down the road.

The weedy yard around the house was littered with broken bottles and old boards, so Michael had to watch his step. At the door, he debated whether or not to knock. He turned the knob; it wasn't even locked. He walked into the house.

The windows were incredibly filthy. Even though it was mid-afternoon, the entry hall was as dark as night. He fumbled a hand along the wall until he felt the plate of the light switch. But only the plate—the switch had been broken off.

Eventually his eyes grew accustomed to the dark. He located a stairway a few feet to his left and began to ascend. What was that sound—that high-pitched hum? He thought for a moment. Telephone wires in the wind? That hardly seemed possible. It was a windy day, but he hadn't heard the hum outside the house.

On the top floor, he found an empty hallway awash with blue light from an open doorway. The humming sound issued from the room beyond. A floorboard popped as he moved toward the door.

"Who's there? I have a gun." A voice from the room—young, male, tremulous.

"Don't shoot. I need to talk to you." He paused for a moment, thinking how best to explain his reasons for this intrusion. "Someone we both know said you could help me."

There was a creak of bedsprings. "Fine. Cover your face and come in."

Michael dug a handkerchief from his pocket. "My whole face?"

"Do the best you can. You don't have to cover your eyes. I'm not a Gorgon."

Michael tied the handkerchief robber-style across his lower face. He wasn't quite sure what a Gorgon was. One of those batwinged things on old churches? No, those were gargoyles. He walked up to the door and looked inside.

The blue light came from a tinted bulb in a shadeless lamp. Thin copper wires were strung across the room at various levels; every piece of furniture seemed to be caught up in the tangle. The breeze from a fan on high-power made the wires hum. On a brass bed in the center of the room reclined a pale man, bundled in quilts and pillows. His long black hair was thick and coarse, like a horse's mane. He wore a tattered bathrobe over a gray sweatsuit. Michael decided the pale man was probably twenty-five, just a few years younger than himself.

Michael brushed a hand over the lump in his pants pocket. He had a roll of bills totalling three-hundred dollars, in case the pale man had a price. "I met somebody in a bar—a mechanic. He'd told me you made his wife go away." It dawned on Michael that the mechanic might have violated a trust. "You can't really blame him for talking. He'd had a lot to drink and...well, I bought him a few drinks, too. He seemed pretty miserable."

The pale man shrugged. "No worry. I appreciate references, if discretion is observed. I'm sure Mr. Curtis has selected well. My name is Card."

"I'm Michael. I guess you don't really want to know who I am, though, since you told me to cover my face." He twanged at one of the copper wires. "What's with the spiderweb?"

"Be careful, will you?" Card nodded as Michael stilled the vibrating wire with a fingertip. "Yes, it is like a spiderweb, isn't it? Except there's no pattern. Still, do you see the appeal? Everything connected to everything. Beautiful, like a work of art."

"Can I get through?"

A brief, worried look crossed Card's face. "I suppose so." The pale man watched intently as Michael threaded his way across the room. "Careful there, a wire is snagged on your coat. And your handkerchief is coming loose. Don't let it fall off. If you should ever show me your face, I would want it to be a conscious choice."

At last Michael reached the brass bed. He turned away for a moment to pull the handkerchief tighter and retie it. Then he climbed over the pillows and sat cross-legged next to Card.

"I don't really have a gun," the pale man said. "I don't need one." He shifted on his pillows. "So tell me. How did you know that Mr. Curtis wasn't lying to you?"

"I remembered reading about his wife's disappearance in the papers. They found a pile of dust in her bed. Real weird." Michael studied Card for a moment. The pale man had fine wrinkles around his eyes. Perhaps he wasn't so young. "This thing you do. With people. What are you?"

Card looked up. "A man in a room." The look in his eyes was intense. Almost feral. "You are having problems with someone. Someone who should go away. A lover, perhaps? Isn't it odd about lovers? So beautiful when you meet them, so horrid when the love grows cold?"

* * * *

The next morning, Michael didn't go to church. After examining the newspaper, he threw it in the trash. What did he expect—a front page headline? HOMELESS MAN DISAPPEARS: DUST HEAP FOUND IN ALLEY. Of course not. He knew that no one would be too concerned about Mr. Linfield's disappearance. If anything, a few of the shopkeepers downtown would be glad of it.

He flopped down on his sofa, turned on the television and flipped through the channels. Sermons, news shows—at last a cartoon popped up. The show, a teenage space opera, was poorly drawn and woodenly animated.

If only *Doc Feisty's Cartoon Cavalcade* was still on the air—a great show with great old cartoons. Each week, fat Doc Feisty would have a different child as his co-host. At the beginning of each show, the lucky boy or girl would pop out of a giant rabbit hole and Doc Feisty would playfully grab the child by the neck. Michael's mother had sent in his name, but he never got to be on the show.

Too bad the real-life Mrs. Doc Feisty had to spoil everything. She'd killed herself by drinking something awful. Drain-opener or oven-cleaner. Something incredibly caustic. Something that made for an incredibly colorful death.

After that, Doc Feisty was no longer funny.

Michael had been nine when the show was cancelled. It wasn't until he was seventeen that a friend of his pointed to a confused old man on the streets and informed him that this was old Doc Feisty: real name, Corliss Linfield. His friend went on to tell him that Doc had spent the last few years in an institution.

Mr. Linfield had changed. The fat Doc Feisty belly had swelled into a bag of sickness. The wavy Doc Feisty hair had become a matted rat's nest. The bright, expressive Doc Feisty eyes had dwindled into twin pits of despair.

The cartoon's credits rolled, and Michael sighed. Maybe the next one would be better.

Card had asked for a picture. Of course, Michael didn't have one. The pale man then pulled a sketchpad from under the bed and told him to give a description. In twenty minutes, Card produced a realistic drawing of Mr. Linfield's face.

"Is this man so beyond hope?" Card had asked. "Are you doing this for him or for yourself? Not that it matters to me."

The question had momentarily weakened Michael's resolve. Was his request a mission of pity—or scorn? Maybe both: he often felt obligated to give alms to the homeless; and yet, the sick temptation to kick at them, to laughingly pile them with trash, was also there.

His was a mission of liberation. Time would erase any doubts on the matter.

He had not questioned Card too closely; he hadn't even asked what void would house the vanished Mr. Linfield. He only knew that the old man's torment on earth would soon be over. Or possibly, was already over; the pale man had not specified when the disappearance would take place.

The next cartoon was about a little girl whose imaginary playmate, a giant wise-cracking caterpillar, was always getting her into trouble. He had to admit that the animation was of a slightly higher quality than the previous show. Strolling through a park, the girl sat down on a bench next to a tramp sleeping under newspapers.

The caterpillar crawled after the girl and—what was this? The tramp tore away the newspaper and began to cackle insanely; his swollen belly shook with each laugh.

It was not an animated figure. It was Mr. Linfield.

The mad-eyed old man pulled a length of wire out of his pocket and wrapped it around the girl's neck, tighter, tighter—

Michael grabbed the remote control. On another channel, Mr. Linfield was strangling the Reverend Tillson Parker with a ragged handful of copper wires.

Michael turned off the television. For a moment, he simply sat and stared. Then he went to the door and opened it a crack.

He could hear faint sounds from the other apartments. People talking. Televisions blaring. But no panic. No screams of horror.

* * * *

That afternoon, Michael went to the mall with a group of friends.

Walking from store to store was a nightmare. He never realized how many televisions were on display. Some store windows were completely filled with them. There were cameras and monitors everywhere, to discourage shoplifters. And on each screen loomed Mr. Linfield for only Michael to see. Mr. Linfield, eyes shadowed with hatred, strangling anchormen, sports figures, shoppers.

At one point, Michael saw his own image on a store monitor. He ran out of camera range when he saw an approaching figure on the screen.

Outside of a shoe store, an elderly woman in ragged clothes asked him for spare change. He dug up a few coins from his pockets—eighty-five cents, total. He gave her a dime and hurried on.

* * * *

The next morning, Michael did not watch the news.

Fortunately, there were no TV sets in the office where he worked. Even so, his boss complained that he seemed distracted. So he concentrated—concentrated on the bland invoices and shipping orders with a fervor that made his head pound. He needed this job and could not afford to slip up.

* * * *

Cross moved his pillows to make room. "I didn't expect you back."

"You didn't say that I would keep seeing him." Michael was about to scratch an itch on his cheek, then stopped when his hand touched the handkerchief. Briefly, he recounted his experiences at home and at the mall. The wires hummed incessantly.

"I don't understand," the pale man said. "What you have told me is impossible."

"Why? Where is Mr. Linfield now?" Michael looked to the dresser, then to the nightstand. There were no photographs of Card in the room. "In Hell?"

Card reached under his mattress and pulled out handful after handful of sketches and photographs. "Fodder," he said, piling them on the bed and on Michael's lap. "Mere fodder. He's within me, forever. They all are. Now tell me who's in Hell."

Michael stared at the faces. Thin-skinned old women. Young, hard-looking men. A boy with bad teeth. A deformed infant. A girl with dark, blank eyes. Dozens of faces, many ugly, many mean-spirited. The un-loved. The unwanted.

Most of the sketches were discolored and brittle. Some of the photographs were faded with age. Michael swept the faces off his lap. "What are you?"

"You've asked me that before," Card said, "and my answer remains the same. A man in a room."

Michael pointed to the sketch of Mr. Linfield. "I don't want to see him again."

Card sighed wearily. "There's nothing I can do. It's just in your mind."

* * * *

Michael pulled the cord out of his television. He stayed out of the mall. Even so, he could not help but catch glimpses of his friends' sets, or those in businesses.

In the weeks that followed, Mr. Linfield's video image grew more violent. After strangling his victims, he would begin to gnaw at their faces.

Once, while walking home from the grocery store, Michael was ac-costed by a streetperson in a ragged sweater. He cried out—but it wasn't Mr. Linfield. The old man grabbed his coat sleeve and offered to carry the groceries for a dollar. Michael set down the sacks and shoved him out of his path, into a row of hedges. There was a can of insecticide in one of the sacks. For one frenzied moment he considered spraying the old man's face. Instead he grabbed his groceries and ran off.

Michael began to wonder. Was Card more or less real than himself? Was this all a game? The pale man was clever, like a demon. He had a pained, kind face, but still, a demon could wear a mask.

* * * *

Soon Michael's dreams were filled with televisions. Televisions de-picting moments from his life, like scenes from home movies, always with Mr. Linfield lurking in the background.

In one dream, Michael watched a huge TV screen floating through space and saw himself as a boy, talking with Mother on the front porch of his parent's house. Mother was cross with him: he hadn't finished cutting the lawn. She explained that he had to learn responsibility. Why, if he didn't, there was no telling what would become of him. Lecture over, Mother gave him a big hug. His face was smothered against her bosom; her lilac perfume made his nose itch. But then the smell of lilacs was overpowered by a hot, meaty smell. He tore free of Mother's embrace and screamed. Mother's throat was wrapped in a bloody snarl of wire, and Mr. Linfield was biting into her cheek.

The dream-scenes all ended that way. Mr. Linfield would appear with his wire to devour the face of a parent. A sibling. A coworker. A lover.

Michael stopped seeing his friends. He stopped going to work. He felt sure that Mr. Linfield had been sent by Card. A puzzle filled his mind, and he needed time to work it through. His continued existence depended on the answer.

He sat home alone, frightened, thinking. He didn't use the phone or answer his mail. He kept his life to a precarious minimum so that the evil threatening him could find no new avenue for intrusion.

* * * *

Card's brow wrinkled with alarm. "You didn't cover your face. What are you doing?"

Michael moved in a straight line from the door to the bed. In the yard of the gray house, he had picked up an old board. He used this to pound and snap the wires. His foot caught the cord on the electric fan, pulling it to the floor. The hum of the wires died. "He's in my dreams now. I haven't slept for days. You've got to call him off."

"It's just in your mind," Card cried. "There's nothing I can do. Don't break the wires. Go away or...or..."

The pale man began to—swell. His flesh seemed to be billowing out from the muscle and bone.

Dust sifted before Michael's eyes, and he put a hand to his face. His skin was softening, turning to dust. Already his nose was half gone. "Stop it, Card," he whispered. "Stop playing games with me. Don't you have any feelings? What's inside of you? What are you?"

Card said nothing. So Michael rushed forward, lifted the board and brought it down on the pale man's head.

Card's flesh began to tear from the pressure within. Eyes peered out through the widening fissures. Then the skin split open, spilling a nightmare cloud of faces. Michael sank to his knees. Mr. Linfield's face emerged from the cloud, confused and pathetic. Completely harmless, even after death. Card had been right.

Michael turned to leave, then stopped. He could not see the door. Or the walls. The man was gone and so was his room. All that remained was an infinity of mad faces and tangled copper wire.

OUR ANNE, PAXTON CATAFALQUE, AND THE INFANTE SARKAZEIN

I must have a word with Our Anne.

She's not quite right: bony body, bonier face, and what teeth she has left resemble a sickly rabbit's stools. The poor girl's health is twig-fragile, and her mind—That snapped years ago. Yet we love her, yes? We love our miserable darling, Our Anne of Green Molars, Ms. Anne Thropic, Ms. Shapen, Ms. Creant.

Oh *why* must she tug around that loaded-up, rickety shopping cart? To think: she used to be so fashionable, so accommodating…used to chainsmoke black clove cigarettes, used to make all the tabloids. Such talent! Painter, sculptress, chanteuse extraordinaire! But then she met *him*.

They say she found him reading his bleak blank verse to chic neo-Goths in a warehouse. She gazed into his predatory eyes and with a wee sigh, fell into the flame-lick'd cauldron of her own sweet candyfactory. How she adored the poet's sharp, fierce face, his needle-teeth and piebald flesh and incessant, monkey-shrill blabber. Truly he was monster-gorgeous, delectably repugnant—a ranting, chanting demogorgon of desire. And his name was Paxton Catafalque.

Our Anne took him out for espresso and was soon driven mad by all things little and big: the touch of his lean little fingers (she didn't mind the occasional scratches from his curved black nails), the little ear nips and neck nibbles, and of course, the big tingly barbarism slung between his lanky legs.

The gossip columns made much of their nonstop goings-on. Our Anne and Mr. Catafalque traipsed about in tiger-striped sunglasses, from club to club, island to island, for a glorious season—during which, five Movies of the Week were released based on their saucy intrigues and misadventures and general joie de vivre. Surely theirs was a union destined to make history, to create mad wonders—and after months and months of glowy earthmother bulbousness, Our Anne plopped out the maddest wonder conceivable: the Infante Sarkazein.

They say he was born with the cuticles already pushed back. That squealing bundle of fuzz cried out for goat's milk laced with cigarette butts; he draped his own shapely ass with perfumed pages of fin de siécle melodrama; he paraded about in frilled pirate shirts and silky pantaloons and a gilded monocle. At three months of age, he received a grant to publish a deliriously campy arts journal. Within a year, his first novel became a riotous bestseller and his paintings were displayed in galleries so trendy, no one was allowed admittance.

The boy grew fast, and soon, supermodels and millionaires and glamorous criminals were vying for his affections. Media vultures circled his summer cottage in smoke-churning chug-a-bug helicopters. And sad to say, no one even bothered to turn an eye toward Our Anne or Mr. Catafalque. Their careers were now the stuff of yawns.

Paxton without the paparazzi is merely a shallow beast; and Our Anne needs too many flash bulbs to brighten her day. They grew dull and dowdy in the shadow of their magnificent urchin; and likewise, the assorted glitterati and ne'er-do-wells clustered about the Infante gradually lost their zest, their style, and even some of their hair. Wrinkles crinkled 'round their drab eyes; their hands curled into spotty, shaky talons. They dwindled and kept on dwindling—none died, but who knew they were alive? One by one, they could no longer keep up with the Infante's breakneck schedule; as each fell away, a fresh new celebrity was drawn into the fold. Thusly did each sweet rose surrender its bloom.

Our Anne learned to accept her curiously *reduced* state; she loved her dapper boy and could not bear to be parted from him. But Paxton—! He decided to set the lad straight…such a sad mistake.

What's worse, Mr. Catafalque initiated the confrontation before the cameras on a public TV telethon (the Infante Sarkazein, for all his faults, did support the arts whenever possible). I happened to be watching and I must say, it was a rare moment indeed. Paxton cried out against his son, calling him a leech, a praying mantis, a crazy-ass vampire. The poet's shrill monkey-voice grew louder, faster, higher—a spray of spittle sizzled from his thin wry lips. I could not tear my eyes from the screen! The Infante simply smiled and gently put a hand to his father's cheek. And he said, so sweetly, "I love you, Daddy!"

Paxton Catafalque shut his mouth.

The boy said it again—"I love you, Daddy!"—and the poet began to *fall in upon himself*—as though someone had stuck a giant syringe in his bottom and drawn out a gallon of blood. Once more the words rang out—"*I love you, Daddy!*"—and a look of surprise popped into Paxton's eyes—then bliss, then excruciating *rapture*—

Sarkazein, no longer an Infante, is now more beautiful, more powerful than ever. And still Our Anne orbits her glorious son. Oh, she is a bony, horrid thing. It's not quite right—and to make matters worse, she insists on towing around that shopping cart and its reeking cargo.

I *must* have a word with her. Even if she wanted to keep the cart, surely no one would fault her for dumping that vile load: a loose, leathery sack of wretchedness that can only twitch its long black nails and whisper, faint but still monkey-shrill, "That's my boy."

SOFT BONES

THURSDAY

Last night in bed I thought really hard and tried to get my bones to turn into metal so I could walk. I imagined all the shitty calcium being replaced atom by atom with cast-iron, or bronze, or stainless steel.

Gopher thinks he's such a hotshit writer. Well, I can write too. Someday I'll write a novel and make lots of money and he'll be real old and have to depend on me, and he'll want to go out and I'll say fuck you, Gopher. Sit in your wheelchair and rot.

I'll be out of my chair by that time. They'll come up with some kind of artificial bone made out of metal. When I'm a big bestselling author, I'll be writing mysteries and spy stuff and not those shitty romances Gopher writes. And mine will be real books, not cheap-ass paperbacks.

There's this dizzy woman with fake eyelashes on the back of all Gopher's books. My first book will be a big shocking thing about how Veronica Blakely is really my stupid dad, a potbellied guy with hairy ears and buckteeth. Real romantic.

Gopher and his new girlfriend Mona have been going out for a couple months now. Mona's way too good for him. She's going to be spending the weekend with us while her apartment's being painted. She's real pale and about five years older than me. She wears lots of black and all kinds of necklaces with crystals and weird stones on them.

Now why would a hot love monkey like Mona go out with a saggy old pusbag like Gopher? Maybe it's because of that big sexy lump in his pants. Yeah. That fat, juicy wallet.

Not much of a day. Not much of a life. Tonight I'm going to concentrate on my bones again. Cast-iron leg bones, warm bronze finger bones, and an indestructible stainless steel spine. Chrome ribs, copper hips and a platinum skull.

FRIDAY

Mona showed up after lunch carrying an overnight bag. Gopher had to go to a meeting with his publisher—it was *soooooo* gross watching him kiss Mona goodbye with his big floppy lips.

After Gopher left, Mona helped me onto the couch so I could get comfortable.

"Gordon told me some more about your bone thing," she said, all serious and pouty. "I really hope they find a cure, Jacob."

"It's all Gopher's fault," I said. "His genes are screwed up. His whole side of the family has all kinds of bone disorders."

Mona wrinkled up her nose. "Eeuw. Like what?"

"Like, my aunt Sandra has bone spurs. My grandma's fingernails are real thick and soft. And there's something wrong with Gopher's jaws. That's why he can't wear braces."

She bopped me lightly on the nose with the tip of a finger. "You shouldn't call him Gopher. Gordon's very sensitive about his overbite."

We watched TV for a while. Next we played chess and I won. Mona got out her bag, pulled out a metal box and opened it up.

I looked inside. "What's all that junk?"

"It's not junk," she said. "My mentor gave this to me. Brother Star-wind. The greatest genius in the cosmos."

My first thought was that Gopher's little sex puppy was into New Age. But then I realized her toys were way too weird.

"These are the Candles of Knowledge," she said, holding up a handful of thick stubs with dead beetles embedded in the wax. Then she gave me three milky crystals. "These are Moon Eyes. They're really, really important. I think they can help you. You have a strong sense of concentration." She handed me a diary-sized book bound in oily-looking green cloth. The title was inked in big old-fashioned curlicues across the cover: *Banefulle & Wyck'd Unctions Of The Insekt Moste Effluvious*. "And this is the book that says what to do. Sort of."

"Sort of...?"

Mona shrugged. "It wasn't meant to be a manual, but it's got all the information."

Suddenly Gopher's car pulled into the driveway. Mona packed up her weirdbox. "Hang onto the Moon Eyes. We'll talk later."

* * * *

Later, in my room, I looked over the Moon Eyes. Each had a cloudy oval in the center. Like, well, an eye.

I held one of the Moon Eyes up to the lamp on my nightstand. There were bugs inside the crystal—four tiny, hairy worms.

I laid back on my pillows and rested the crystals on my forehead. Just to see if the Moon Eyes worked.

Nothing.

The crystals kept falling off my forehead, so I arranged them in a triangle on my chest. I concentrated on metal bones again but all I could picture was a giant cockroach, sucking the neck of a cut-off head like a baby with a bottle.

I shook the sight of it out of my head and sat up in bed. I looked down and the crystals were still stuck to my chest. When I pulled at them, they came off with a little sucking noise. They even left red marks on my skin.

It's midnight now, and I'm still not sleepy. I hope I can get some rest tonight.

SATURDAY

After breakfast, Gopher went to his study to work. As soon as we were alone, I told Mona about what I'd seen.

She was about to give me a hug but I stopped her—one good squeeze would break all my ribs. "You saw Brother Starwind! You're so lucky, Jacob!"

"Brother Starwind's a cockroach?"

Mona shook her head. "No, no, no." She ran upstairs. She came down a moment later with her weirdbox. "Brother Starwind gave himself to the Bug King two weeks ago."

We looked at the green book together. Mona told me that during the Salem witch trials, Cotton Mather's scribes had written down all of the testimony. The book contained the testimony of Goody Clay, accused of making maggots appear in the neighbor's porridge. She'd been only too happy to share the details of her spells and rituals with the court. While she was being led to the hangman, a cloud of flies blotted out the sun and in the confusion, she disappeared.

"She wasn't really what you'd call a witch," Mona said. "Witches are actually wise-women who use their spiritual energy to help others. Goody Clay observed the Way of the Swarm. Like me and my friends."

She rummaged in the box and found a huge amulet shaped like a grasshopper.

"Gordon's going golfing with his agent this afternoon." She smiled with her little cat's teeth. "Free this afternoon? Care to pencil a little ritual into your schedule?"

"You're psychotic, Mona. Does Gopher know you're into bug worship?"

She placed a pale hand under each breast. "Do you think he'd even care?"

* * * *

Gopher took off for the golf course at two. At two-fifteen, Mona began the ritual. She wanted to call some of the other members of her cult, but I talked her out of it.

It was strange, but I wasn't really worried. At worst, the Bug King would suck me down like a popsicle. Not like I had anything else planned.

I watched as Mona scattered cicada skins across the floor. When she finished, she whisked her hands together like a housewife shaking off flour. "Okay," she said. "Now let's get you ready."

She noticed the red marks on my chest as she undid the velcro on my shirt. "You did pretty good," she said, "but you messed up on the positioning."

After my clothes were off, I stretched out on some large throw pillows on the floor. She put the amulet around my neck and placed one crystal over my heart, one over my liver, and one at my crotch.

Mona stared down at me. "Relax your body. Concentrate. Focus on your desires."

I desired Mona, yes—but not as much as I desired strong bones. Rigid bones. Shining metal bones.

What can I say? I saw The Insekt Moste Effluvious, slopping up Brother Starwind's brain. And this time, I could smell the roach-god: he reeked like a bucket-sized cocktail of baby-shit, motor oil, and moldy green meat. I saw a crystal pyramid with translucent millipedes flowing out of the entryway. I saw a harem of dancing hermaphrodites with praying mantis eyes and puffy pink scorpion tails. I saw a sky filled with dog-sized copper wasps with yellow venom dripping from their mandibles.

When I awoke from the visions, the crystals were gone. In their place I found three purple sores. Mona told me that the Moon Eyes had been absorbed into my flesh, worms and all.

SUNDAY

Even though he usually sleeps in on Sundays, Gopher woke up early and made breakfast. Before wheeling me to the kitchen, he asked if we could talk.

"I don't spend enough time with you, Jacob. You know—quality time."

"That's okay, Gopher. Veronica's a busy guy."

His long, sad face got even longer and sadder. "Since your mother died…" Blah blah blah. Mother died right after I was born, so Gopher's mom speeches meant nothing to me. Sad but true. I faded out on him as I felt the heart-sore under my pajamas. After a while I tuned back in. "…That's why I think it's time for me to remarry."

"Remarry?" I was blown away. "You can't mean Mona."

"We've been seeing each for quite some time now and…" On and on with all the soap opera caca. "She makes me feel young…" More precisely, he liked feeling her young goodies. "She'll never replace your mother, but…" But the worst was yet to come. "…And wouldn't you like a little brother?"

"Mona carrying your baby?" I turned my chair away from him. "In your dreams. You've got some heavy evolving to do if you want to match her chromosome count. You know, Gopher, I always thought I looked a little like the TV repairman…"

"Now you stop that!" Gopher grabbed me by the shoulder. "The name is Gordon. G, O, R, D, O, N! I am your father and I will not have you making fun of me in my own house!" Before I knew it, he was all red in the face and shaking me and slapping me. Enough to break every bone in my body.

A look of horror spread across his face. His eyes looked like they'd pop right out of his head. "Oh my God Jacob I'm so sorry what have I done oh my God are you all right please say something!" He babbled on and on but the funny thing was, I was okay. No cracks, no snaps, no broken-pencil agony deep in my muscles.

I spit in Gopher's face. What a moron. A miserable hack with a pumpkin-head full of shit and cliches. "I'm okay, you rat's ass with teeth. Now get out of my room."

* * * *

Mona came up with my breakfast a half-hour later.

"Your dad told me what happened. He's completely freaked." She looked at me suspiciously. "Did you ask for anything yesterday?"

I gave her my best *duh?* face. "Ask who?"

She set the breakfast tray on the bed and stared at me.

Finally I nodded. "Sure. I asked for strong bones. Maybe I got them."

Mona felt my arms, my legs, my neck. She stopped by the door before she left. "What does the Bug King know about bones? He doesn't have any."

* * * *

The sun hasn't even set yet, but I'm midnight tired. My skin feels different—it slides on top of the weird rubbery muscles underneath. Better get some sleep.

MONDAY

I don't know what came over me when Gopher stepped into my room this morning. He may have been an utter jackass, but still, it was awfully petty of me to lop off his head with my new mandibles. I said to myself, *Franz Kafka, eat your heart out.* Then I picked up Gopher and carried him down to the kitchen. For breakfast.

I'm not complete yet. My hands are still human enough to hold a pen. They have a few bones left in them, but those will melt away after the skin grows thick and rigid.

I wonder what Mona will do when she sees me? I'm sure she won't scream. In fact, I think she will be proud.

After all, she's bound to admire my shell. It's as hard as nails. As hard as cast-iron. Bronze. Stainless steel. And how it gleams.

HER HORRIBLE APARTMENT

As soon as she came through the door, she told us she'd found an apartment at the mall. This didn't seem to make any sense, but everybody smiled and said how lucky she was, and so we made plans to see the place after work. We even decided to make a little party of the occasion.

I liked my job—computer graphics—but the workload was very boring that day: plopping copy into the same old newsletter formats. She walked by my desk on her way to the copying machine, and I thought: *she's so skinny. She's starving herself like one of those scrawny fashion models.* She was a pretty girl, and a very nice person, but I didn't find her attractive. Her skinny neck and nervous eye movements were too birdlike.

At break time, I went down to the vending machine area and there she was, sipping steaming black coffee from a styrofoam cup.

"So. The mall." I gave her the most encouraging grin I could muster. "You'll be shopping like crazy."

She rolled her eyes. "I'm right next to my favorite store, The Bracelet Hut. It's like heaven."

I looked at her wrists. She was wearing dozens of thin bracelets—plastic, copper, gold, beaded. Had she always worn so many? Probably so.

"Lot of food places at the mall… Hope you don't have a pest problem." I meant *rats*, of course, but I didn't want to scare her.

"There *are* some bugs, but that's okay." She shrugged. "Nothing's perfect. Only stupid people expect things to be perfect."

After work, I drove to a discount liquor store for some wine, then headed for the mall. I was pretty proud of myself: the wine I'd bought was a dirt-cheap German vintage with a long name. Everyone at the party would think it was so chic.

The shoppers were out in full force, and I had to park a long way from the mall entrance. As I walked across the lot, a heavyset blonde woman sneered at me, and I suddenly realized that I probably looked like some kind of bum, carrying around a bottle in a paper bag.

Inside, I located The Bracelet Hut on a directory display (it was practically at the other end of the mall) and began walking again. After a while, I noticed that people were staring at me. Staring with looks of disgust. Of pity. I slipped into a menswear store and found a mirror.

My suit was all dirty and torn. My face was covered with dark stubble. There were dark circles around my eyes. I thought to myself, *Oh, this must be a dream*, and tried to wake up. And—

Nothing happened.

I left the menswear store and said "Damn!"—because men swear. Well, I was dirty and a little scary, but no matter: I was only dreaming. Probably. I hurried along to the party, the silly little party for her silly little apartment at the mall.

I passed Doughnut Heaven and Makeup Madness and and Love Them Computers and a lot of other stupid stores. I stopped for a moment to look through the door of a store called Measure Your Pleasure: inside, naked men were gauging their privates with golden rulers.

I just laughed. Oh, I HAD to be dreaming!

Finally, I found The Bracelet Hut—and next to it, a dusky-pink door with the words *Her Apartment* on it. I knocked and she let me in.

The apartment was nothing more than a converted men's room, complete with urinals (she'd planted flowers in them). A dozen or so middle-aged men in blue coveralls were standing about, laughing, drinking, gobbling hors d'oeuvres, pretending they were going to pee on the flowers. Each man was holding a blue lawn rake.

I turned to her and said, "Who are these guys? Where are the folks from work?"

Her eyes were very sad. "These are the exterminators. I had to cancel the party because of the bug problem. But please, don't let the snacks go to waste." She crossed to a side table and returned with a trayful of cocktail weenies. "So why aren't you wearing any clothes?"

I looked down in utter shock: I was naked, caked with dirt, and my toenails needed trimming. Everyone in the room turned toward me and laughed. Except her: she simply sighed.

Suddenly, fat, moist-looking iridescent bugs began to scurry around the room. They had way too many legs and bulging compound eyes. They seemed to be talking to each other in a shrill little buggy language. As I watched them, I realized that a form of nausea very close to car-sickness was building inside of me.

One of the exterminators, a tall man with red hair and a redder face, handed me a rake. "Make yourself useful, ya bum," he said.

I looked around and saw that all the other men were chasing the bugs, slicing them to bits by passing the rake-teeth over them. I sliced up a few of the slower bugs, and hated doing it. Sure, the slimy freaks were utterly loathsome, but they were still living beings. My nausea became so intense that finally, I had to crouch in a corner and breathe deeply to keep from vomiting.

"Don't do that," said the red-haired man, pulling me to my feet. "Are you crazy, letting your butt drag so close to the floor? One of those bugs could have crawled up there, and *then*..." He made a face—a disgusted yet smirkingly *knowing* face—and returned to the task of bug-raking. More and more of the creatures were crawling about. Soon they were joined by frogs, scorpions and lizards, all multi-colored, all dewy with slime. Thin rivulets of steaming ichor flowed across the floor as more of the little horrors were sliced up. A hot, farty smell filled the air.

My skinny hostess took my hand. "Let's go," she said. "We don't want to get in their way."

As we were heading out the door, I looked back for a second, just in time to see an iguana force its way down the red-haired man's throat. The look in his eyes was—well, I suppose it was one of pleasure. There are so many different kinds of pleasure, and oddly enough, some of them aren't all that pleasant.

She led me next door to the Bracelet Hut, where the clerks were fighting off glistening Komodo dragons. She loaded down her wrists with gold and platinum, pearls and diamonds. Then we zipped across the corridor to Chick-Chick-Chicken, where we helped ourselves to some tasty hot wings. The fry-boys were too busy to stop us: they had their hands full, smacking rainbow-hued crocodiles with brooms.

We sat by the fountain in the middle of the mall's Food Court, licking wing-sauce off each other's fingers.

"I can't believe we're doing this," I said. "It's not like we love each other or anything like that."

"Well, we *are* friends, aren't we?" The tone of her voice was borderline frantic. "Everything's going to hell and it would be nice to face the end with a friend."

I looked—really *looked* at her. Sure, she resembled a sad, skinny little bird, but this particular bird needed me. Needed my support. My understanding.

I cradled her face in my hands. "For a while now, I've been thinking that this whole day has been one big bad dream. Not mine, not yours... Maybe the God of Slimy Things is taking a nap. Why don't we just wait and see what happens? It sure can't get any worse."

She flashed a cheery smile, revealing hundreds of thin, sharp iridescent teeth. "Okay."

WHAT THE NERVOUS OLD LADY ON THE BUS HAD TO SAY

Oh, good. I'm so glad you sat down next to me.

You look so normal and friendly and clean, which is more than I can say for most of these…people.

I'm on my way to Baltimore to see my daughter, Denise. I started out in Sioux City—it feels like I've been on the road forever! I hate these buses, but there's no way anyone is ever going to get me into one of those awful planes. What if the one with me in it crashed and burned up? I'd be strapped in my seat, as helpless as a baby, screaming with pain. No thank you! Denise bought me my bus ticket. Wasn't that nice of her?

You wouldn't believe some of the people I've had to sit *right next to*. So close, they could have just stuck out a finger and touched me! These buses really should have little walls between the passengers. Little walls that go up and down. If you want to be left alone, you can just make the little wall go up.

There was this one guy who sat down right next to me—I swear, he smelled like a dead animal. I wanted to ask him, "Do you need a bath, or are you carrying around something dead in one of your pockets?" Of course, knowing my luck, he probably would have pulled something right out of his pocket to show me—some stinky, sliced-up little dead thing.

He was one of those Asian fellows, so he probably wouldn't have understood me anyway. Why do people come to this country if they aren't even going to bother to learn the language? Those Asian men, they have a real passion for white women, you know. The age doesn't matter to them. I didn't say a word to him, not a single word. I wasn't about to do anything to excite him, I can tell you that!

White female skin, it drives them insane. That's why I'd never eat alone in one of those Asian restaurants. My goodness! Suppose they put something in my food to make me pass out, so they could—well, you can imagine. They have all sorts of ancient Asian herbs, passed down through the centuries from Genghis Khan and awful people like that. I'm sure they know how to make a white woman go into a deep sleep so they can do their dirty business.

It makes me shiver just to think about it.

Why, what if I was abroad and had something to eat in one of their restaurants right in the middle of China? I'd probably pass out and all those awful, awful Asian men—millions of them! There are quite a lot of people in China, you know. They would have their way with me, one right after the other. For years! I'm sure I would die from the abuse—I'm just a tiny thing. But that wouldn't stop them, I'm sure!

I suppose you must think I'm one of those prejudiced bigots, but I'm not. Actually, what I'm saying probably applies to all men. White men aren't that different. I hate to tell you this, but it is a sad fact that when I was very young, I was raped by my own father. And he was a man of the cloth—the kind that can marry, of course, not one of those Catholics. My own father! Men are such pigs, they really are. Not all men, but most.

Well, here on a crowded bus, I'm safe. And you're so good-looking, you're probably one of those funny men who like to play with other men's thingies. Sometimes I wish all the men in the world were gay homos, so they would just leave me alone.

My goodness, it drives me insane sometimes, it really does, walking around outside and seeing some yellow devil-man looking at me—or one of those black fellows. I've never talked to one in my whole life, but I think I'd die five times in a row if one of those black fellows tried to have his way with me. I hear their private gender organs are quite huge—I'm sure it would split me right in half.

How is a poor old woman like me supposed to survive in today's world? That's why I carry a gun, you know. I have my gun with me right now, right here in my pretty pink purse—just in case some sex-mad rapist tries any funny business with me. I'm not afraid to pull the trigger!

I really wish I could take a little nap, but I'm just too nervous. I do tend to get nervous, particularly around a lot of people. But it's just as well that I stay awake. If I fell asleep, I'd probably have one of my awful dreams.

Sometimes I dream there's been a world war, and the entire Earth is covered with ashes and flames. And in the smoking ruins, all these little scorched cradles are rocking back and forth, back forth, and all the poor babies inside are crying—screaming, really. They're all sliced up, all slashed and gashed. Some of the babies are white, some are yellow, some are a little of both. They all have beautiful dark eyes—looking at them makes me so sad, knowing they'll never grow up and be happy. They'll never say, "I love you, Mommy!" No love. Just pain and death.

Then I find a door that leads into a wonderful dining room, with a big table covered with dishes and trays, loaded with the tastiest food anyone could ever imagine! So I sit down and eat all those wonderful sausages and bratwursts and bananas—but then the ceiling opens up and God and my dead mother are looking at me, calling me a dirty, shameful whore, and then a nuclear bomb filled with knives falls on me and blows me apart, slicing me to ribbons, so there's nothing left but a few bloody strands.

I was seeing a psychiatrist for a while, and he used to spout all kinds of gobbledy-goop and say it was all in my head—but my own father well and truly raped me, and so did those millions of yellow devils. They all drugged me and had their way with me. A long time ago. But they'd do it again in a second, if I gave them the chance.

It's true.

Why are you looking at me like that?

You're squinting at me. Are you part Asian? Are you thinking about raping me? Remember, I have a gun in my purse, right next to my pill case. The case is empty, though. I can't afford my medicine any more—it costs so damned much. I do take it whenever I can afford it, even though I worry sometimes that maybe it was made by those Asian monsters. My sister used to say I was a prejudiced, but my father would tell her, "No, she's not—she hates all men."

That was so long ago, back when he said that. I was very young. The summer before, a boy got me in trouble—his family lived across town. What was his name? The last name was Chang, but the first name—what was it? My goodness, why can't I remember? I should remember something like that. He had such beautiful dark eyes. And he spoke perfect English, not like some of those others. I loved him—of course, back then, it was wrong to love somebody who was a different color. So I had to use all my saved-up money, and some money I took from my mother's purse, to pay that back-alley doctor to make the baby go away, before it started to show. He didn't do a very good job, though. I was in so much pain, bleeding for days, and eventually I had to go to the hospital. It was terrible. Terrible. Terrible.

And that boy, that boy with the beautiful eyes—he didn't even visit me in the hospital. A devil, that's all he was. I mean, maybe nobody let him know, but still—it would have made me feel a little better, if he'd have told me he was sorry. But nobody—nobody in the whole world—felt sorry for me. My mother told me I was a disappointment. My own father told me I was going straight to Hell for causing him such shame. He screamed at me and didn't have any pity for me at all, even though I was in so much pain. There was an infection, you know. Infection. What an awful, filthy word. How could my own father tell me I was going to Hell? He pretended he was so holy, but he was just a man with one of those thingies, just like all men. I know he raped me. My psychiatrist said it was all in my head, but I remember pain—deep, deep pain. My father filled me with pain, that much I know. And even if it wasn't rape, it was something just as bad, because it made me feel dirty and cheap and miserable.

A few years later, I moved away to Sioux City and met a good man. Bill. He was always very kind and eventually we got married. He was very patient with me, one of the few good men who ever lived. He never yelled at me when I'd wake him up in the middle of the night with one of my nightmares. They made me scream, you know, those nightmares.

We tried to have a baby—we tried and tried—but I couldn't get pregnant. We went to one of those special doctors and he took a look at things down there. Oh, I was so embarrassed. It turns out my lady parts had been damaged by that other doctor—though now that I think about it, I bet he wasn't even really a doctor. Good doctors don't ruin lady's parts. I should hope they don't.

I felt so bad, knowing I would never be able to make a beautiful baby for my Bill. He'd been so good to me. So kind. He deserved a baby. Maybe I didn't, but Bill did.

But we did eventually find our beautiful baby. We had to wait a long time, but finally, we were able to adopt Denise. Her mother didn't want her, but we did. I love her so much. I'll never understand how her mother could have given away such an angel…such a precious, precious angel. But I'm glad she did. I don't know what I'd do without her. These days, I think my love for Denise is the only thing holding me together.

Denise has no idea she's adopted. She doesn't know any of these things. Nobody does, these days—except that psychiatrist, though I can't afford the visits any more. Oh, and you! You know, now. I have no idea why I'm telling you all this. You do have a kind face. I suppose that's why.

And it does help to talk about it.

All my old problems were so long ago, everybody's passed away since then. My parents both died over twenty years ago. Bill, just about three years ago. My sister died last year.

Oh, now stop looking at me like that. Stop squinting like some damned Asian devil. I didn't kill them, if that's what you're thinking. There aren't any bullets in my gun. Even if I was being attacked from all sides, I couldn't afford to load it. I don't have any money. Bill was a good man, but bless him, not the best provider in the world. He was a janitor. Didn't make very much. I guess he thought he'd live forever, because he never bothered to take out life insurance. His funeral used up a lot of his savings. Though I didn't skimp on the coffin. I bought him one of the best. Beautiful wood. That man deserved a shrine. So I did the best I could.

So I'm going to see my daughter. She's going to find me a nice little place to live where someone can look in on me every now and then, and make sure I always have enough food and clean laundry and pills.

I haven't had my pills for three or four days now.

Out of pills.

Out of money.

Out of everything, really. Out of—

What did you say?

I heard you. You said something. I believe you said I was out of my mind.

That's very funny, mister funny-man.

Sometimes I wish I *was* out of my mind.

Because it's hell being inside of it.

EYE DEW

On Sunday they got married and became completely different people. Even though they had lived together for ten years before the ceremony.

That happens, sometimes.

They had decided not to go on a honeymoon, to save money. And really, after ten years, most of the lust was gone anyway. They'd only married because they were tired of relatives griping at them. "When are you two going to get married? The state probably considers you married anyway—that whole common-law deal—so you might as well just get it over with."

As soon as they arrived home that night, she peeled herself out of her wedding dress and flung herself into the shower, to wash away her make-up, hair gel, even the fine golden body-glitter lightly sprinkled on her shoulders and cleavage. He just stripped off his tuxedo and flung himself straight into bed. Though most of the lust had departed, a bit of random randiness remained.

She emerged from the bathroom with an oatmeal-based beauty mask caked on her face and her hair up in curlers. "Oh, honey," she said, glancing at the manmade tentpole jutting up under the covers. "I don't have the energy for that tonight. I'm completely exhausted. Weddings are hard on a bride. Be a dear and bring in the gifts from the car. We don't want burglars breaking into the car during the night and stealing all our wonderful gifts. Can you do that? Right now?"

So he threw on some clothes, went out and brought in the gifts from the car. When at last he returned to the bedroom, she was already asleep, snoring like a trumpeting elephant with a sinus infection.

He wasn't tired, so he went out to the living room and watched the cartoon channel for four hours, until he fell asleep slumped in his armchair. He dreamed of wide-hipped cartoon wives with crying babies clinging to their meaty legs. The wives kept chasing their scrawny, crazy-eyed husbands with rolling pins, screaming orders at them. "Take out the trash, you bum! Wax the car! Do those dishes! I'm too tired from raising these damned brats of yours!" The husbands could only reply with frenzied cries of "Yes, dear! Yes, dear! Yes, yes, yes!"

In the morning after shaving, he weighed himself—he did so every day—and was shocked to see that he'd lost six pounds. He used to have a little bit of a paunch, but now his stomach was quite flat.

At the kitchen table, she was eating a huge breakfast of bacon, eggs, toast and orange juice. "You'd better hurry up," she said. "You're going to be late for work."

"Work?" He stared down at the bowl of cereal in milk she'd set out for him. The cornflakes were now cornmush. "We're on vacation for the next two weeks, remember?"

She waved a strip of bacon at him dismissively. "Vacation? What for? The wedding's over. I called your office and told them you'd be in, same time as always. I gave my office notice two weeks ago, so I'll just stay home preparing our future. That's what wives do."

She got up, grabbed his breakfast bowl and poured its contents down the garbage disposal. "You won't have time for that if you want to make it to work by eight."

At the office, he found his black plastic in-box piled high with financial reports to prepare—plus, his boss wanted him to work on increasing the internet traffic of the company website, even though he'd never worked on that sort of thing before and had no idea where to begin. He wanted to cry, but what kind of a man does that?

"You have a family to feed now," his boss said. "Once you become a family man, you have to work harder than ever before. That's the way of the world."

When he arrived home after three hours of overtime, she greeted him at the door, waving a paint scraper in front of his face.

"How am I supposed to prepare our delicious future meals looking at those awful off-white kitchen walls? That terrible color is sucking the life out of me." She put the scraper in his hand. "Be a dear and paint the kitchen Springtime Periwinkle Fantasy No. 12."

"But I just got home from work and haven't had a thing to eat since lunch," he said, slapping his belly, which was now not merely flat, but actually sunken. His clothes felt loose, almost oversized. He slapped his empty belly again for emphasis, and the vibrations sent his pants flying down around his ankles.

"Oh honey, we don't have time for that now," she replied, gnawing on a roasted turkey-leg. Where did that come from? "Now please, get started on that kitchen. I'm going to look at new bathroom fixtures on the internet."

By two in the morning, he had the kitchen walls all scraped clean. He slept on the couch and dreamed of Amazons in aprons. When he woke up, he found himself seated behind the wheel of his car with his business clothes piled on the passenger seat. He managed to struggle into his shirt and pants—he couldn't get dressed in the driveway, what would the neighbors think?—then slipped on his socks and shoes and drove off to work. His clothes were looser than a circus clown's jumper, but there was nothing he could do to fix that. He certainly didn't have time to go shopping for new clothes—he was already five minutes late for work.

He spent the whole day working on financial reports and internet matters, and only had time for half a chicken-salad sandwich for lunch. He was so tired, he just wanted to curl up in a corner and cry himself to sleep, but that sort of thing takes time.

He painted the kitchen that night while she ate doughnuts and looked on the internet for a new mailbox—maybe one that had a pattern of baby ducks around the edges. Ducks were so cute.

He finished painting around three in the morning, then fell asleep on the kitchen floor and dreamed of bulldozers in Eva Gabor wigs. When he woke up, he was fully dressed at his desk, already working on a new batch of financial reports. His suit was so loose, he felt like a child playing dress-up in adult clothes.

Springtime Periwinkle Fantasy No. 12 turned out to be a nightmare, absolutely hideous, so she told him to scrape all that off and start over. He also washed all his shirts and pants in hot water that night, so they would shrink and fit him better.

The company website's traffic figures just weren't increasing fast enough, so that meant spending some weekends working on that, and the new kitchen color, Dainty Daisy Delight No. 7, turned out a little too greenish, too queasy, so he had to scrape it away, and he lost more weight and that meant boiling his clothes until they'd shrunk enough to suit him, and she ate chicken nuggets dipped in zesty barbeque sauce as she surfed the internet for pretty hand towels, and a new batch of financial reports came in and the car needed an oil change and Warm Autumn Ochre No. 8 looked like crap and so did Cool London Mist No. 10 as well as Enchanting Aqua Surprise No. 43 and his clothes needed more boiling and she bought more housewares and home improvements on the internet while eating pastries and pastrami and tacos and roast beef and one day, she turned to him and said, "Honey, we need to talk."

By then he was just a wizened, palsied little monkey, spattered with paint and dressed in crumpled, shrunken doll clothes, gnawing hungrily on some old paint chips—they looked so pretty and tasted so sweet, so yummy. But the toxins in the chips made him drowsy, sooooo drowsy. He felt himself falling asleep, and before his mind drifted into a black-velvet beddy-bye tunnel, he looked up and saw his five-hundred pound wife standing over him, her jowls flecked with pancake crumbs and dripping with maple syrup. And she whispered, "I'm bored. This whole marriage thing just isn't working. I want a divorce."

As his mind wended its way down into darkness, he pondered the fact that he could still feel his cheeks. He couldn't feel any other part of his body…not even his lips…but yes, he could still feel his cheeks, warm and wet with tears.

* * * *

He woke up three weeks later in a chrome hospital bed. About a dozen thin plastic tubes spooled into or out of his body, nourishing him or removing wastes.

By the side of his bed sat a handsome, red-haired, thirtyish man with kind blue eyes.

"You're awake!" the man cried. "My prayers have been answered."

Confused, he stared at the red-haired man. "Who are you?"

The man sighed. "Poor thing. You're still delirious. Just rest. I'm so happy you're awake! Soon you'll be all better. You'll see."

"I must be having trouble with my memory," he said. "I remember getting married to her and painting the kitchen…painting it more than once…and…"

The red-haired man laughed. "You really are delirious! But no wonder, after all you've been through. You must be starved—you've lost a lot of weight, so we'd better buy you some ice cream on the way home."

"Yes, I'd like that," he said.

"You've never been married," the red-haired man added, "and certainly not to a woman. You were painting our kitchen and you forgot to open some windows. The fumes got to you. The doctors were worried about brain damage, but I knew you'd be okay. Still, that didn't stop me from worrying night and day, and praying, too. I've been by your side this whole time, crying for you. Now you're better and we have so much to look forward to."

The red-haired man then began to cry. Copious tears of relief flowed down his face, landing on his lap and the floor with syrupy plops. He shed tears of Springtime Periwinkle Fantasy No. 12 and Dainty Daisy Delight No. 7 and Warm Autumn Ochre No. 8 and Cool London Mist No. 10 and Enchanting Aqua Surprise No. 43 and pretty soon the nurses rushed in to see why the patient was screaming.

FINE PRINT

Once you hit twenty-seven, it becomes practically impossible to make friends; better to become self-absorbed and content. Hector Derhake decided this as he stirred up his yogurt. No fruit came to the top—this one was plain, although he'd grabbed it from among the fruit-flavored selections. Next time he would read to make sure.

Hector had belonged to a small group of friends in college, but over the years they had all moved away. Now he was an entire week into his twenty-seventh year and basically friendless. He was an assistant art director at a small advertising agency. Sometimes he had lunch with others from work, but his co-workers always felt that this time together had to be used as a brainstorming session. The agency folks were too fickle, he felt; if he quit tomorrow they would all become instant strangers.

The problem was that he wanted to make friends. He didn't really want to retreat into himself. Whenever he saw one of the agency people with a group of friends, at a restaurant or out shopping, he would wonder what he was doing wrong. Why weren't people clustering around him?

It was early Saturday morning and Hector had nothing to do until the afternoon; then he was going to drive into the country to look at some property which, evidently, now belonged to him. One of his uncles, Ezekiel Derhake, had died recently, leaving him a house in a nearby semi-rural community.

Hector's paternal aunts and uncles were scarecrows—bachelors and spinsters, all old, thin and gangly. His parents had died in a car accident several years ago. He imagined that he would end up with a number of houses eventually. The entire scarecrow clan lived apart and hated one another, and even though they probably didn't cherish Hector, there was really no one else to name in a will.

Hector went into the living room to watch TV. The only shows that looked even halfway interesting were cartoons. The animation on these shows was incredibly poor. The mouths moved while the eyes stayed still and dead. Did children actually enjoy this?

On the table by the television, he had placed a packet of paperwork relating to Uncle Ezekiel's property. In this pile was a letter from Uncle that he had never bothered to open. Ezekiel had been the liveliest of the scarecrow clan: tall and thin, but with some color to his cheeks and a horsy smile. He had been something of a traveler, and was actually an expert on—what? Some odd topic. Starfish? No, but it had reminded Hector of marine life. The last time Uncle had stopped by to visit, about three years ago, he had rambled on and on about some strange project, constantly repeating himself like a stuck record. Also, the old boy had given him a pencilled map to the house. Hector dug through the odds-and-ends drawer of his desk, found the map and paper-clipped it to the letter.

Hector decided to try calling Uncle's lawyer again. He had called earlier that morning but no one had answered—probably still asleep. Even so, he had some questions he needed answered before he went out to the house.

Mr. Pierce sounded raspy and annoyed. "It's Saturday morning. Not even nine yet. What can I help you with?"

"I'm going out to my uncle's house today, remember? I told you yesterday when you gave me the key."

"Is something wrong? Did you lose it?"

Hector started to chew on a thumb-nail, but stopped himself. "No, I just wanted to know if the power switch would be on."

The lawyer sighed. "The power switch, as you put it, isn't in my bedroom."

"But will anything be on? Electricity, heat, phones?" Hector could hear Mrs. Pierce's birdy little voice chirping in the background.

"I doubt it," Pierce said. "And there isn't a phone. Evidently you never tried to call him. Is there anything else?"

The birdy piping was getting louder. Clearly Mrs. Pierce wanted peace and quiet. Not that it mattered. Hector had once met the woman and she was too far gone for beauty sleep. "Refresh my memory. I'm trying to remember what the old thing did for a living."

"Haven't you looked over any of the papers I gave you? He was a writer. Which reminds me—there was a book he'd wanted you to read. I put a copy in with those papers. Yes, dear, I know." This last comment was directed at the bird-woman. "Your uncle did leave you practically everything he owned, Hector. He wasn't a thing—he was a person. A very generous person. Now if you'll excuse me, I'm going back to bed.

* * * *

Later, as he was getting ready to leave the apartment, Hector did glance through the packet of papers. Tons of small print, of course. Even his uncle's book was small print, and nonfiction at that: *Mind, Matter and Life: Legends of the Aquastor*. That last word rang a bell. Ezekiel had mentioned it in his ramblings; it was what made Hector think of the sea.

The book's cover art depicted a gaunt, shadowy figure with glowing yellow eyes. Under the author's photo on the back was a list of other books by Ezekiel Derhake. There were at least a dozen, all concerning the occult. Hector took the letter and map with him, as well as the book to look over when he stopped for lunch.

On the drive to Ezekiel's town, Wajno Grove, he had a cigarette, his first of the day. In a little while he had another. He was trying to quit, and even though he was cheating, he felt that he was making progress. In the past, he'd have gone through half a pack by this time.

He really had no idea what he would do with a house in the middle of nowhere. Wajno Grove was something of a bedroom community. Maybe he could rent it out to newlyweds—or better yet, a retired couple. He stopped for lunch at the Fat Granny Cafe. The painted wooden cutout above the door certainly didn't encourage an appetite. It depicted a large elderly woman with a stirring spoon, but the colors were lifeless, and the spoon was too thick and phallic. Probably some backwoods Picasso's idea of subliminal advertising.

He thumbed through the book as he ate. From what he could make of it, an aquastor was like an imaginary playmate, except that it actually existed. Someone thought it up, performed a ritual, and voila!—it came to life.

He noticed that a paragraph under the heading of *The Aquastor in Muslim Demonology* had been highlighted in yellow marker:

> In ancient times such a being was known as a jinni. This creature was the mental spawn of a sorcerer, who brought it forth from primal darkness. Spacial constraints limited the powers of the jinni; even so, it could still exercise control over the workings of time and space, and command a multitude of minor demons...

Here Hector stopped. The book was a complete waste of time. He laid it aside and broke open Uncle's letter.

After reading some of the letter, Hector looked back at the postmark date. Ezekiel had mailed it two weeks before his death. The old boy's mind had been on the blink, no question. The content was fragmented and, like Ezekiel's style of speech, repetitive to the point of being meaningless.

> Dear Hector,
> Mr. Pierce stopped by the other day so I gave him a book for you to read. I couldn't trust the mail with it. The book is

important to you. He said he would drop it by your office but he may forget. It was nice of him to visit. I think he worries about me. The book is important to you.

I am not well at all—I am completely drained. After you read the book you'll have a better idea of what I'm talking about. It took years of study—years and years. But now it has finished me. The room at the end of the hall. I'm finished and soon will be gone. Read the book from cover to cover.

The book is important to you. I want you to do this for me. I'm finished and soon will be gone. Pay heed and you can take control. The room at the end of the hall.

Ezekiel D.

Hector crumpled up the letter and stuffed it in his jacket pocket. His waitress, a stocky woman in her fifties, came to the table with his bill. "Never saw a man with fake nails before," she said.

"I bite my fingernails. It's a nervous habit." People were always looking at his nails. They were too thick and a little too glossy. "My doctor told me these artificial nails would stop me from biting. They're as hard as rock."

She shrugged her big round shoulders. Hector noticed she was wearing heart-shaped earrings and a matching necklace, all far too delicate for her. "I wasn't accusing you of being funny," she said. She reached for his plate, practically thrusting her breasts in his face. She saw the book and picked it up instead. "You got one of Zeke's books. You kind of look like him—any relation?"

"He was my uncle. My name is Hector." The scarecrow had a girlfriend?

"I'm Myra. I'm awful sorry your uncle passed away. He used to come in all the time. We'd drive down for steaks in Springfield whenever we felt like having some real food." She studied the photograph on the back cover for a moment before handing the book back. "But then he got sick—all skinny and wrung-out. He'd throw a tantrum whenever I mentioned doctors."

Myra sat down next to him. The manager, leaning in a doorway across the room, looked annoyed but could hardly complain. There were no other customers.

"Now if I were you, Hector," she said, "I'd check to be sure none of your uncle's things are missing. I think he had someone in that house who was making trouble for him."

What did this mean—another girlfriend? Hector could hardly picture his uncle entertaining a harem. "I don't follow you. His lawyer never mentioned any companions."

"Lawyers don't know everything. I'd stop by every now and then to bring Zeke something to eat. We'd be talking in the front room and, sometimes, I'd hear someone else in back. Shuffling around. And typing! I always heard typing, no matter what time it was. I think there were dogs, too, because I could hear…" She thought for a moment. "Something running around. Claws clicking on the wood floor. No barking, though."

By now Hector was completely baffled. "So why would this person, this *typist,* make trouble for my uncle?"

"I'm not sure. It's just that if I ever brought it up, he refused to talk about it. He died not too long after that. I told all this to the sheriff, and he did say that things were a little weird out there. He found something… Was your uncle religious?"

"Not that I know of. Why?"

"Well, I didn't see it myself. The sheriff said one of the rooms was set up weird. I suppose you'll see when you go out there. You *are* going out to the house?"

Hector nodded. "I need to find out what kind of shape the place is in. I really don't know what I'm going to do with it."

Myra got up from the table. "If you want, I can stop by when I get off work. I'll even bring some pie if we've got any left." She gave him a wink and smiled. Hector hoped that she would drop in. She was too old for him, but she would be company.

Hector wasn't too worried about the noises the waitress had mentioned. His uncle probably had a secretary who was just as odd as her employer. She might have brought a dog with her now and then—one of the copywriters at the agency was always bringing in her old Persian cat. Hector was more worried about his uncle's mental state. In the bathroom of the cafe, he tore up the letter and flushed it down the toilet. It wouldn't do for anyone to know that Ezekiel's mind was going. Pierce might even make trouble.

After lunch, Hector's drive to the house led down a rustic stretch of road. The crickets here were practically ear-splitting. The sound was like nails on a blackboard, he thought: not all the nails at once, but one finger at a time, in an odd little rhythm. Ee-*ee* ee-ee-*ee* ee-ee-*ee*. Ee-*ee* ee-ee-*ee* ee-ee-*ee*.

Then it struck him. The sound was echoing a phrase out of Ezekiel's letter: the *room* at the *end* of the *hall.*

He tried to remember the gist of the letter. It had taken his uncle years to create something, and now it was complete—but the process had finished him. But what could it be? A collection of some sort? A new manuscript? The only thing he could recall word for word was that phrase. The *room* at the *end* of the *hall*.

At last Hector came to the "X" of the map. The Derhake house was an ugly grey structure, flanked with weeping willows. The ivy growing on the walls made it difficult to tell where the house ended and the trees began. The front door was open, swinging with the wind.

The house looked like a dead thing left to rot. Some day it would probably fall in on itself. He remembered from the letter that Pierce had called upon his uncle to check up on him. Was it actual worry on the lawyer's part, or did he know something about this *room* at the *end* of the *hall*? Hector didn't doubt it; something extraordinary was hidden there.

He took a flashlight from the car and walked up to the front door. From another part of the house he could hear—a typewriter? He called out as loud as he could, but no one answered. As he crossed the threshold the door slammed shut behind him, plunging him into darkness. Startled, he dropped the flashlight before he had a chance to turn it on. He could hear it roll across the room.

Thu-*thuk* thu-thu-*thuk* thu-thu-*thuk*.

Immediately Hector turned around, only to bump into a solid wall. He called out again, but the typewriter still chattered away without pausing. Couldn't whoever was typing hear him? He felt along the wall for the door. Where was it?

Arms stretched forward, he moved cautiously about the room. A table corner gouged his thigh; a strip of what felt like lace or cobweb brushed over his face. It was strange, but he found himself wishing he had Ezekiel's book. But the *book* was *outside* in the *car*.

An animal of some sort rubbed his ankle—a cat? It smelled horrible, like rotten meat. He reached down and flung it away. It was covered with short, stiff hair and a slime that reminded him of earthworms.

"I *want* to get *out* of this *house!*" Hector muttered. As he wiped his hands on his trousers, he came across a small square lump in his pocket: his matches.

Hector pulled out the matchbook and fumbled it open. He could feel three matches left. He tore one out and lit it. He scanned the floor but could not see the flashlight. In front of him was a large bookcase spotted with fungi. The shelves were filled with hundreds of typed manuscripts, crudely bound with wire. The ceiling above the bookcase was discolored and swollen. Either a pipe had once burst or the roof was desperately in need of repair. Some of the manuscripts had suffered water damage, and were crinkled from uneven drying.

The match burned down almost to his fingers and went out. Tearing a handful of pages from one of the manuscripts, he rolled them up tightly and lit them with his second match. The sound of the typewriter was louder now. Clack-*clack* clack-clack-*clack* clack-clack-*clack*.

Hector's paper torch was slightly damp, and its flame crackled fitfully. He glanced at the cover page of one of the manuscripts: it was entitled *The Room at the End of the Hall*. He looked at another, another, yet another. The titles were all the same.

Dozens of boxes were stacked throughout the room. The furniture seemed to be arranged in a sort of labyrinth. It was impossible to walk three feet forward in any one direction. He could not see the door; his light was so dim that the walls were lost in shadows. A few manuscripts were scattered across the floor. He noticed one that had fallen open— something about the arrangements of the words seemed strange. He knelt next to the manuscript and read part of a page:

> The end of the hall has a room. The room at the end of the hall. The hall has a room at the end. The room at

He turned the pages to another section.

> the hall has a room at the end the end of the hall has a room the room at the end of the hall the end of the hall has a room the room at the end of the hall the hall has a room at the end the room

Hector stopped—a door had slammed. He stood up and listened. Had someone called his name? Then there was another sound. Closer. Overhead.

Something thin and angular was crawling along the mouldering ceiling. It dropped down onto the bookcase with a dry rattle. Reaching down with a long groping arm, it drew out a manuscript, tore off the last page and flung it to the floor. It then sat and watched him with eyes like slivers of glass.

Hector picked up the torn page. There were no margins; the words filled the paper completely from side to side:

> THERE WAS NO ESCAPE FOR HIM NOW THE ROOM AT THE END OF THE HALL THE FOOLISH ONE SOON WOULD BE GONE THERE WAS NO ESCAPE NO ESCAPE THE ROOM AT THE END OF THE HALL THE FOOLISH ONE SOON WOULD BE DEAD NO ESCAPE

The sound of the typewriter stopped. Hector's torch flickered and died, leaving him in darkness.

From the depths of the house came shrill laughter. Hector cried out as papery wings flapped against his face. In his surprise, he dropped the page and his paper torch. The laughter grew louder and higher, echoing in eight shrill syllables.

He still had one match left; this time he would make a bigger torch. He would set the manuscripts, even the house on fire if he had to, so long as there was light. He groped around him—where did the bookcase go? He stumbled through the cramped furniture. Then his foot hit something soft. Was it that horrible animal again? No, whatever this was, it smelled like perfume. He reached down and felt—a face. Here was a mouth, a chin—a necklace? Yes, and a little metal heart.

The waitress had come by after all. But was she alive? He tried to feel for a heartbeat, but below the shoulders there was—nothing.

Screaming, Hector scrambled to his feet, backing away from what he had found. His cries seemed suddenly magnified, as if he had just entered a small room—or a narrow hall. A door clicked open behind him in the darkness. With another click, the door eased shut, this time in front of him.

Hector was in a different room now. It appeared to be some sort of chapel. Flickering candles were scattered about, on chairs and on the floor. The walls were covered with sheets of black cloth. In the center of the room stood a tall platform: a pulpit, carved of dark wood. Beyond the pulpit was darkness.

But was it a pulpit? Normal pulpits were not crisscrossed with hundreds of deep gashes, like claw marks. He walked closer. There was something on top of the platform. A typewriter, surrounded by stacks of manuscripts.

He sat down in a chair and waited. His parents had never taken him to church as a child. On those few occasions he had accompanied his college friends to Mass, the experience had left him unmoved. Now as he sat before the dark pulpit, he surely felt—what? Something new to him. He began to chew and grind on his artificial nails. When the darkness of the room behind the pulpit began to solidify, to condense, he felt that he was indeed in the church of his own heart. And not alone.

Tall, lean, bestial, the shadow stepped down from the pulpit. An entourage of creatures followed, all small and twisted, some leaving tracks of blood. Their claws clicked against the hardwood floor. The shadow held a book in its hooked, gnarled fingers—a copy of *Mind, Matter and Life: Legends of the Aquastor*.

The shadow grinned, revealing fangs like those of a deep-sea carnivore. It read from the book in a shrill voice, vastly amused. "Thought brought to life. What would it look like? How would it act? What limitations would nature impose upon it?"

Something spidery, with a jumbled multitude of limbs, parted from the swarm. It leaped onto the pulpit and began to type in a cadence now quite familiar to Hector.

The shadow turned to the center of the book and read on. "The creation of the jinni was a lengthy, grueling ritual. In bringing the creature into existence, the sorcerer would concentrate upon a singular rhythm: the mantric pulse of the jinni. The sorcerer could very well perish, for his soul served as nourishment for the gestation of the beast. Although the stakes were high, the rewards were immeasurably great; the jinni could grant boons transcending the very limits of reality. But first, it was necessary to take control of the jinni by..."

Here the shadow tore a page to shreds.

So. Uncle Ezekiel was a sorcerer, and this being was his final creation. A thought occurred to Hector: in some mad sense, the creature was his kin.

"Bound within bottles?" The shadow cried mockingly. "Yes and no. A jinni is a contained explosion of mental energy, needing a vessel, a receptacle, to keep it from slowly dissipating to nothingness. But some of these creatures were far too powerful for mere bottles..."

The jinni flung the book to the floor. The spidery demon at the pulpit typed out the pulse of its master, louder, faster. Hector's eyes swept to where the door should have been, only to find a blank wall.

The jinni continued to speak as it lunged for Hector's throat. It knew the book from memory.

"Some filled rooms."

YOU SHALL HAVE THIS DELICACY

From *The Fine Art of Living*, the unpublished autobiography of Erika Finlay Pennywhistle Nelstrom Wong Vultaine:

It's hard to believe I was ever a baby. I'd like to think I simply popped full-grown out of my father's forehead, like Athena, but birth is never that tidy. And of course, if I had gone the Athena route, I could have avoided my mother entirely.

Father was a warm, albeit nondescript teddy-bear of a man. Mother was loud, needy, and a terrible drinker. No, wait—technically, she was very good at drinking. But it made her a terrible person.

I learned about addiction from her. She was addicted to booze, a variety of drugs, and stupid men. Losing her looks was the best thing that ever happened to her. I've fallen in and out of addiction many times. You know how it goes: you discover a new thrill, so you try it every now and then. Before you know it, you are starting and ending the day with it, until it sickens you. At one point, I was addicted to dried Peruvian spiders—I would chew them, make coffee out of them, and spend the whole day in a silken spider-buzz. My fifth husband Osbo helped me through that whole mess. Osbo, what a wonderful man. The very mention of his name brings back such delicious memories.

Whereas mother was not a picky person, I have made it my life's work to be as discerning as hell. I'm a survivor, and survivors should be rewarded. If others won't reward me, well then, I'll just pamper myself. So I have allowed myself one special addiction: the need to be surrounded by luxury. Exquisite jewelry. Fabulous outfits by genius designers. Exotic taste treats from strange lands. Rare books. And of course, the ultimate luxury: magic.

There will come a day when I will have to give up the clothes and the jewels, but the magic will always be a part of me. My last two husbands—one of whom was dear Osbo—were leading experts in that particular discipline. Since it is a secret discipline, they had to live in the shadows.

But they lived well.

* * * *

Mrs. Vultaine had invited six to dinner; invited them with crisp black cards, the message embossed in gold leaf. Each guest had been instructed to bring one companion. Thirteen at table did not fret the hostess: this was a woman who had survived strange diseases, stranger travels, and far too many years of perilous existence. Thirteen? Pshaw. Just another number.

The widow walked tall through the dining room, observing, correcting, at times praising her servants during preparations for the evening. She wore black silk pants and a matching blouse with the shoulders cut out. She knew this was a very young fashion, but no matter. She had a beautiful face, regally angular and as pale as milk; long, silver hair; even, white teeth; and soft, fine-boned hands, anointed with expensive creams. And she still had smooth, lovely shoulders: this the world had a right to know, and she refused to hide them.

A sad-eyed maid with delicate features poured nuts into a crystal dish.

"Just a moment, my dear," Mrs. Vultaine said, her voice an imperious warble. Her right hand fluttered at eye level, punctuating, emphasizing. "Cashews? Oh, no, no, no. Certainly my guests would not care for cashews."

"We're out of morroka seeds," the maid whispered. "I found these in the servants' pantry. They're very good. And they look the same."

"And you look like a melancholy puppy. Does that mean I feed you scraps and make you do your business outside?" The widow rolled her eyes and sighed. "If you like them so much, take them to your room. And set out praku berries for my guests. I know we have buckets of them somewhere."

The maid picked up the dish and walked a few paces. Then she stopped and turned around. "Please don't fire me. I know I'm common. But I can't help it."

Mrs. Vultaine stepped forward and placed a cool hand on the girl's cheek. "Your tastes are common. But you…you, Vexina…are not common." She ran her fingers lightly over the servant's coiffure—a pinned bundle of thick auburn hair. "I would never surround myself with common sorts. Now off with you, puppy. There's work to be done."

The maid flashed a nervous smile and hurried off.

The widow turned her attention to the table settings. Five forks, five spoons, three knives per plate—and such plates. Plates of glass, gold, silver and polished bone: no two were alike. Green lizard-fat candles. Napkins with a pattern—goats, moths and daggers—matching that of the tapestries on the walls.

She entered the great hall to make sure the display was in order. The curious objet, or perhaps objets, d'art would amuse and surely disconcert her guests. This pile of gleaming metal appeared to be composed of parts from a disassembled golden harpy. A wing and a ribcage topped the pile; around the edges, one could detect a spine, a hip, and some extravagant clockwork organs.

She went into the library and strolled down a long row of books. How she loved books; they were her sturdy, silent friends, always willing to share. Many of these were first editions, signed by the authors. Here was an especially rare one—*Listen to the Weeping Dead*, a book of poetry by Augustus Fygg, the cannibal. And here—*The Hidden Power of Maps*, by Benson Phelps. How ironic that he died while lost on safari. There was only one cookbook in the library: *A Pinch of This, A Smidgen of That* by Jacob Nelstrom, her third husband. And then there was the privately published *Worlds of Splendour: The History of the Family Vultaine*, by her last and most beloved husband, Osbo. His love had made her the happiest woman alive. Would she ever be that happy again? Perhaps, perhaps. She was not one to rule out any possibility.

Mrs. Vultaine settled in the lace-draped corner of an overstuffed couch by the fireplace. On a small table by her side rested a stack of small boxes, a roll of black wrapping paper, tape and scissors. She picked up a box and smiled as she shook it by her ear.

That tiny squealing was absolutely precious.

2.

From *The Fine Art of Living*:

I did a lot of traveling back when I was an adventurous single girl, and one of my boyfriends was a spy named Nicos. We never talked about marriage, but we became very close. Nicos sold secrets to the highest bidder, regardless of the consequences. I helped him on a few of his assignments, just for the thrill of it. But it was a dangerous game, even by my extremely liberal standards. He was found disemboweled in the backroom of a French bakery. I later found the microfilm in a croissant.

I learned a lot from him, and my efforts eventually turned from espionage to politics. I met and trysted with many powerful men, most of whom were married—and I kept records. A tiny camera was hidden in my loofah sponge.

Ah, when it comes to romance, men of power are merely puppets. They can be weak, foolish. I went through a rather long phase where I delighted in pulling their strings. I wasn't even using magic.

These facts help explain why I do not pay taxes…why I do not need a passport to travel the world…why there are no public records of my marriages, or even of my birth. I am a woman of countless secrets. Even the address of my luxurious home is a secret. That particular secret was devised and maintained by the Vultaine's. His family created a sort of visual labyrinth around the house—quite an achievement, when you consider that the building is bigger than most cathedrals.

Of course, my friends all know how to find the House. Most also know how to keep quiet. Friends who become too loud…well, they learn to quiet down soon enough.

I do want to stress that I don't use magic every day. Months can go by without my even thinking about using it. I can be resourceful in my own right. I like solving problems and figuring out why people do the strange but interesting things they do.

Of course, magic doesn't give a person permission to do absolutely anything. There are limits. Magic is nothing more than a reality booster. I can't tap an evil person on the shoulder and say, "You are now good." I can't just point up and say, "Let all the money in the world rain down upon me." No, no, no. I must first find a way, set the wheels in motion, turn up the dial on the old booster—so to speak!—and then hope for the best. Nothing is absolutely certain for *anyone*.

* * * *

The guests—all pale, darkhaired chainsmokers—arrived on foot. They all had to leave their cars parked a mile away, inside an abandoned warehouse. Each guest received a glass of reddish-gold champagne upon entering the basalt immensity of the House of Vultaine. They mingled, laughing and gossiping, in the great hall. Overhead, a full moon shone through an enormous skylight. The window had been levered open to let in the night air.

Vexina refreshed the plates of praku berries while her sister, Osmette, hefted a large platter of hors d'oeuvres. Osmette was a thick-waisted cherub with small dark teeth. She had no idea what sort of delicacies she carried, and had no desire to taste them.

All eyes turned to the grand staircase as Mrs. Vultaine made her entrance. She still wore the silk blouse and pants, and her hair was piled high into a shining nimbus, with wispy tendrils snaking down along her slender neck.

She circulated among her guests, listening to speculation regarding the golden display. "My dear Silhouetta," she said to a sliver of a girl with limp black hair and nervous eyes. "So good to see you. Hope you've brought an appetite. You *are* eating these days…?" For six years, this wee girl had lived off of various ointments smeared onto her skin.

Silhouetta snatched a brandied trilobite from a tray. "Afraid so. I found out the hard way that intestines, like muscles, need their exercise."

The widow spotted a tanned man with a white streak in his reddish-brown ponytail, and tapped him on the arm. He smiled enormously as he embraced her.

"It's been years, Erika," he whispered into the pale shell of her ear. "Can't we just send all these awful people home?"

"Tinder, you are incorrigible," she whispered back. "Imagine, flirting with a woman who will soon be gone."

Tinder gazed into her eyes, shocked. "What are you saying?"

She shrugged. "Nothing less than the truth." She put a finger under his chin and shut his gaping mouth. "Now come to dinner."

The silver-haired woman walked to the table, arms outstretched, beckoning with her fingers. The others followed instantly—even those whose backs had been turned to her.

Mrs. Vultaine took her place at the head of the long table. Once the guests were seated, the servants brought out, per instructions, baskets of black bread and small bowls of grasshopper bisque. They filled the wine glasses with a vintage as clear as water.

For a few minutes, the widow watched her guests dip chunks of bread into their soup.

Silhouetta nodded toward the widow's glass. "Look, she hasn't touched her wine." A reedy giggle fluttered from her lips. "Maybe she has brought us all here to poison us."

The old woman sighed. "I never hold a dinner party without an occasion. But mass murder is not on tonight's agenda. I haven't touched my wine because alcohol no longer thrills me." She smiled alarmingly. "I have gathered you all here to say goodbye. Soon I will be gone. I will be done with this world, and this evening, I shall share my arrangements with you."

3.

From *The Fine Art of Living*:

I remember something very unusual, and absolutely *pivotal*, that happened to me during my childhood. We were living on a outskirts of a small town, near a wooded area. My parents had gone off on some errand, and had left me alone. Back then, parents weren't worried about things like "bad strangers." And it was the afternoon: bad stuff only happened at night in those days. At any rate, what happened to me wasn't bad. It was meant to happen. Some men—or rather, manlike beings—came up to me while I was playing in the backyard.

Based on what I have learned over the years, I now think they had once been human, but years and years of magical living had made them quite different. They told me that they could tell I was a very special young lady. I was flattered by this, but also a little scared. I saw one of them had a lump moving around under his skin, and I remember saying, "Oh, are you sick?"

"Oh, no. We each have one. See? We gave them to each other." And so I sat in the backyard, looking at the busy lumps as they moved around their arms and across their chests.

They seemed very happy with their lumps. They then told me exactly what the lumps do. The explanation would be too hard to convey in words—their expressions told most of the story—but the entire experience can be summed up by saying: some gifts are more special than others.

* * * *

As Mrs. Vultaine enjoyed her bisque (with a spoon: no dipping and dripping for her), she noticed many of her guests casting small glances about the room, taking in the paintings, the statuettes on the side tables, even the chandelier of pale rose crystals and rubies. She didn't mind.

"I have one possession," she stated, "that is exceedingly dear to me…one that should be bequeathed to a special someone. If any one of you can prove you are that someone, why then, you may have it."

"I cannot believe what I am hearing," Tinder said.

"Incredulity is the calling card of the simple-minded. Or so some say." Mrs. Vultaine finished her last spoonful of creamy bisque, then deftly pointed a pinky toward her empty bowl. The servants cleared away the soup course. They began to bring out salads made from seven-pointed leaves and strands of pink seaweed.

A young man with a round face and shaggy eyebrows turned in his seat toward Tinder. "Are we to assume you are more worthy of Erika's affection than the rest of us?"

Tinder flashed his large-toothed smile. "Erika and I know each other quite well, Moyan. You wouldn't understand."

The young man returned his smile. "Oh, but I would."

With a cry of outrage, Tinder grabbed a knife and sprang across the table, upsetting wine glasses and toppling salads. Moyan yawned, pulled a small pistol from a jacket pocket, and shot the toothy man in the left eye.

At the widow's sign, the servants cleared away the doomed salad, carted off the body, and presented petite servings of flavored ices.

"After that unpleasantness," Mrs. Vultaine said, "we must cleanse our palates."

More courses were served after that, and the guests took pains to compliment her at length on the selections. She simply nodded and observed.

At one point, Osmette brought out a tray piled high with boxes wrapped in black. Vexina helped by setting one box in front of each guest. Many packages remained.

"My servants also may take one each," the old woman said. The maids and butlers moved quietly but eagerly to claim their gifts.

"Now, unwrap! Unwrap!" Mrs. Vultaine clapped her hands like a delighted schoolgirl.

Shreds of black paper sailed through the air. Box lids flew open. A few gasps were heard, then many screams.

The widow continued to clap. She giggled as thumb-sized larvae with human faces and crablike pincers sprang forth to burrow into their recipients. The faces of these tiny creatures resembled that of Mrs. Vultaine in all but one detail: the silver-haired woman did not have the ringed, razor-fanged mouth of a lamprey.

Chairs fell backwards and bodies toppled. Before Silhouetta slumped to the floor, she forced a wretched smile and cried "Thank you" to her hostess.

"You're welcome," the widow said. She then tiptoed past the writhing bodies and out of the dining room.

4.

From *The Fine Art of Living*:

It makes me sad, whenever I meet some poor young woman who feels she will never be able to catch a man.

Men! Men are notoriously indiscriminate. Given the right set of circumstances, men will link up with—you name it. Produce, household appliances… There are men who are desperately in love with hot water bottles. Marsupials. Cacti.

Catching a man is about as hard as catching a cold. Let us look at how I caught some of my hubands:

Mr. Finlay: At this time of my life, I was still a little too much like my mother—too needy, too man-hungry. I used sex to snare this one. I basically just tossed myself at him. We had a few good years, but then I started concentrating on magic and we grew apart. I still feel sad about—and yes, somewhat responsible for—the way he died. We'd had an argument, so I told him to go to Hell. I may have been using a little magic without realizing. And, he may have had a buried self-destructive streak, which I'd inadvertently unearthed. The next thing I knew, I looked out the bedroom window and saw he was pouring gasoline all over himself in the backyard. I shouted for him to stop, but that only caught the attention of our nosy next-door neighbor, who came over to see what was wrong. And she was a smoker.

Mr. Pennywhistle: He was very handsome and very rich. I captured him with elegance and attitude. He was also very work-oriented, and spent a great deal of time at the office. We had servants, so I was able to concentrate on my own interests, and of course magic. He had no idea: he was wrapped up in meetings and reports and mergers and cocktail parties. I was his beautiful trophy wife, and he never knew that his trophy could work wonders. He had a terrible heart attack, and as he sat by his hospital window (he refused to stay in bed) dying, I told him everything about myself. He said, "Darling, don't be silly," and then he was gone. So I brought him back and kept him alive for a few seconds, just to show him a thing or two. That took some effort, but it was worth it.

Mr. Nelstrom: He was a very serious fellow. He was a chef, and he taught me a great deal about the art of food preparation. One begins with the finest ingredients, and then works from there. Timing is also incredibly important. That flavor peak won't last forever! But as the years passed, my Mr. Nelstrom began to miss a few dinners, and my eyes and ears in the community told me he was seeing a crude young thing with an enormous bosom and tiny brain. Can you imagine how that made me feel? My dining room gourmet was a bedroom gourmand. Unthinkable. So I told him in a very stern voice to go away. But, there was a problem much like the episode with Mr. Finlay. He walked away—and never *stopped* walking. Again, I must have tapped into some sad inner defect of his. Eventually I divorced him. I caught up with him on a road in Italy—he was just a scrawny thing, walking, always walking—and trotted by his side, holding the papers as he signed them.

Those were my first three husbands, and I will admit, I had a small advantage since I am a person of magic. But really, every person—every living creature—has some degree of magic. They just have to learn to find it. To embrace it. And of course, to *use* it.

* * * *

Four hours later, Mrs. Vultaine came back into the dining room. She smoked a clove cigarette as she waited for her party to resume consciousness. When at last the guests returned to their chairs, she instructed five of her groggy servants to fetch the main course.

"I had to prepare the entree myself," she said, "and I don't mind saying, it took a bit of doing."

Vexina leaned against a sideboard. She put a shaking hand to a raw, bloody hole below her collarbone. "What have you done to us?"

"Oh, that," the old woman said. "A little something to remember me by."

The maid pressed a finger tentatively against the wound. "Oh! I think it has healed up already." She took a deep breath and said to her employer, "I'm frightened."

The widow laughed. "Fright is simply a symptom of ignorance. Note that I am not calling you 'stupid.' Rather, I am bringing to your attention the fact that there is much you do not know. You are young and inexperienced. You must learn to trust. Certainly you can trust me. I have no reason to destroy you. I am too jaded to do it for amusement! Therefore, if I do anything *to* or *for* you, it will probably help you. Do you see?"

Vexina nodded slowly. "Yes, I think I do. I'm still scared, though." Her eyebrows raised a little. "But please, don't worry about me. The fear will go away eventually."

Mrs. Vultaine smiled warmly. "You are trying. Genuinely trying. I like that." She then addressed her guests. "Next is the main course. The specialty of the house! After that, you may all take whatever of my gewgaws and trinkets you like. Load them in your cars. Call for trucks. Fight over them if you must."

"I must say, this is all very…" Silhouetta searched for a word. "… impromptu!"

"For all of you, yes. But I have been planning this evening for quite some time," the widow said. "I suppose I do have a weakness for springing surprises on others. And why not? I've had enough sprung on me over the years, and they've all made me a better person. And speaking of surprises: there is an utterly enormous safe in the basement. You will find the combination etched onto the handles of the dessert forks. For my treasure, dear ones, is your dessert. But first…"

She clapped her hands lightly, and the servants brought out several covered trays, which they set at intervals on the tables.

"Bon appetit," whispered Mrs. Vultaine.

The servants raised the tray lids, revealing large, steaming chunks of roasted meat. Vexina and Osmette began slicing at the savory mounds with curved knives.

"As for my most cherished possession…" The widow studied her guests. "I still don't know who should have it."

5.

From *The Fine Art of Living*:

So how did I catch my last two husbands—the magical ones?

Mr. Wong: A very handsome, exotic man—half Chinese, one-fourth French, and the last fourth…! His grandmother on his mother's side was a circus reptile woman. He had wonderfully sculpted features, and a slight greenish cast to his skin. He was always hungry, so I captured him by making him wonderful things to eat. I will admit, most of the recipes were Mr. Nelstrom's. Mr. Wong preferred raw meat, so I had to make a few adjustments.

Mr. Wong showed me how to make animals understand human words, and also, he taught me to slow-dance. That second skill isn't really magical, but no one had ever shown me how to do that before. It was fun. Sexy. It made me feel young.

But in time, I tired of Mr. Wong. He became more reptilian with the years. He grew bigger—not fatter, just proportionally larger. He was still good-looking, but huge, and cold to the touch. Eventually, all he wanted to do was eat and bask. So we separated. I hear he now has a tail.

Mr. Vultaine: Ah yes, Osbo! He was the only one who ever caught *me*! I met Osbo Vultaine at a film festival. He saw I was a woman of power and he simply had to have me. He was a fantastic man, and very handsome and virile for a fellow of three-hundred. When he showed up at my door with the Book of Thoth, I knew that he was the one for me. We traveled to lands which most people think are mythical, and met people who had no business being alive. Did you know there is a valley in Canada where everyone has yellow eyes, and a plateau in Argentina where the women have four breasts? They say technology is making the world smaller—don't you believe it! It's still big enough to have plenty of hidey-holes. Osbo and I had many exhilarating adventures. But best of all, we could talk, share concerns, figure things out—and laugh! We had seventeen marvelous years together. And then the Night-Birds came and carried him away.

I tell people I'm a widow, but I'm still not sure. Someday, I will go to where the Night-Birds roost and see what I can discover. The thing is, that's not the sort of place from which one can return. But for Osbo Vultaine, I would do anything. Even the impossible.

* * * *

A murmur arose among the guests. Suddenly Moyan stood up. "I have killed to prove my love for you! Your cherished possession should be mine."

Silhouetta cleared her throat. "What about me? At least I say 'thank you' when I receive a gift."

Other guests voiced their reasons, their desires, their concerns. The widow simply nodded. So much greed. So many social climbers. But still, she had to pick one, and soon.

"Maybe I…" murmured a small voice.

Mrs. Vultaine looked about the room. It took her a moment to realize it was Vexina who had spoken. "You? Tell me more, puppy."

The sad-eyed servant slid a slice of meat onto the nearest plate. "I've worked so hard for you. Even though you scare me to death."

"True." The widow rose from her chair. "You are a survivor, and survivors should be rewarded."

Slender metallic wings ripped through the back of Mrs. Vultaine's silk blouse. She tore away her clothes, slowly, delighting in the sharp *rrrrrrip* of the fabric. She stood naked before her guests, revealing golden arms and legs, golden breasts and hips. The display from the grand hall was now her body, new and improved. Of her own flesh, only her head, shoulders and hands remained.

She picked up a rounded lump of meat from a tray and offered it to Vexina. "Take it, my dear. Take my heart."

As always, the servant did as she was told.

Mrs. Vultaine stared into her servant's eyes. "A trite gift, but the right gift. You are a sad, sickly creature. You shall have this delicacy and it shall nourish you." She brought her lips close to the servant's ear. "There is a manuscript in my nightstand drawer. It contains all the dreams and secrets of my life. Read it, learn from it, and then burn it."

She then spun round to face the table. "As for the rest of you…my useless old body is yours." She gestured toward the meat. "You must forgive me for foisting that little nap upon you earlier, but in meal preparation, timing is everything. Try the roast and I think you will agree: one cannot accuse me of being tasteless."

The widow's metal wings flapped slowly, once, twice. Then they began to beat in earnest, speeding to a golden blur. Protective golden sheaths slid over the hands, and shields rose up from her back, covering the shoulders.

"I'm coming, Osbo," she said.

More curved shields sprang up, sliding together as a sleek helmet around her head.

Erika Finlay Pennywhistle Nelstrom Wong Vultaine soared out of the dining room, into the great hall, and up through the open skylight.

Vexina sat on the floor, chomping on her gift as though it were an apple. But yes, oh yes, it was sweeter by far. She removed the pins from her coiffure, shook out her long, lustrous hair and laughed and laughed and laughed.

THE SLIMY ONES

Michael Jarvis blinked his eyes once, twice, then opened them wide and rolled them around in their sockets. His new contacts were killing him—but anything was better than wearing those horrible glasses. The lenses were so thick they made him look all fishy-eyed.

His mother would be pleased that he was wearing contacts. She had always hated his glasses. "I bet they cut those lenses off the bottoms of pop bottles. You look like Aunt Edna with her big googly glasses. How are you ever going to get married? What kind of woman would want a guy with big googly glasses? I just want you to be happy." She used to say that all the time, and it was true. She wanted him to be happy. Unfortunately, he'd never found the right young lady to help bring about that happiness.

He'd been lonely after his mother passed away, if you can call getting hit by a bus "passing away." She'd been such a caring woman—and very frank, too, always one to speak her mind. Well, he now had his investigations to help him not feel so lonely. And he still had the family house.

People had told him to sell it, saying a single man didn't need such a big place. But he couldn't do a thing like that: the new owners might not take care of it. He kept it looking nice, every little thing in place, just the way Mother would have wanted.

Eventually his eyes felt better. He looked at the clock—time to turn on the radio. Soon, it would time to call-in.

Thank God for talk radio. The George Flicker Show was the perfect forum for talking to the River City, letting the people know about The Slimy Ones. He realized that people thought he was being a pest, a crackpot, but he didn't care. The people—the world—had to know.

After the show's opening music, George went into his usual spiel about every little thing that was ticking him off these days. Then it was call-in time.

Michael already had the first six numbers dialed—he still used Mother's old landline. He hit the last number.

A moment later, he was on the air.

"Hey, it's our old friend Fishboy," George said. "How ya doin', Fishboy?"

"Please don't call me that. My name is Michael. I have some more information for your listeners, George. About the Slimy Ones."

"Ah, yes. The Slimy Ones." A note of amusement crept into George's voice. "A little background information for our first-time listeners. Our friend Fishboy—Michael, I mean—has been collecting information on a race of giant catfish people living at the bottom of the Mississippi. He has described some photos he has on file: slimy handprints on the sides of the riverboat casinos, and some webbed footprints around the Prescott Bridge area. What else, Michael?"

"Well, let's see..." Michael thought for a moment. "I've mentioned that the Slimy Ones have been in touch with alien visitors, whose ships have left crop-circles in certain fields in the area. The visits of these aliens coincide with the Mississippi's highest flood levels. I've also told you about the time I glimpsed one of the Slimy Ones skulking outside the River City Public Library—and now, I think I know why. Tonight I will tell you why a horrible catfish humanoid wanted to get into the library."

"They've got DVDs there. Maybe he wanted to check out *Jaws*," George said as the movie's theme music blared forth: *da-dum, da-dum, da-dum, da-dum!*

Michael bit his thick lower lip. George must have prepared that sound-bite in advance for the next update on the catfish people. Michael didn't like being set up—but still, he had to let the world know about the menace lurking and growing in the muddy depths of the Mississippi.

"Lately, I've been doing some research on some of the families that founded River City." Michael shuffled through his notes—photocopies of old documents and pages from diaries. "There was a family back then called the Thraggs. Hecuba Thragg and her daughters, Rose and Lavinia, came to this country from England because they were on the run from the authorities."

"Hey, now wait a minute," George said. "There are some Thraggs on my mother's side of the family. You won't be pulling old George's leg now, would you?"

Michael's eyes itched, and he started blinking again. "Certainly not. I didn't know that about you. I'm part Thragg, too. That's why I have some of these old diaries. When my mother died, I started looking through all her old boxes in the attic, and there they were. I think she got them when my grandmother died. So you're part Thragg? We must be related."

"Great. I'm related to Fishboy. I mean *Michael*. So tell me more about these three Thragg babes."

"Well, they were wanted for witchcraft. They worshipped the ancient sea-god Dagon. So when they came to this country, they eventually settled in River City and—picked up where they left off."

"But River City's nowhere near any ocean. Did their sea-god swim upstream to meet them?"

"He didn't have to. He holds power over catfish and all bottom-feeding creatures. They are his evil spawn."

"Yeah, evil—and pretty darned tasty. Have you ever been to Mississippi Mama's Catfish House? I hear they put shredded ginger on—"

"As I was saying," Michael continued, undaunted. "The Thraggs started a coven of Dagon worshippers here in River City, and during the river's flood stages, they would walk into the water to commune with the catfish. It's all here in the diaries. And after a while, some of the worshippers began to take on the physical characteristics of their river brethren."

"Those are the catfish people. Right?" George played that snip of movie music again.

"Right. Their lifespan is now measured by centuries. They hope to eventually rule the land dwellers—but in order to do that, they will need The Book of Old Wisdoms, which used to belong to Letitia Thragg. That copy—the only one in the world—is under lock and key at the River City Public Library. And they don't even know it."

"Wait a minute...." George actually sounded interested now. "How can they have a book locked up there and not even know it?"

"Because it's a very small book—no bigger than the palm of a child's hand and as thick as a pencil. There are less than one hundred pages. Letitia hid the book inside the thick leather binding of a much larger book—but I don't know which one. All I know is that the larger book had been donated to the library, along with a lot of other old volumes."

"And what would happen if these catfish people ever got their webbed hands on this book?"

"Ultimately, they'd be able to change our world into the perfect environment for themselves and their alien friends. Unfortunately, that sort of swampy hellhole wouldn't make much of a home for humanity. We'd all be reduced to slaves or livestock."

"So what do these aliens look like, anyway?" George asked.

"They can look like who- or whatever they want, so long as it helps them to meet their purpose. In old times, they used to take on the appearance of Indians to fool people of European descent. And vice versa. They always appeared as a stranger to whoever they met, in case their 'disguise' was a bit off."

"There you have it, River City. We're all doomed to be eaten by the very catfish we so love to charbroil. We'll be back after this commercial break. Michael, please stay on the line, we'll take up where we left off."

On Michael's radio, a snappy commercial jingle for a muffler shop started up.

"Ya still there?" George said on the phone.

"Sure I am." There was a moment of awkward silence. Michael looked over at a small table covered with little figurines that his mother had bought, years ago. Fragile little statues of barefoot farmboys and freckle-faced girls with pigtails. He smiled. "You probably think I'm a big nutball, huh?"

"Oh, I don't know." George said. "I've seen some weird stuff myself. And when you think about it, we live on a pretty weird planet. I mean, take TV for example. We've all got little boxes that show what's going on all over the world. Cavemen would have thought that was pretty freaky."

"Yeah, I suppose you're right."

Suddenly there was a loud rattling, crunching sound—it seemed to come from the back porch. Michael couldn't help but think, that side of his house faced the river. "I've got to get off the line, George. Something's going on outside."

"Like what?"

"It's probably just a dog or something—but I've really got to check it out."

"Oh...okay." Was there actual concern in George's voice? "Well, call back as soon as you find out what it is, okay?"

"Will do, George." He hung up and looked around for something to use as a weapon. He wanted to call the police, but he was always calling them for information on his various investigations, and they never seemed to take him seriously. They sure weren't going to break their butts to rush and help him.

In his odds-and-ends drawer he found his dad's big old fishing knife. He grabbed it and moved down the hall toward the porch, listening. Somebody was moving around on the back porch—the screen door had been locked, so whoever it was must have broken through it.

Usually, the back porch light was always on, since there were several large, shady trees lining that side of the house, and it was always dark back there. But now, no light shone through the curtains of the window looking out onto the porch. But he could see a larger shadow that seemed to shift uneasily through the darkness. The rest of the view was obscured by a thick, swirling fog.

"Who's out there?" Michael called out.

The shadow moved directly in front of the darkened window. It was shaped roughly like a huge person with some sort of shaggy mane around the head. A surge of bile rose up in his throat. His stomach always acted up whenever he was worried. Or nervous. Or scared out of his mind.

"You should not…" A thick voice, full of phlegm, murmured. At least, Michael supposed it was phlegm.

"What shouldn't I do?" Michael called out, moving a little closer. There was a hammer on the table by the couch. He'd been fixing a bookshelf in that room earlier that day. He didn't want to get too close to the window, but the hammer would make a good weapon, if needed.

"No more talk. Why are you saying these things? You are one of us." The voice had an odd, halting accent to it—either that, or the speaker just wasn't used to speaking. "You are a Thragg. Forever."

As Michael's hand closed around the handle of the hammer, something dawned on him.

A picture. I should get a picture. It would be proof.

But where was the camera—? Then he remembered. It was outside, in the glove compartment of his car, along with his mother's old tape recorder. He'd taken them to a UFO symposium in Peoria the week before, and had forgotten to bring them back in the house.

A ripe, fishy odor seeped into the house. It was so strong that Michael soon began to feel nauseous.

"You must be quiet," the shadow murmured. "Do not destroy all we have worked for. In time you will join us in the water. In the mud and decay and darkness. You are a Thragg, and you cannot escape your destiny. You cannot escape … this."

Something hit the window with a wet smack. A hand had emerged from the fog and was now pressed against the glass: a wide hand with long, clawed fingers and veined, scaly webbing.

"This shall be you," the voice chortled, bubbling with slime.

Michael blinked repeatedly. Yes, his own fingers were very long, but he'd never given it much thought. After all, his mother's fingers were long, and so were his grandmother's on that side of the family…the side that traced back to…the Thraggs.…

"We have friends who have been telling us about your…" The voice paused. "…your treachery. We do not like what you have been saying. But there is still time for you to undo your foolishness. Then the way will be cleared for both of you, and we will embrace you when at last you are ready."

"Both? Who else are you talking about?"

"The other Thragg…the one who speaks to everyone.…"

"George Flicker?"

The being on the other side of the window pulled away its hand and chuckled. "Yes. He is older than you, he will be joining us soon. How surprised he will be when his gills open up and his fingerwebs begin to grow ... when his skin grows cold and slick...."

The creature then pressed, for just a moment, its face against the glass. Or rather, it pressed one side of its face; perhaps to get a better look at Michael. And he was shocked by the fact that the face was—

Beautiful.

Yes, it was unmistakably the face of a beautiful woman, with sculpted cheekbones, a well-shaped patrician nose, an imperious forehead and full, pouting lips. True, the sky-blue eye that ogled against the glass was huge and watery, and thin fleshy whiskers dangled from the top lip, but still, there was no denying that this was a face of ancient, unspeakable beauty.

"Who are you?" Michael said. Then he remembered a name. "Are you Hecuba Thragg?"

The voice bubbled with laughter. "Mother is much too huge to leave the river's depths. No, I am Lavinia." The hand slapped against the glass once more. "You can still undo the damage you have brought about. You must call that program again and tell the people that you were..." The hand half-rubbed, half-clawed at the glass. "...joking. Tell them it was all a sort of amusement."

Michael shook his head. "Never!"

"Simple-minded dolt!" the creature bellowed. "It would be easy... so very easy...for us to kill you and then ask one of our friends...the creatures from the stars...to take on your voice and appearance and tell everyone it was all a game. But we are giving you a chance to redeem yourself. Go to the phone. Do it. Do it now."

Michael raised the hammer, preparing to give it a good strong throw, right through the window. But then that beautiful sky-blue eye pressed up to the window again. The full lips parted and a low, rhythmic murmur— a timeless and compelling song—poured forth from that slime-coated throat.

Michael stood completely still, listening, transfixed. One single, all-encompassing thought oozed through his brain:

Obey ... obey ... obey...

He turned and moved back down the hall.

Obey ... obey...

Behind him, he heard the sharp crash of breaking wood, but he did not turn around to see what had happened. He already knew. The thing on the porch had burst through the porch door, singing with triumph.

Obey ... obey...

When he reached the phone, the hammer and knife dropped from his hands. He found himself picking up the phone receiver and punching in numbers. He did not want to … but he had no choice. He had to *obey* … *obey*…

He was about to punch in the seventh number when he paused. Someone was now by his side. He looked up at the grotesque creature standing next to him.

The beautiful, unearthly face was surrounded by a tangled mass of thick, writhing tentacles. The body was thick and powerfully muscled, with a slick, leathery tail that whipped around savagely. The lashing tail upset a small table, sending figurines crashed to the floor.

Michael gasped and slammed the phone receiver down. "Look what you did! Those were *Mother's!*" He stared at the beast and realized, with a sudden rush of exhilaration, that the hypnotic spell had been broken.

Lavinia Thragg stopped singing and let loose with a piglike squeal of rage.

His hand swept down, snatched up the hammer and swept back up, as high as he could reach. He then brought it down with all his force, right on top of the creature's head.

Lavinia collapsed to the floor, writhing in pain. After a moment, she stopped moving.

Michael suddenly realized that the radio was still on. And of course, George was still talking. The guy never shut up.

"Well, we still haven't heard back from Michael," George said. "Call in, dude. Please. I promise I won't call you Fishboy. I just want to know if you're okay out there."

Yes, it was time to call in. Michael took a deep breath—and then vomited. The fishlike reek of the dead creature was overpowering. It looked even slimier in death than it had in life. In fact, it seemed to be turning—liquescent. Greenish-yellow rivulets of rank liquid flowed down the oversized carcass.

Soon the floor was awash with stinking, oily fluid. The body was quickly turning into a pool of rot. He couldn't allow his mother's house to turn into a fishy slop-pit. He found some buckets and a mop and began to clean away the mess. He poured it all down the sink, letting the garbage disposal take care of the larger, semi-solid chunks.

Four hours later, he realized that the call-in show was long over.

Five hours later, when the clean-up was finally finished, he realized he had discarded the best evidence he'd ever had in his possession.

At least his clothes were still coated with that ungodly fish-juice. Maybe some scientists could analyze that. He took them off, dropped them into a garbage bag and stuck that in the freezer.

God, but he felt itchy. No surprise. His skin had been soaking in that smelly goo during the entire clean-up. He examined his skin to see if that horrible ooze had given him some sort of rash.

He shook his head wearily. No, not a rash.

Something else. Something worse.

His skin was turning grey and slimy … leathery, too, like the hide of a catfish.

He trudged to the shower and turned on a nice cool stream. He let the water pour over him. Nice, very nice. As he changed, his growing eyes protruded from their sockets, and the waters washed the contacts right off of them.

When at last he emerged from the shower, it was midnight. His finger-webbing had grown in completely.

He looked around his mother's house. There was no way he could stay here, stinking up the place with his heavy fish-smell.

He fumbled open the door, looked around, and shambled off into the night....

Toward the river.

The beautiful river.

WHY THE CATHARTOLEPTIC APPROACH IS NOW LOOKED UPON WITH DISFAVOR

"Your mother, Peter. It would be good for us to talk about her," Dr. Matapathamos said. "Is she large-breasted? Passive? Docile?"

"What rude, ridiculous questions!" Peter cried, biting at a nail. "My mother has nothing to do with my problems. And you shouldn't be asking about such personal questions about her! But for the record: she is small-breasted and bitchy."

"Very well then…" The psychologist tapped his full lips with his silver pen. "Tell me about the cows."

"Do I have to?" The boy fingered a bruised patch along the front of his throat. "You know I don't like talking about the farm."

"And that is why you *must*." The doctor raised an eyebrow. "One must probe. Explore. One must lift the rock to see what crawls beneath."

Pale, thin Peter reclined on an overstuffed couch. The flesh around his dark eyes was finely wrinkled, though he was only fifteen years old. The doctor sat by his side, taking notes.

Peter looked about the room, desperate for a distraction. Anything, anything at all to take his mind off of the cows. How cruel that Dr. Matapathamos actually wanted him to focus on the horrid beasts. He took in random details as he scanned the office. Books bound in red and black buckram. A brass and crystal clock, clack-clack-clacking on the mahogany desk. Diplomas in dusty, mismatched frames.

"Tell me about the cows," the doctor repeated.

"They were big," Peter sighed, defeated. "They were black and white and they smelled bad. They were cows. That's all."

"No, that is *not* all." Dr. Matapathamos extended a finger toward Peter's throat, then pulled it back just before making contact. "You tried to hang yourself in the barn. Your suicide note read…" He took a manila folder from the desk, shuffled through its contents, then pulled out a ragged piece of paper. "Here it is: *The cows want me to die. I cannot help myself.* Do you still believe that these cows—these big, foul-smelling, black and white cows—await your demise?"

Peter turned away from the psychologist and caught a glimpse of the word *Meat* on a bookshelf. He tried to find the word again, but failed.

The doctor leaned over to his desk and pressed an intercom button. "Some refreshments, please, Muti."

"I suppose I'll have to tell you about the cows eventually," Peter murmured, "though you'll probably have me locked up until I'm really old. Then I'll become one of those stinky bagpeople."

"My dear boy. The Institute of Cathartoleptic Research is not in the business of manufacturing the homeless."

Muti, a thin, dark-haired young woman, entered the office carrying a glass of water and a brown ceramic mug. She handed the glass to Peter and the mug to the doctor. Just before closing the door on her way out, she turned and gave the boy a small sad smile.

The psychologist took a long pull from the mug, then wiped a slathering of milk from his moustache. "When your father and uncle brought you here, I told them I would do my very best to help you, and so I shall. I am here for you, my boy. Now about those cows…"

Peter took a deep breath. "I didn't want to spend the summer with Uncle Viktor, but my father said that I had to because it would make a man out of me. Uncle Viktor has a huge dairy farm with about two hundred cows. My Aunt Flora died a month before I got there. It happened during a thunderstorm. A cow had jumped a broken fence and she was helping my uncle to chase it back into the pasture. The cow was scared by the thunder and it trampled her." He glanced toward the bookshelf again and spotted the title: *The Trauma of Meat: The Cathartoleptic Perspective*. The author? Emil S. Matapathamos, Ph.D.

"How awful. Your uncle must have been devastated. Consumed with guilt." The doctor's heavy spectacles slid down his nose. He pushed them back in place with a ring finger. "I've seen it happen. 'The highway of life is filled with motion-sick drivers.' That's my little joke, Peter. And as with most humor, it has a basis in truth. Please continue."

Peter wished that he could take the book down from the shelf and skim through it. Would there be pictures? What sort of trauma was the book about? And what sort of meat? "Uncle Viktor told me that the cows hated Aunt Flora," he said. "Whenever she wanted more beef, she would take a big orange grease pencil, walk up to the pasture fence, and mark the nearest cow for death. Uncle didn't approve, but what could he do? He'd never learned to read or write, so Aunt Flora did all the paperwork. She ruled the checkbook, so she ruled the farm. Uncle didn't bother to wear black for her funeral. He just wore his overalls and a feedstore cap. I had to do all of Uncle's paperwork during my stay.

"Uncle Viktor began talking to his herd. He would forget his chores and walk for hours in the pasture. After a while I joined him on his walks, even though I hated the cows. I knew that nothing would happen to me in his presence."

"And just what did you think would happen?" Dr. Matapathamos asked. "Were the cows going to do something to you?"

"Oh no, they were going to make me do it to myself. By staring at me. By *thinking* at me. They didn't want to share Uncle with anyone. Aunt Flora's death started the process and Uncle's reverence completed it. He was their priest, you see. The cows had gained a sort of power, and they used that power to make me attempt suicide."

"Do you know where your Uncle Viktor is now? We haven't heard from him since your admittance to the Institution. I'm concerned about him, too."

Suddenly there was a fierce pounding at the door, followed by an earsplitting bellow. "The cows are after me!" Peter screamed. "The cows! Help me, doctor!"

"You are in no danger. One of my other patients is early for her appointment. That is all." The psychologist pressed the intercom button. "Muti? Poor Peter is distraught, so I want to show him that there is nothing to worry about. Please show Mrs. Pronka in."

Muti opened the door and led a heavyset elderly woman into the room. The mottled flesh of the vile old thing was horrid to Peter. Her skin reminded him of the hide of a Holstein cow, with irregular black splotches on a living field of white. Or perhaps rivers of white carving islands out of a black plain.

"Get her out of here, doctor. Please! She's staring at me!" Peter covered his eyes with his hands. "Oh, she's staring! Make her stop!" He began to utter short high screams.

"Yes, Peter—scream! But don't cover your eyes." Dr. Matapathamos reached out and pinched Peter's wrists, but the boy would not uncover his eyes. "Look at her. Look at her and scream. Mrs. Pronka claims that she is the living incarnation of Hathor, the Egyptian cow-goddess. What do you think of that? Scream! Scream and heal yourself, Peter."

Mrs. Pronka stared at Peter with dull cow-eyes. Then she reached for the doctor, but Muti turned her toward the door. Muti whispered an unintelligible phrase as she pushed the old woman out of the room.

Peter's screams faded to whimpers. He finally stopped after a quick peek between his fingers. Then he sat up on the couch. "You did that on purpose," he shouted, kicking the doctor in the ankle.

The doctor winced, but did not cry out. "Whatever do you mean?"

"The old woman…you and your girl arranged for me to see her. I know you did. You wanted to scare me."

"You scared yourself." The doctor wrote for a moment in his journal. "Mrs. Pronka bore a resemblance to a certain sort of cow, yes? You think that she is an avatar of dread; *she* thinks that she is a deity. But thinking does not bring these delusions to life. The woman has a pigment disorder. It's as simple as that." The psychologist patted Peter on the cheek. "Cathartolepsy: a revitalizing frenzy of release. We are progressing nicely. I await the moment when your screams shall purge you of your rage and self-horror. We shall talk more tomorrow."

* * * *

That evening, Peter dreamed of tall, ungainly creatures that lumbered across a midnight desert. The moon was veiled in clouds. The creatures wore shining capes and tall headdresses. Their forelimbs swung forward awkwardly. Their huge guts shook with each cumbersome step.

The clouds parted and the figures were bathed in moonlight. Cows they were, strutting impossibly on their hindlegs. Their eyes were golden and unblinking. Dreary low voices bubbled in Peter's mind: *Die, stupid boy. You are too fragile to live without pain. Kill yourself. Your dead body can nourish grass. Die, little fool.*

With a shrill cry Peter awoke, drenched in sweat in a narrow bed. His sleeping quarters at the Institute were completely utilitarian. The room was dimly lit by a small blue bulb over the door. The furnishings consisted of a white plastic chair and table, an empty wooden bookcase, and the wooden bed with its patternless blue quilt. The security glass in the single round window was more than an inch thick.

The boy sat up in bed. From this angle, he was able to see out of the window. In the yard outside, the cow-woman was crawling naked on her hands and knees. The thick glass distorted her image, making her appear grotesquely bloated. She bowed her head and bit into the grass. Peter slapped a hand over his mouth to keep from screaming.

This horrid grazing couldn't be part of the old woman's therapy— she enjoyed it too much. Peter guessed that this was the doctor's doing.

The night wore on and Mrs. Pronka continued to feed. Peter found himself wondering how the doctor would make the cow-woman scream.

* * * *

Dr. Matapathamos flipped through pages of notes, lost in thought. Suddenly he looked up. "Your father, Peter. Was he a well-endowed gentleman?"

"How in the world would I know? Why do you bring up such idiotic questions?" On the couch, Peter tore a jagged bit of nail off his thumb.

"Did you sleep well last night, my boy?" Dr. Matapathamos coughed lightly…perhaps to cover a small chuckle.

Peter said nothing. Instead, he got up from the couch and took *The Trauma of Meat* from its shelf. He started to skim through the pages.

"Put that book back where you found it," the psychologist said, alarmed.

A picture in the book caught Peter's eye. It depicted an obese man with a thick, piggish nose squatting, naked and terrified, in a meat locker. A half-dozen hog carcasses hung on hooks around him.

"About your Uncle Viktor…" The doctor's tone was peevish.

"What about him?" Peter said. "Do you want to throw him in a meat locker? Just to hear him scream?" He slapped the book shut. "Count his livestock. Maybe there's an extra bull in the cowyard."

"You think that your uncle has transmogrified into a bull? We are delving deep. I see a thread at the door of the labyrinth, leading inward. But even so, your uncle is not a Minotaur. My people found him last night, a few hours after our session. Put the book away, Peter. It's time to see Uncle Viktor."

The boy did as he was told.

Dr. Matapathamos stood up and led his patient out of the office. Muti left her rosewood desk to join them.

The three walked down a long corridor, past a number of black metal doors. From beyond these doors, Peter heard hysterical laughter, mindless babbling, and screams: high screams, hoarse screams, screams of horror and screams of delight.

The doctor stopped in front of one of the doors. By the side of the knob was a small panel covered with buttons, each a different color. The doctor pressed three buttons—red, blue, then purple. He turned the knob as he pressed a green button and the door opened.

Peter was amazed. The room was huge, more than eighty feet across. In the center was a pit surrounded by a wire-mesh fence. On the nearest post of the fence was another panel of colored buttons. He stepped up to the fence and looked down.

Twenty feet below, muddy sod was piled on the floor of the pit. The sod looked fresh—the grass was succulently green. Something white and puffy rested amidst the chunks of earth; its pallor reminded Peter of a nightcrawler. But it was far too large to be any sort of worm.

It was Uncle Viktor, fast asleep.

Dr. Matapathamos and Muti joined Peter at the fence. "He was found in the pasture, burrowed under the turf," the doctor said. "As you can see, we've tried our best to accommodate him."

Uncle Viktor opened his eyes. He looked up with a wide, stupid smile.

The psychologist removed his spectacles and, taking a tissue from a packet in his pocket, wiped at the lenses. "Ordinarily, I would need more time to make inquiries. In this case, however, I believe I have enough information to venture an opinion. It would appear that your uncle wishes to meld with the grass. To *become* grass."

One of the lenses popped out of his spectacles and broke on the floor. Muti knelt by the doctor's side to pick up the bits of glass.

"I don't understand," Peter said. He heard Muti inhale sharply and saw that she'd cut her thumb on the glass.

"Muti!" The doctor slipped his spectacles into a coat pocket and helped his secretary to her feet. "Are you all right, my dear?"

Muti uttered a few strange syllables: "Ugh ha k'ma." She held pieces of the lens in her uninjured hand. Peter realized that he had never heard her speak a word of English. He noticed a tattoo on her palm, but could not make out the pattern under the broken glass.

"Oh, that's not bad," the doctor said, examining Muti's thumb. "A mere scratch. We'll put a bandage on that in minute. For now, this will do." The doctor took a fresh tissue from his pocket and wrapped it around Muti's thumb. He took the broken glass from her and threw it in a nearby waste can.

He then turned to Peter. "Your uncle has developed a truly unique mania. No doubt he yearns for the cows to devour him so he can be as one with his deities." The doctor touched four buttons on the fence's panel—green, purple, blue, then red. "I have been presented with a marvelous opportunity, Peter. An opportunity to affect four cures at once."

A hidden door opened up in the wall of the pit. Mrs. Pronka crept through the opening, sniffing loudly. She saw the sod and bellowed with delight.

"All her talk of needing a sacrifice!" the psychologist said. "When it comes down to it, she simply won't go through with it. Her self-horror will be too great. You'll see."

Peter turned to ask the doctor what he meant. The boy saw that the doctor was in fact talking to Muti.

"You and your mother shall scream your way to normalcy, my love. We can then put this entire nightmare behind us and get on with our lives." The doctor leaned toward to kiss his secretary's forehead.

Below, the cow-woman pounced on Uncle Viktor and tore at the old man's face and shoulders with her teeth.

"Stop her!" Peter cried. "She's going to kill him!"

"She'll stop, she'll stop," the doctor said nervously, squinting into the pit. "Viktor will be screaming very soon and so will Muti and her mother and you too, Peter. You'll all be screaming and screaming and very soon you shall all be well."

The cow-woman gnawed at Uncle Viktor's head, tearing up chunks of hairy scalp. The old man's smile never faltered.

Muti started to laugh. Peter found himself fascinated by the beads of sweat covering the doctor's face.

"I realize that this may seem extreme," the doctor whined, "but believe me, Peter, soon each and every one of you shall be screaming. Everyone shall be screaming as the sublime healing power of cathartolepsy takes control. The sexual and emotional tensions of a traumatic life cannot be contained without sporadic bouts of verbalized release. My methods are infallible. Soon you shall all be screaming. Soon. Soon."

The cow-woman beat Viktor's head against the wall of the pit. Most of the old man's features had been bitten away.

Muti raised her hands, palms forward. The bloody tissue around her thumb came loose and fluttered to the floor. On each palm was tattooed a golden cow's-eye—one was smeared with red from her cut. She chanted in a throaty tone: "Ul'ka r'hama horti. Ul'ka r'hama gont. Um'na Hathor. Um'na Hathor. Ul'ka r'hama Hathor."

The cow-woman's skull swelled and lengthened into a ponderous horned structure. Her chest and belly expanded rapidly. Her arms and legs grew thicker, bonier. More limbs sprouted from her bulging, mottled abdomen.

Peter took in the events around him with a surprising degree of serenity. True, it did seem odd that the blood-streaked eye on Muti's palm was now rolling and shedding pink tears, trying to wash out the irritant. And yes, it was disconcerting to note that Mrs. Pronka now resembled a cross between a prize Holstein and a giant tarantula. Still, he was able to accept the chaos around him because he knew just what to do.

These were matters best left to a professional. He would simply let the doctor sort it all out.

Peter backed slowly out of the room. He waved goodbye to Dr. Matapathamos, who was screaming so violently that ribbons of blood and spittle flew from his lips.

REGARDING THE SITUATION ON CLOVE STREET A REPORT AND AN ADDENDUM

REPORT 6C.:

Clove Street is lined, not with clove trees, but with catalpa trees. But then, cloves only grow in the tropics, and this street is not known for its warmth. The weather here is capricious and yet rarely pleasant. Swirls of frost can be found on windows on early summer mornings. A clear, sunny day can bring hailstones as large as cats' heads. The lawns here suffer heinously: most are dotted with brown spots and dead patches.

And what of the green house with the yellow door? The neighbors are not sure what to think. The old woman who lives in the green house is named Letitia Clover. Mrs. Clover claims to be a widow, yet no one in the community can remember ever meeting or even seeing a picture of her late husband.

Mr. Tremayne, who has lived next door to Mrs. Clover for thirty-six years, insists that she always has appeared to be in her late seventies. He adds that she always has lived alone; always has owned numerous cats; and always has worn the same copper-rimmed spectacles (which always have been specked with dandruff or, to be kind, perhaps just dust).

Mrs. Lamb, who lives on the other side of the green house, wonders if perhaps the street had been named after some member of Mrs. Clover's family, or even the old woman herself. Could it be that the "r" had been dropped or misplaced with time? Or maybe some manner of city planner had smeared the ink after filling out a work order. One never knows. Inquiries shall be made and a report shall be filed.

The white trumpet flowers of the catalpa trees fill the air with a scent not unlike vanilla, but sweeter. In time the fragrant blossoms drop, and turn to pale brown slime on the cracked sidewalks.

Why does Mrs. Clover pay the neighborhood children to scoop up the slime—with silver spoons!—and deposit the noxious ooze in little pine boxes? She pays the children with silver dollars (she has been heard to say that paper money is a ludicrous concept). What does the old woman want...what does she *do*...with those wet, rancid petals?

Mrs. Clover's exceptionally large cats roam the Clove Street area freely. They all wear little silver chains about their throats. Her cats smell of catalpa petals.

Here now is the situation: many of the residents of Clove Street are disturbed by various low hums and throbbings and utterances that seem to issue from Mrs. Clover's green house.

The hums could be caused by a motor of some sort.

The throbbings are more often felt than heard—felt through the soles of one's feet.

The utterances are limited to this muted, unintelligible exchange: 1.) An exclamation in the voice of an elderly male; and 2.) A shout, presumably in response, from Mrs. Clover.

Passersby on the sidewalk are frequently startled witless by these baffling sounds/sensations, which can be discerned within a ten-yard radius of the Clover house. Only Mr. Tremayne and Mrs. Lamb have sufficient reason to file a complaint with local authorities, and they dare not—for one must not alienate one's nearest and undearest neighbor. Suburban tranquility is a sacred ideal; plus, Mrs. Clover has a strange, almost feral way of staring down others through her dusty lenses. At first, Mr. Tremayne and Mrs. Lamb were reluctant to share their experiences with our fact-finding agent, Community Member X. Luckily, both of Mrs. Clover's next-door neighbors have a fondness for white wine.

It would seem that Mrs. Clover (who, one must remember, claims to be a widow) and an unknown senior gentleman are working together on some project or process that involves a machine. Neighbors state that Mrs. Clover keeps her drapes drawn at all times. Mr. Tremayne believes she has never had a job...or at least, an occupation outside of her home. Furthermore, Mr. Tremayne's niece works at the local department store, and she claims that Mrs. Clover always pays for her purchases—even upscale major appliances—in silver. As for the shocking account given by a local paperboy: that shall be saved for the last, as an addendum, since one cannot be sure if the youth should be considered a reliable source.

Listed below are the prevalent theories, and their variations, regarding the situation on Clove Street:

A.) Mrs. Clover and her undead/deformed/insane husband are manufacturing toxins with which to poison neighborhood housewives/children/dogs.

B.) Mrs. Clover and an unidentified elderly alchemist are brewing catalpa-based aphrodisiacs with which to seduce postal workers/meter readers/door-to-door salespeople into complex sex rituals. Once the trysting is completed, the seduced individuals (through the application of some form of dark magick) are transmogrified into large cats.

C.) Mrs. Clover is an alien/Martian invader, working with a certain long-thought-dead scientist to build a death-ray and/or legion of murderous automatons. Individuals from Mrs. Clover's world subsist on decayed catalpa blossoms.

If theory A. is correct, one could assume that Mrs. Clover's activities are being financed by a foreign power. If B. is indeed the answer, the alchemist certainly might be using his paranormal pseudoscience to generate not gold, but less conspicuous silver to fill the widow's coffers. And in the case of C., Mrs. Clover's alien comrades would be the so very generous providers of her heretofore inexplicable wealth.

As Pi, with all of its eccentricities and little-known dangers, is to mathematics, so Mrs. Clover is to the security of Clove Street and ultimately, our sector. The noises and sensations issuing from her residence—the low hums, the throbbings, the muffled utterances—continue to vex and confound the populace.

Mystery must be monitored. Surveillance shall be maintained through Community Member X. More reports shall be filed.

In the meantime, all involved should exercise caution.

One should regard the green house on Clove Street with suspicion and certainly, dread. One should make discreet hand signs to avert the Evil Eye when Mrs. Clover turns her filth-speckled lenses in one's direction. One should pray to the stars while walking widdershins to curry cosmic favor. And above all, one should advise one's children not to fall into the practice of collecting dank, dead catalpa flowers with silver spoons.

ADDENDUM 1A

To ensure exactitude, the account given by a local paperboy (name withheld) has been condensed and itemized into a comprehensive sequence of events. Transcripts of the paperboy's verbal account are available upon request to agents with 3H.a. security clearance.

At this time, the reliability of this account is in doubt: several months before the alleged Mrs. Clover occurrence, the youth had experienced a severe concussion as the result of a motorbike accident. The boy's doctor has stated that the paperboy had recovered completely from the accident—but can even the most adroit of physicians be truly sure in such matters?

The sequence of events detailed in the paperboy's account is as follows:

- Paperboy knocked on front door of Clover residence.
- Paperboy heard low hums and felt ground-throbbings.
- Mrs. Clover answered front door.
- Paperboy requested delinquent funds.
- Mrs. Clover withdrew into residence to procure funds.
- Paperboy required use of restroom.
- Paperboy noticed front door ajar.
- Paperboy opened front door to call for Mrs. Clover.
- Mrs. Clover did not respond.
- Paperboy entered Clover residence.
- Paperboy searched for restroom.
- Paperboy passed through halls filled with large cats.
- Paperboy passed stacks of small pine boxes.
- Paperboy found closed pine door from behind which issued loud, low hum.
- Paperboy opened pine door.
- Paperboy discovered glowing void filled with outsized clockwork of silver.
- Paperboy noticed pale brown grease lubricating clockwork.
- Paperboy speculated that low hum might be caused by multiple hidden motors, turning the countless gears.
- Paperboy could not discern source of throbbing.
- Paperboy noticed giant elderly man chained to clockwork.
- Paperboy noticed gaping incision in belly of elderly man.
- Paperboy noticed clockwork parts (silver axles, gears, springs) and gleaming coinage steadily pouring from incision.
- Paperboy noticed numerous large cats floating through abyss.
- Paperboy closed pine door.
- Paperboy retraced path through Clover residence.
- Paperboy met Mrs. Clover in hallway.
- Mrs. Clover offered payment to paperboy.
- Paperboy accepted twenty silver dollars.
- Mrs. Clover led paperboy to front door.
- Paperboy heard scream of *Please* (elderly male voice).
- Mrs. Clover laughed.
- Mrs. Clover cried *Never.*
- Paperboy exited Clover residence.
- Mrs. Clover closed front door.

DROOL TOOL: THE MELTDOWN MIX

What? You've never been to the Black Box?

It's delicious, my dear. Black walls, black carpeting and a black marble dance floor. I'd be there tonight if it weren't for—Well, they're going to be closed for a week or so.

This club is *interesting* enough, but the music? Absolutely dreadful. They don't even play the Psychonauts.

You've never heard of them? Do you live in a cave? On a farm? I have all their CDs: *Monkey Boy, Slurp It Up, Robot with a Whip...* Surely you've heard their latest single, *Drool Tool*?

You have some lipstick on your teeth. Right there. You're quite pretty. You shouldn't bleach your hair, though. You should dye it black, like mine. Then we could pass for sisters.

Yes, I know I'm a bit older than you. Your older sister. Older but wiser.

The lead singer for the Psychonauts is Tarot Mandrago—an absolute god. I met him a few months ago. I'm an account executive at *Raw Hits* magazine and—

Hmm? Didn't hear you.

Oh, that just means I sell ad space. The magazine threw a huge party and that's where I met Tarot, with his long black hair and big black eyes. He rambled on and on about Haitian music, aborigine music, even dream music. I had no idea anyone in a dance band could be so *erudite*. Unfortunately he was standing to my left and I'm practically deaf in that ear. The other one's a bit weak, too. If the party got too loud I couldn't catch everything he said.

Soon Tarot's backup singers came to whisk him away and I was whisked right along. We all piled into a stretch limo. We drove for the longest time before we pulled up in front of a gorgeous mansion with stone gryphons on each side of the door. And inside—!

The walls were draped with blood-red velvet curtains. There was sound equipment everywhere. Some sleepy young things were lounging about on huge pillows in the main hall. An absolute Adonis wearing nothing but a leather mask was leading a monkey on a leash.

Tarot explained that the mansion belonged to an elderly millionairess who desperately needed a hobby. He pointed to a metal booth hanging by gold chains about twenty feet above the floor. The old girl was in there, watching. The masked Adonis whistled and a rope ladder shot down from the booth. He and his monkey shimmied right up.

The Psychonauts began to rehearse, so I went over to the pillow people. They were smoking the most obnoxious substance: ground-up African beetles mixed with dried seaweed. I sat with them, smoking and talking to a strange young thing from Cat's Ass, Illinois. I asked her what was on the agenda and she gave me an odd little smile.

"Tarot will be treating us to his latest masterpiece," Miss Smalltown said. "Put these in when the time comes." So saying, she gave me a pair of foam-rubber earplugs. I asked: why would I want to wear earplugs while listening to music? She just tapped my nose and said, "Trust me."

Tarot then announced that the group would be playing their forthcoming release. What was I to do? I wanted to hear it, but Smalltown had been terribly specific. I decided to put in one earplug. When in doubt, compromise.

As I put in my one earplug, I saw that everyone else was putting in two, including the group. Then they began to play. A few weeks later I heard the same song on the radio—*Drool Tool*. But they weren't playing the radio mix that night. They were playing the dance version: the Meltdown Mix.

Of course it was wonderful—what little I could hear of it. I shouted to Smalltown: Can you hear *anything?* She answered by holding her thumb and forefinger a quarter-inch apart.

Suddenly I felt a small splash on my head. I looked up and saw that something was dripping from the booth. It was like the coffee stupid housewives make on old sitcoms: all gooey and brown. And the smell! A clot of the stuff fell right on Smalltown's face. The group stopped playing, and Tarot went to a control panel and lowered the booth to the ground.

Inside, they found three intertwined bodies. One was extremely small. They were in sad shape, my dear. In fact, they hardly had any shape at all.

The skin and muscles had dissolved into a sort of chunky brown syrup. The organs looked like rotten fruit. The bones had liquified. Adonis' spine was little more than a soggy pink stick.

The groupies and the band members were a bit shaken, as was I. Tarot was utterly ecstatic! The look in his eyes…like a crow admiring a nice bit of roadkill.

Excuse me, my dear. I have a quick errand to run.

* * * *

Now, what were you saying?

The bodies? Well, it's all rather complicated. You see, Tarot just loves to experiment. With music, drugs, reality—you name it. He later explained that particular experiment to me.

The Meltdown Mix contains dream-rhythms that send a powerful subliminal message to the brain. This message lulls the brain into a waking dream-state. In this blissful dream, the body's cellular structure relaxes—to a truly *alarming* degree.

But you're safe if you can't hear the entire sound spectrum of the message. That's why they'd put in earplugs—to block out the higher frequencies. The old girl and her boyfriend hadn't been told to do so: one never informs the guinea pigs. As it turned out, I didn't need my earplug. Tarot said my hearing problem was all the protection I needed.

The radio mix is doing quite nicely, but the Meltdown Mix won't make the charts. Only two copies were made. Tarot kept one CD for further experimentation. The other was snatched up while no one was looking.

I can't say that I envy the cleaning ladies at the Black Box. And my dear, I certainly don't envy you. Your mascara is running…or is it your face? The DJ is playing the Meltdown Mix right now. I gave him my copy just a minute ago.

There's a certain satisfaction in being the prettiest girl in the room, don't you think?

PRINCE OF THE DARK GREEN SEA

A fisherman and his wife lived by the sea in a shack of rotted boards and driftwood. Each morning the fisherman cast his net into the dark green waters, and each afternoon his wife carried his catch to the village to sell. Each night, she gutted a fish and boiled it in a copper pot for their dinner. Work and sun and salt air toughened the skin and grizzled the hair of the fisherman and his wife. What time they spent together was used to collect grass and sticks for their fire. When they spoke, they spoke of tides and wind and petty village intrigues. So they lived for many years.

One morning, the fisherman caught a most frightening fish. The vile thing had black scales and filthy needle teeth. He was about to slap the monster against a boulder when he noticed that its eyes were brown and sorrowful and strangely beautiful. The fisherman put the fish back in the water, saying, "Swim away, my sad little friend."

When he returned to the shack, he told his wife about his catch. The old woman smoked a pipeful of dried blue seaweed as she listened.

"Surely I am married to a fool," she said. "That was a magic fish, and you should have made a wish."

"What would I have wished for?" the fisherman asked.

"Such a stupid question. Do you want to live in this worthless hovel forever?" His wife blew a cloud of smoke in his face. "Go back and ask the fish for a fine warm cottage."

"I should like to sleep in such a cottage." With this, the fisherman left the shack. He returned to the boulder and called out, "Swim back, my sad little friend."

The water rippled and the black-scaled creature appeared. The man gazed into its beautiful, melancholy eyes. He then noticed that the fish's mouth had changed. It now had a beautiful mouth, too. The lips were red and the teeth were even and white.

"My wife told me to come and wish for a fine warm cottage." The fisherman held out his hands. "She is a hard worker, my wife. No one deserves happiness more."

"Go home, catcher of fish," said the monster in a low murmur of a voice. "The Prince of the Dark Green Sea is indebted to you. I know what you want and I know what you need. Your wife has her cottage."

The fisherman returned home and found a cottage of pink stone where the shack had been. Around the cottage grew bushes abundant with fragrant pink roses. He lifted the gold latch on the cherrywood door and went inside. His wife smiled at him from the rocking chair by the fireplace. He believed the woman to be content, and returned the smile.

But in a week's time, she again blew pipe-smoke in his eyes. "You gave that miserly fish back his life and how does he repay you? With a paltry cottage. Go now: I desire to be a queen in a castle."

The fisherman nodded wearily and returned to the boulder. "Swim back, my sad little friend," he said.

Again the fish poked its head out of the water. The creature's black scales had turned to beautiful milk-white skin.

"I thank you for the cottage, good fish," the man said. "But my wife must be a queen in a castle. She is a hard worker, my wife. No one deserves happiness more."

"The Prince of the Dark Green Sea is indebted to you." The fish blinked its sorrowful brown eyes. "Your wife has what she wants."

Upon his return, the fisherman saw, instead of the cottage, a castle of silver bricks. The trees and shrubs surrounding the castle were adroitly trimmed to resemble fabulous beasts: harpies, satyrs, rampant griffins and more. A lady-in-waiting led him to his wife's chamber, where the old woman sat before a mirror of polished silver. She ignored him as she styled her stringy grey hair around a glorious silver diadem.

The fisherman's wife drank royal jelly liqueur and pomegranate wine from the castle's mazelike cellars. She ate roast lamb and delicate pastries from the well-stocked larders. She slept on cushions filled with the down of baby swans. And by the end of a month, she considered these luxuries woefully lacking.

"Truly I must become an empress, in a palace befitting my rank," she said. "Take this wish to the magic fish. I am sure that he would think nothing of such a small request."

The fisherman went to the boulder and called for the fish. The Prince of the Dark Green Sea now had long black hair and the face of a beautiful young man.

The old man stared in admiration at the fine features of the Prince. He then made his request. The creature said, "I am indebted to you. Your wife has what she wants. Go now, catcher of fish."

The fisherman walked home. The castle was now an exquisite palace of gold. About the grounds were scattered towering golden statues of the fisherman's wife, all more than flattering. In the sky, guards garbed in golden armor rode roaring bat-winged chimeras.

The fisherman found his wife seated on a golden throne. Around her thin shoulders was draped a robe of spun gold; on her head was a filigreed golden crown, graced with cunningly crafted amber plumes. On plush divans lounged smirking pleasure-boys who regarded the aged fisherman with disdain.

In her callused palm, the fisherman's wife held a box carved from an enormous yellow sapphire. She opened the box and dipped a wee golden spoon into the crystalline powder within. With a languorous moan, she snuffed the sparkling powder up a nostril.

"Ah, the life of an empress..." The woman frowned hugely. "So very boring."

"But—" The fisherman's eyes opened wide. "I've only just returned from the shore. I thought you would be happy for at least a year."

"A year? A year of this utter tedium?" She dismissed the notion with a wave of her hand. "You must be mad."

A young handmaiden entered the throne room carrying a tray of beauty ointments. She began to massage a mixture of honey and lily oil on the old woman's sere cheekbones.

"There's no need for that," said the fisherman's wife with a bitter laugh. "You might as well rub your fancy balm onto a chunk of granite."

The handmaiden studied the face of the empress. "If you like, I can brew a clever skin-softening unguent, made from the fetuses of rare albino alpacas."

The old woman pushed the handmaiden away. "The pretty fool has given me a marvelous idea," she cried to her husband. "There is certainly no need for her silly creams. Inform the magic fish that I wish to have control over time. Then I shall turn back the clock and make myself young again." She glanced toward her pleasure-boys and simpered.

The fisherman could not believe his ears. "Control over time?"

"Yes—and space, too. I should like to make my palace larger." She looked up into the far shadows of the throne room's ceiling. "This miserable closet is so close, I can scarcely breathe. Now do as I say, before I summon the guards and have you tossed into an oubliette. I am aging needlessly even as we speak."

The fisherman hurried out of the palace—but gradually his steps slowed to a crawl, for he was reluctant to ask the magic fish for yet another wish so soon. It was twilight by the time he reached the boulder. "Swim back, my sad little friend," he said.

This time, the Prince of the Dark Green Sea walked out of the water. The creature now had a human body, well-formed and desirable. The fisherman was so enthralled that for a moment, he forgot why he had returned. But at last he remembered his errand. "Forgive me, good fish, but my wife desires even more. She must have control over time and space."

"I am indebted to you—indeed I am. I know what you want and I know what you need." The beautiful young man stepped forward and placed his cool palms on the fisherman's chest. "Your wife is now back in the wretched shack. And you shall come with me, catcher of fish. You are a hard worker and no one deserves happiness more."

So saying, the Prince of the Dark Green Sea pulled the fisherman beneath the waves.

SOMETHING IS COMING

In the dream, he somehow knew: *something is coming.*
Something strange. Something wrong.
Something filled with ageless malice.
Something is coming.
It emerged from the darkest corner of the universe in a vessel crafted of black metal, racing at a speed that made the passage of light seem as sluggish as sap oozing from a broken tree limb. He had no idea how he knew these things. He just did.

Closer the horror came, closer, ever *closer*.

Suddenly the dream was ripped to shreds by noise, bright noise—

He awoke and swatted the ringing thing off the nightstand. What was it? Why was it making so much noise?

In the bathroom, he switched on the light, but the bulb only made an odd sizzle. Sitting on the toilet, he realized that he needed something, something, but what was it? What?

Desperate and confused, he used a washcloth instead of toilet paper.

He wandered naked through the house. Each time he came to a window, he wondered why the sky looked so sickly and strange. He put his hand on a window in the living room. The glass had turned yellow and it felt soft. Damp yet crinkly. He checked a light bulb in one of his lamps. The bulb was yellowed and slightly misshapen. Could glass go bad, like milk? He tried to remember what glass was made of...

But then, the concept, the very thought of glass seemed to dim as he considered it. Glass? What was glass? It was a thing, yes, but what sort of thing? A thing you can look through. A look-through-it thing.

It occurred to him that perhaps there was something wrong with his...his... The word eluded him, but he found himself touching the side of his head. Yes, the thing inside his head, whatever that was called. He decided he should call someone. Find someone who could help. A moment later, he looked at the phone and wondered what *that* thing was.

He moved to the flat thing in the front hall and concentrated: he knew that this was a very important thing. He reached out and slapped his hands against it. He started to panic. He fidgeted with the round shiny thing sticking out of it until—the door? Yes, that was it! The door! The door thing! The thing! Until the thing opened, and he walked outside.

The millions of skinny green things under his feet were all limp and watery. And the flat green things high up in the tall dark things hung down all slimy. As far as he could see, every green thing was dead and wet and icky.

He tried to gather his thoughts. Something had made the things you can look through into soft, yellow things. Something had made all the green things into rotten, oozy things. And worse of all, something had made him not know what things were or what they did. Everything was wrong. Every … thing. A thing is a thing is a thing.

He looked down at the things he stood on, those two pink things, each ending in five stubby little things. They sure were funny-looking—but how did they work? When he tried to move them, he fell down. The long things on each side of him flopped uselessly. He breathed heavily and muttered, "Thing—thing thing—*something is coming*—thing thing—"

Suddenly, he saw a pair of huge, brown blubbery things floating above him.

The brown things looked silly. They resembled the messy, lumpy things that came out of the back of barking things. But these brown things were big, much bigger than he was, and they had many of those wet, round things that you see with.

Both of the brown things held long shiny things that went *buzzzzzzzz* when they pointed them at things. The brown things squealed as they drew toward him.

He suddenly realized that these things were to blame, these horrible, disgusting THINGS, these, these—

For just a moment, sheer terror cleared his foggy mind, and he was able to recall one last succinct word:

Aliens.

The invading things wrapped their warm, slick selves around him. Though they looked soft and harmless, they were in fact incredibly tough and infinitely cruel. He screamed again and again as they opened up and began to gnaw, gnaw, gnaw....

On his things.

AGATHA SAYS

Dear Irene,

Today was the worst. Poor Bernice was so embarrassed. Pete's wife Vonda came by to visit wearing a leather skirt and a tube-top. And she brought the brood! The woman must be half-crazy to bring four children to a nursing home.

Bernice was trying to take a nap, but how could she with all those children running around and coughing? You should have heard them coughing—they'll give us all pneumonia with their germs. I asked Vonda if she gave them vitamin C and she just looked at me. Well, Bernice offered to keep an eye on the kids while Vonda visited. She was playing some game with them when the youngest boy, Kevin, started going on about the smell. Bernice just burst into tears and left the room.

I went looking for her and found her in the rec room. There were only a few others in there but they were all watching her. Bernice has been having trouble with that bag she has to wear and she thought that was what the boy could smell.

Of course it wasn't the bag—it was Vonda's baby girl. Sometimes I think Vonda just let's that diaper go for a couple rounds. Poor Bernice, she can't smell a thing with that dry nose of hers and she's so paranoid about that bag. And the fact that everyone was looking at her only made matters worse.

It took me half an hour to calm her down. The poor thing—she'll die with that damn bag on and they'll probably bury her with it. She once told me that when she passes on she wants me to make sure they take the bag off. I bet they wouldn't, though. I'd just do it myself.

So! Thank God every time you use the toilet, Irene. Some people aren't so lucky.

—Lucy

Dear Irene,

Bernice is much better today. She even got out some polish and did our nails. I've still got pretty hands. Bernice says I could be one of those hand models on the commercials. Most of the other gals here are jealous of my hands.

A new lady moved in today. I say lady because the nurses were treating her like royalty. I think she's got bucks. Wonder what she's doing here!

You should have seen her. You'd have thought she was some movie star, what with all the make-up and jewelry she was wearing. She has a long thin nose and the largest brown eyes. I think she's Italian.

This lady had the nurses laughing with some story she was telling. Those big eyes of hers were just dancing. She's quite pretty—not as pretty as you, though. If there was a beauty contest for women our age you'd win for sure. This new lady would probably get Miss Congeniality. They'd have to add a new category for me: Miss Prettiest Hands.

Maybe I should be a vixen and have Bernice polish up my toes. Then again, my feet look so awful I'd probably be better off not drawing attention to them.

—Lucy

Dear Irene,

I'm sorry to hear about Mr. Naps. At least he passed away in his sleep and not at the vet's office, like Boots did. Mr. Naps was such a good kitty. I've always wished they'd let me have a cat here. You ought to get a kitten. Maybe a longhair, because they're more of a lap cat. A Siamese will tear the house up.

I guess the new woman isn't Italian—her name is Agatha Stone. Still, she has a weird accent. I'll bet she was raised in Europe somewhere. When she talks her little voice goes up and down. It's so funny to listen to her.

You should have heard her talking to Bernice. One of the nurses must have told Agatha about the bag, because she went right up to Bernice and said if she ever saw Bernice's doctor, she'd cut *him* a new hole! I was so shocked. But I guess Bernice liked the idea, because she laughed a little and started talking about the operation, which isn't the easiest thing in the world for her to do.

Agatha was carrying a plate of these little cookies. Agatha says her nutritionist sends them to her. She must be rich to get that kind of treatment.

Again, I'm so sorry about Mr. Naps. Write if you get a kitten.

—Lucy

Dear Irene,

No kitten yet?

Well, I was half right about Agatha—her mother was Italian. And she was raised in France, England and Belgium. Her father taught piano to rich people.

She's not so bad off herself. I still don't know what she's doing here. She has a private room and they're letting her redecorate. She even had bookcases brought in. Remember the fuss they made when I wanted to hang a picture?

Time for dinner. Oh, the wonders of cornstarch.

* * * *

That Mr. Cushman! One of the servers gave him some lip and he poked her with a fork. Right in the elbow. He didn't draw blood, but I bet it'll hurt her for a few days. Still, serves her right for being so sassy. It was that red-haired girl I was griping about a while back—the one who's always making fun of Bernice's lisp.

I got a chance to talk to Agatha. She was handing out her little cookies all during dinner. I could tell the supervisor on duty wasn't too happy about it but he didn't say anything—and I know why. Agatha's going to be the new boss!

Agatha is trying to buy the place. She told me that her lawyer is negotiating the deal, and once the papers are signed, she's going to change everything. She says that she wants to get to know everyone at Fern Hill so she can spend the rest of her life among friends. When I told Bernice all this, she just laughed. She doesn't think Agatha has that kind of money. We'll just have to wait and see.

—Lucy

Dear Irene,

I just adore that picture of your new puppy. Those wrinkly doggies are so cute. I told Agatha what you spent on it and she said $350 was a steal (still seems like an awful lot for a dog).

One of the supervisors confirmed it—Agatha really is going to buy Fern Hill. Imagine, owning a nursing home so you'll always have company. Of course, it's an investment, too.

Vonda stopped by today. Bernice had another run-in with Kevin—she gave him a little slap for rummaging in her nightstand drawer. He said he was looking for gum. As if any of us have chewed gum in years!

I told Bernice she was getting as bad as Mr. Cushman. He poked another server with a butter knife. He said this one was moving too slow.

—Lucy

Dear Irene,

Thank you for the lovely present. I'd almost forgotten my own birthday! I just love brooches—I'm wearing it right now. The cat in the design reminds me of Mr. Naps.

We got a little snow last night. You do remember snow, don't you? I could live without it, but I think I'd miss it at Christmas. Do you string lights on the palm trees?

A couple of the nurses quit last week. So did that red-haired server.

Agatha is such a joy. Now and then I catch her splashing a drop of rum in her tea out of a little flask. I wonder if her nutritionist sent her that, too.

The other day Agatha was telling me about a party she threw in Belgium thirty years ago. She was living with a group of artists and poets at the time. I can't remember everything she said because it was so interesting just watching her talk. Her hands were flying all over the place. They're not as pretty as mine. Her fingers have little patches of black hair on them.

Anyway, I was so busy watching her hands that I stopped listening for a moment. When I tuned back in, I realized she was talking about a murder—a fellow was killed at her party. The police came by to quiet things down and somebody stabbed an officer in the back.

Agatha has a beautiful car. It's big, black and foreign and she parks it out back. She has one of the servers cover it with a canvas if she's not going to be out for a while.

—Lucy

Dear Irene,

Bart had to be taken to the hospital today. He's the fellow who was leaving little notes for Bernice last year. Agatha says she's going to see how he's doing tomorrow.

One of the new nurses was giving Bart a hard time because he didn't want to take his medicine. He said he didn't need it any more. After a while she tried to force the pills into his mouth. So Bart bit her finger right down to the bone and wouldn't let go. Can you believe it! So she took his cane and hit him in the shoulder. That's when Bart's roommate Carl came in. He grabbed the cane and broke it over her head.

It's hard to forgive violence but you know, Irene, it serves that awful woman right. Some nurses think they can just bully us around. She dislocated Bart's shoulder, too.

Time to go eat. How's your wrinkly doggy doing? You never told me what you were going to call it.

* * * *

After dinner Bernice and I had tea with Agatha in her room. She offered, but neither of us had any rum. Agatha has so many old books. I bet they're worth some money. She says that once the place is hers, we can all have pets. She'll even hire a boy to help take care of them. I told her I wanted a cat and Bernice said she would like a bird. I hope pets in nursing homes aren't against the law. Still, that wouldn't stop Agatha. Rich people can find loopholes.

Agatha served us some of her delicious cookies. They're black and very sweet and minty. They even have little pieces of mint leaves in them.

I think Agatha has been to Africa. She has the most bizarre wooden mask hanging by her bed. The face is catlike but the mouth looks like a shark's, with rows and rows of teeth. She called it a zoo—does that make any sense?

Here I am going on and on about Agatha. Don't worry, Irene— you're still my best friend, ever since third grade. Followed by Bernice and then maybe Agatha. If I go on about Agatha it's only because she's so unusual.

I was telling her a little about you the day. I told her how well you played the piano and she found that so interesting. Did I mention her father taught piano? I showed her that poem you wrote for my birthday a few years back, too. I hope you don't mind.

What are you getting Joseph for Christmas? Agatha's taking me and Bernice to the mall for an hour or two tomorrow to do some shopping. Bernice in the mall! I think she's finally starting to get over her little worry. Myself, I'm thinking about that long drive. It's a good twenty minutes to the city and you know me and my peanut bladder.

By the way, at dinner I thought up a name for your dog—Pruneface!

—Lucy

Dear Irene,

Merry (belated) Christmas, and thank you, thank you, thank you for the new gloves! Sorry I haven't written for so long, but so much has been going on.

Bart got out of the hospital just in time to make the Christmas party. Did I mention that the nurse who hit him had to go to the hospital, too? For stitches in her hand and her scalp. Carl opened her head up with that cane. No charges were pressed against him. What are they going to do—send a 78-year-old man to prison? Needless to say, the nurse is not returning to Fern Hill.

For the party, the music teacher from Sloane High School brought down some kids to sing carols in the rec room. While they were singing I looked around and realized that Agatha wasn't there, so I snuck back to her room to fetch her.

When I got to her door I forgot to knock. I simply walked right in and there she was, stark naked and wearing that cat mask. She was standing in the middle of the room, mumbling some made-up song and moving her hands around, like she was conducting an orchestra or something. She'd drawn all kinds of funny little pictures on the floor in chalk, too. Of course she had to be drunk—her and that rum. What else could it be? I was about to say something—what, I don't know!—when I saw there were no eyeholes in the mask. She didn't even know I was there, so I backed out and shut the door. I'm sure she'd die of embarrassment if she knew I saw her carrying on like that.

I'll tell you this: for a woman in her late sixties, Agatha has some body on her. None of the chicken skin you see around here. She must have had it lifted. You know that fat they suck out of liposuction patients? I wonder why they can't pump it into skinny people. Bernice's bony old butt sure could use some extra padding. Yours, too—those snapshots you sent have me worried. You're still the prettiest gal I know, but you could stand to pack on a few pounds. Joseph looks like he's picking up weight again (he must be eating off your plate too!). I wish they could take some of Joseph's spare tire and give it to you.

Agatha never did come to the party. I told everyone she was sick. After the students left there was a problem—Celeste slapped the supervisor on duty for telling her not to eat so many cookies. Agatha had given Celeste a whole box of cookies that morning, which was a little irresponsible, since Celeste is on a restricted diet (cancer everywhere, the poor dear). After that slap, the supervisor simply stood there, utterly shocked. Then his nose started bleeding. Celeste just shuffled off with her cookies.

Then—I don't know what got into us!—we were all laughing and laughing while the supervisor stuffed tissues up his nose. He must have quit since that was the last we saw of him.

A few days later, Agatha announced that negotiations were final. Fern Hill was now Stone Manor. After that, everything started to change, just like Agatha said.

New carpeting, a big-screen TV in the rec room—this week Bernice and I are having our room completely redone. And it's not costing us extra! I hope there isn't a catch. Still, Agatha hasn't made us sign anything, and she *is* rich. Didn't Elvis used to give away Cadillacs to complete strangers?

Agatha also brought down that nutritionist of hers. He's going to be working here full-time, fixing our meals. Some health expert—he's as white as a fish-belly. There's something wrong with his eyes, too. They look like blue glass marbles. Agatha swears by him, but I have my doubts.

For one thing, he's always asking us for urine samples and little clips of our hair. He says he's checking us for vitamin deficiencies. I just hope he washes his hands before he starts dinner.

I showed Agatha those pictures of you and Joseph. She thought you were his daughter! She couldn't believe you were my age.

—Lucy

Dear Irene,

Agatha says that Mr. Sartok, the nutritionist, is an albino. His eyes are pink under those tinted contacts.

I've talked to him a few times since my last letter and he's truly a very nice man. His meals are wonderful, too, although half the time I have no idea what I'm eating. Lots of that mint. I've picked up about eight pounds.

Bernice is doing better. Mr. Sartok seems to be taking a special interest in her.

With all this special care, I think everyone's in fine shape. Sometimes a change in management is the best thing.

Off to dinner. I'll be back!

* * * *

Remember that article you sent me about how older people see certain colors better because their corneas have turned yellow? You clipped it out of one of those tabloids.

Well, that article must be right, because at one point during the meal Celeste dropped her knife (we've got real silverware now) and everyone looked up at the same time. And you know, everyone's eyes looked yellowish. Except Agatha's. She was at the head of the table and her eyes were just big and brown and full of love for all of us. I tell you, Irene, that woman is a godsend.

—Lucy

Dear Irene,

It's funny, but Stone Manor doesn't get many visitors these days. Carl's daughter stopped coming by after he hit that awful nurse. Celeste says she flat-out told her son never to visit her again.

Vonda stopped coming by after I called Pete about three weeks ago. I don't think I've told you about that. I called Pete and said if he was too busy to come see his own mother then he shouldn't send over his good-for-nothing trashy streetwalker of a wife.

I shouldn't have gone on like that but I couldn't help myself. I started talking and I kept on thinking, he doesn't have time for me, he probably doesn't even love me any more, he loves that sleazy wife of his more than me, his own mother—my mind was just spinning.

But you know, Irene, maybe it was just as well. I don't need him any more. Just last night, Agatha was telling us how much we mean to her. She said that we could all stay with her forever, no matter what. That made me feel so good. Agatha gave each of us a special gift, too. A funny cat mask! Then the new nurses poured the wine and Mr. Sartok brought out dinner. Later, we all sang a little song that Agatha taught us.

Agatha is getting us a litter of kittens! Some of us have been hinting for cats, so she answered a newspaper ad. Agatha says pets keep you young—it's a fact. Mr. Sartok is going to pick them up some time next week.

—Lucy

Dear Irene,

I'm so sorry to hear about Joseph. I was just thinking about Mr. Naps the other day and now this happens. You poor thing. Joseph was the dearest man. If only he'd watched his health. When I lost my Roger, I thought the world was going to end. I didn't know what to do with myself. I was still wearing black when Pete and Vonda put me in this home.

Now, I love it here. Agatha has given us lots of cats. I adore my little Tiger Kitty. Sometimes I'll put a ribbon on his tail and he'll go round and round chasing it. Bernice got a bright-green parakeet, too. She named her new birdy Arabella. Fancy name for a fancy bird! We don't dare let her out of the cage—not with all these cats!

I don't know where we'd be without Agatha. She sees to our every need and all she wants from us is love. And we do love her dearly.

Don't think that you're alone in the world, Irene. I told everyone about your situation and we're having a meeting tonight. I'll write back very soon and I know I'll have good news.

—Lucy

Dear Irene,

It's decided: we want you to live with us. Now is the time to be among friends. You can play the piano, too—Agatha will buy you one. It's been so long since I've heard you play. Agatha says you can have her old room. She's moving into the new section once it's completed. Of course, you can bring Pruneface—just be sure to keep him away from the cats.

We'd so like to have you here, Irene. Bernice can't wait to meet you. She says she feels like she already knows you. I do talk about you quite a bit. Did I mention? Bernice doesn't need her bag any more. I guess it's all a matter of diet. Celeste's all better, too.

It'll be so much fun, Irene. You and me and everyone. We can talk and play with our cats and look at Agatha's old books. They have the strangest pictures! You can have your own cat mask, too, like the rest of us. We'll do the mask dance and sing the mask song and Mr. Sartok will cook up meals to make us feel so much better.

Agatha says that when Christmas rolls around and the students come back, she's going to try and summon Azu again. And this time it's going to work because we'll all be helping.

You know what, Irene? Agatha doesn't have a cat! And after all her talk about how pets keep you young. Of course, she's so busy looking after us—maybe she doesn't have time for a pet. Or maybe she's just holding out for something special.

Agatha wants you to join us, Irene. It's really the best thing. Agatha says that if you don't, she and Mr. Sartok are going to drive on down in that big black car and get you.

—Lucy

DIAGNOSIS AND TREATMENT
OF OCULAR PARASITISM
AND ASSOCIATED MENTAL DISORDERS

"There is no need to fear," Dr. Seldag said. "I've read about this problem in Professor Puthmoor's text. Puthmoor is the last word in parasitism of the eye."

Pretty Mrs. Thetron nibbled nervously at a corner of her delicate lace hankerchief. "Then there is hope?"

"Of course. Your father will be fine." The physician patted the bald head of the emaciated man seated on the examining table. "As I see it, old Beric must have been napping under a thromba tree. Lich-crows favor thromba trees for their nests. Lich-crows are simply acrawl with the most vile organisms. The worst of these is the eyeworm. A little nap... an upturned face, directly beneath an infested nest...a slight breeze... Most unfortunate. But do not worry, Mrs. Thetron. There is no need to alarm yourself. With the Puthmoor text to guide me, we'll have these eyeworms licked in no time."

In a shadowed corner of the room sat a silent woman, visible only to Dr. Seldag. Her black hair hung down over her face in a solid curtain. Only her mouth and chin could be seen. Her lips moved, but no sound came forth. Her long, twisted fingernails wove manic patterns in the air. The doctor chose to ignore her.

Old Beric gasped. "Am I dead? Get these squiggly-wigglies out of my head. I must be dead 'cause I've got worms in me. Am I dead?"

Mrs. Thetron helped Beric down from the table and wrapped her thin arms around him. "Can we take my father to the Professor?"

"Oh, no, no, *no*. Professor Puthmoor was killed in his Lundyn laboratory during the Great Meteor Rain." Dr. Seldag said. "In fact, the Museum of Abnatural Wonders on Yath Street has a few of the Lundyn meteorites on display. The largest found was the size of a baby's fist... But what does size matter? Eyeworms are small and just look at all the trouble they cause."

Mrs. Thetron bit her lower lip. "The Great Meteor Rain was almost a century ago. Surely his book is outdated by now."

"Professor Puthmoor was something of a recluse. Little is known of the gentleman. But I can assure you of this: Puthmoor was a genius, well ahead of his time. His text is clearly the work of a visionary. That is why I am so proud of my copy of his book—a rare first edition. My bookseller informed me that it came from the library of one of the Professor's pupils...a Dr. Paglio Ferni of Romae." The physician turned to gaze out the window. The sky was cloudless: excellent. A throat-hawk squealed in the distance. "Bring old Beric back to this office this evening. Treatment can only be administered at night."

"I hate to go out when it's late," Mrs. Thetron said. "The city is so full of bad sorts. Terrible people who pinch. Robbers with whips. Killers who bite their victims to death. Can't you do anything for him now?"

Dr. Seldag sighed wearily. Why did this woman doubt him? Was she not impressed with his tastefully decorated office? His delightful paperweights from foreign lands? His many black-framed certificates and articles? These documents attested to his unique alignment with a variety of mind/corpus research facilities: the Zhikago Institute of Psychotic Decay; the Lobe Dome in Zengapoor; even the CerebroSpinal Enlightenment Center (on the campus of the University of Maggakuzzets). "Moonlight makes the eyeworms glow, Mrs. Thetron. Surely you've noticed...? You know what they say: a *glowing* eyeworm is an *easily detected* eyeworm. I cannot remove what I cannot see."

With a nod and a mumbled apology, Mrs. Thetron led Beric to the door. There the old man paused, his pimento-red eyes rolling. "Is this a tomb, little death-lady? Am I dead? Am I dead?"

Dr. Seldag gave them a fond smile and a little goodbye wave. He was a tall, pink-cheeked man with an angular face and not an ounce, not a speck of excess fat adhering to any of his ropy muscles. His silver-grey hair coiled down from his scalp in thick, serpentine locks. He was handsome, yes—but dedicated to his work, and so, never gave any thought to his looks. Looks were only useful for attracting lovers, and he had no need for that sort of thing. He had his work to fill any emptiness that might crop up in his existence.

He saw many other patients that afternoon. Mrs. Aggi required consultation regarding her dreams: horrid, nauseating visions of insects and genitalia. She spent most of her visit crying, tears streaming, spattering all over his nice rose-colored rug. Dr. Seldag wondered if the woman had some sort of obscure lymph-related condition. It was his opinion that folks with bothersome lymph glands had difficulty controlling their various bodily humors. After that, sickly Mr. Pnik's miserable sinuses needed draining. Otherwise, the infection could spread, even to the brain. The man clearly had a poorly formed skull, with inner structures that tended to pool their viscous secretions until they became septic. Then Lystir Norl, the effete young actor, was having sharp pains and tingly feelings in his right ear again. Lystir's bossy mother used to tug on that ear, back when he was a small child. Yet there seemed to be nothing visibly wrong with the ear. But what about the fellow's mind...? Fortunately, the little pink and orange pills always proved effective. Pills to soothe frazzled nerves. Still, Dr. Seldag worried about the poor lad, since the condition refused to go away.

The silent woman with hair in her face stuck her tongue out at Dr. Seldag as he examined Lystir's ear for the seventeenth time that year. The doctor knew that the woman was only a symptom of stress-related madness. His was a difficult field: just last year, in a fit of pique, Dr. Ungila hollowed out a man's head and filled it with some sort of creamy dessert (brandied pudding or poppy puree—reports varied).

Dr. Seldag was determined not to give in. He would not react in any physical way: to do so would be granting the status of reality to this illusion. To hell with his colleagues and their insipid adherence to tradition! In his heart, he knew that to confront a fear was to beckon for madness with an eager, wiggling finger.

Every now and then, the silent woman would attempt to fondle him; hers was the insubstantial touch of a phantom's shadow. And so he ignored her. Ignored her. Ignored her. No matter what. That was the prudent thing to do.

The silent woman mouthed obscenities at him. Her too-long black bangs brushed against her upper lip.

"My good Mr. Norl, I believe you need more pink and orange pills," the physician said. "Take two whenever the pain spasms or tingling sensations strike." He smiled knowingly. "Or simply...whenever."

A single tear rolled down Lystir's white cheek. He took a tissue from a box on a side table. "Thank you, Doctor. Without you...why, I can't imagine where I'd be without you. You are my salvation."

Soon Lystir Norl was gone, and Dr. Seldag locked himself up in his office. The silent woman with hair in her face was infuriated with his indifference. Slicing deep into her abdomen with her twisted fingernails, she pulled forth steamy red lengths of herself and wrapped them around his throat—

But as always, he felt the mere ghost of a touch, and did nothing in response. Eventually the silent woman tucked herself back together. Dr. Seldag then prepared for Beric's visit. When he was finished, he took a blue pill, then a green pill, then a long nap. He dreamed that winged scorpions were tearing out his father's hair.

The doorbell rang and rang. The doctor bid farewell to the scorpions (and to bald, sad, silly dream-daddy) and returned to the waking world. He unlocked the door to let in Mrs. Thetron and her father.

"Am I dead?" shouted old Beric. "These grave wigglies are so itchy but I sure can't scratch inside my eyes."

Mrs. Thetron cleared her throat. "I've always meant to ask…why don't you have anyone to help you? A busy man like you! No assistant? Why?"

The silent woman with hair in her face smiled in the corner.

"I work alone," Dr. Seldag said as he assisted Beric up onto the examination table. "My patients surely prefer the sincere, confidential one-to-one attention." The physician pulled a row of metal bars up from the sides of the examination table. He strapped Beric's arms and shoulders in place (it would not do for the old man to squirm at a crucial moment). He propped open Beric's eyelids with petite but sturdy frameworks of rubber-coated wire. He then reached up and pulled a slender silver chain.

Off went the office lighting. Moonglow streamed in through the windows. Wormglow streamed out of Beric's eyes.

Dr. Seldag opened a metal cabinet by the window. He lit a small candle and placed it on a tray of syringes with curved needles. The tray also held a bottle of pink fluid, an eyedropper, and a textbook—*Diagnosis and Treatment of Ocular Parasitism and Associated Mental Disorders* by A. L. Puthmoor. The physician set the tray by Beric's side and applied several drops of the pink fluid to each of the patient's eyes.

"This contains a soothing local anesthetic," the doctor said, holding the bottle up for Mrs. Thetron to see. "Old Beric won't feel a thing."

Dr. Seldag began to remove the worms one by one, suctioning them out of the old man's eyes with the syringes. He consulted the textbook by the light of the candle. Every now and then he would inject pink fluid into each of Beric's eyes.

"Squishy, squirmy worms," the old man whispered dreamily. "Graveyard glowworms in the moonlight. Am I dead? Are you embalming me? Are you shooting embalming fluid into my eyes? Sure wouldn't want my eyes to rot. Am I a mummy? A squirmy, wormy mummy?"

The silent woman with hair in her face sat by the old man's side. She snaked a hand into the gash in her belly and began to uncoil herself.

Dr. Seldag reached for a fresh syringe and continued with his work. The silent woman began to dangle her damp yardage in front of his face.

"Leave me be," the doctor murmured. "I'm working. Can't you see that? Maybe you should brush the hair out of your eyes." He pulled back the plunger of the syringe and drew the last glowing worm from Beric's right eye. He then realized with a start that for the first time, he had spoken to the silent woman. She grinned hugely as she backed into her shadowed corner.

"Are you all right, doctor?" Mrs. Thetron said. "Who were you talking to?"

Dr. Seldag smiled as he turned the lights back on. "I was merely experiencing a stress symptom. Please, don't mind me. Your Beric is free of eyeworms, Mrs. Thetron. I shall bandage his eyes and then you may take him home. Be sure to keep him away from thromba trees."

As he finished taping gauze over the old man's eyes, Dr. Seldag noticed that Mrs. Thetron was looking at the textbook. She pulled a small nail file from a pocket and began to pick at the inside cover.

"My book! What are you doing?" cried the physician with dismay.

"Oh, I'm sorry. I just happened to notice…" She held the book out to him. "The very first page was stuck. See? Somebody must have been eating and reading the book at the same time."

Dr. Seldag took the book from her hands. There was a brown smudge on the inside cover, to which the page had adhered. A chocolate thumbprint from long ago.

The doctor's pulse quickened. The newly discovered page held a handwritten message in light-green pencil.

> *To Paglio, my naughty monkey—*
> *Bon-bons for your belly, a book for your*
> *brain, and me for the rest of you.*
> *—Agmylia*

Agmylia?

Had A.L. Puthmoor been a woman? Apparently so. And a clever, zesty one at that. Amorous, too. "Me for the rest of you." Such a lusty phrase. Lusty. Lust. The doctor rolled the word around in his brain. *Lust.* It rhymed with must. Ashes to ashes, dust to dust. Professor Puthmoor must have lust. A giggle, tiny but not quite soundless, danced on his tongue and squeezed its way past his lips.

He looked up in time to see Mrs. Thetron and Beric leaving the room, hand in hand.

Then the doctor felt a tap on the shoulder.

He turned to face—

Was this the silent woman with hair in her face? Evidently. Her hair was pushed back now, to reveal one staring, pimento-red eye. A dark, pitted mass was embedded in her other eye-socket: a meteorite, just a tad smaller than a baby's fist.

The woman moved her lips. This time, words came out. "I thank you for granting me my reality. Now let us see just how real I can *be*." She put a hand to the rock lodged in her face. Her red eye blazed with triumph. "A doctor is what I need. Yes, indeed. I know that your caseload is rather heavy. But still, won't you please…take me on?"

* * * *

One week passed.

Two weeks.

Three.

Pleased with the progress of his patients, Dr. Seldag decided it was time to experiment with group sessions.

Lystir Norl wiped at his eyes. "The horrible squiggly ickies scare me so. Will Mommy be at my funeral?"

Mr. Pnik blew his nose. "Bury me deep. Deep in the dark. Down with the worms in the deep dark dirt."

"Wiggle, wiggle, wiggle. It's so funny. It's just so funny. It's just so very funny." Mrs. Aggi said, rubbing drool from her lips with the back of her hand. Lystir gave her the last tissue from the box on the side table.

Dr. Seldag opened his metal cabinet. On the bottom shelf rested a lich-crow nest which held three open tissue boxes.

Groups sessions brought out so many emotions! The physician grinned hugely as he reached down. His long, twisted fingernails speared yet another infested box for his loving, sharing patients.

THOUSANDSKINS

Once there was a goblin king whose wife had shining golden fur and eyes like silver coins. The other goblin women, whose furs were either lead-grey or calico, were quite jealous of the beautiful queen. For that reason, one of the ladies-in-waiting—a spindly beast with bald patches—hid a sprig of parsley in the queen's mold pie. Since goblins cannot abide good fresh food, the queen fell ill. On her deathbed, the queen made her husband promise this: that if he should marry again, he would choose as his bride one with eyes as silvery and fur as golden as her own.

This the king promised.

The king and queen had three female kittens at that time, so young that their eyes were still closed. The queen kissed her babes and bundled more warm spiderwebs around their limbs (for they had yet to grow fur). She then died with a small smile on her lips. The king instructed a nursemaid to take away the mewling babes, for the very sight of them saddened him.

For many years, the king's advisors searched for a she-goblin with silver eyes and golden fur. But alas, one could not be found. In his study, the brooding king busied himself with the affairs of his land.

In the servant's wing of the palace, the nursemaid raised the royal kittens to adulthood. One grew into a fine calico lass; another became the darling of the court, slim and grey with sweet red eyes. As for the third: she was an enigma. She wore a hooded robe and studied in the cobwebbed, neglected palace library. She spent so much time among the old books that her fur was always smeared with thick dust. She ate her meals alone and talked to no one. All in the goblin court called her Princess Shush.

One night (but of course, it is always night in the goblin-land), the king glimpsed a silvery glint down a darkened hallway. He went down the hall and found Princess Shush standing by a window.

"There is something that gleams of silver in this hall," said the king. "Can you show me what it is?"

Princess Shush threw back her hood, and the king saw that her eyes were like two silver coins. He saw too that her fur, under the dark dust, was as bright as gold.

He took her hand and led her to the chamber of his foremost advisor, a lean old thing with two teeth in his head. The king informed the elder goblin that he planned to marry the Princess. The old goblin smiled and nodded, for goblins have no laws against such things. Goblins have but one law: In matters of enjoyment, thou shalt not hesitate.

Ah, but Princess Shush enjoyed nothing. She read the big dusty books in the library only because the fine, faint lettering strained her eyes. She did not want the goblin-land to enjoy a royal wedding festival with feasts of lovely mold and rot. The princess penned this contract and gave it to the old advisor:

> Know you that I shall marry the king only after I have received these fine items of wedding apparel: a gown of diamonds as bright as the sun; emerald shoes as green as grass; and a ruby necklace as red as human blood.
>
> Know you that I shall sleep in the king's chambers only after I have received a fine blanket made from snippings from the skins of one-thousand humans.
>
> Know you that I shall bear the king's young only after I have received these fine kitten toys: a wee metal bird that sings; a wee metal flower that blooms; and a wee metal human that dances.

Princess Shush was sure that these demands would bring an end to the king's wedding plans. The sun was hurtful to goblin flesh, and bird songs pained goblin ears. Grass and flowers were foul-smelling, poisonous things, and furless humans were utterly noxious beings.

These demands repelled the king, and for a moment he thought seriously of forsaking his plans. But he dearly wanted a son to whom to give his throne. He summoned his army and sent them into the world to find and steal the items requested by the princess.

The royal court waited for the soldiers to return. The princess spent many days searching the palace library for volumes on humans. She found just a few very old books, but they told her much.

At last the soldiers returned with the gifts. The ladies of the court stitched together the thousand bits of skin—light, dark, young, old—harvested by the soldiers. The goblin women despised the task, for they found it abhorrent to touch smooth human hide.

The old advisor presented Princess Shush with her niceties. The princess nodded by way of thanks. When she was alone, she gathered her sewing instruments and fashioned a curious garment from the blanket. This strange suit fit her body like a second skin. She slipped into this garment and then put on her hooded robe. Carrying her other gifts in a filthy sack, the princess left the goblin palace.

Down moonstone lanes and through blackwood forests walked Princess Shush, out of the goblin-land and into the realm of humans. The suit of one-thousand skins protected her from the burning sun. Her piebald appearance frightened the humans she met along the way, and they screamed as they ran from her.

Soon the princess came to a human castle. She rang the tin bell at the kitchen entryway and presented a letter to the cook who answered the door. This letter explained that its bearer, Thousandskins, was a sad quiet creature who wanted to be left alone (and surely, this was the truth). The letter went on to state that the bearer was more than willing to labor for the right to be ignored.

"I am a homely thing," said the old cook, "but you, Thousandskins, are homelier still. You may work in the kitchen, so that I may feel pretty when I hand you pots to scrub."

For a good long time, the princess lived as happily as one of her melancholy nature can. She washed dishes and swept stairs and helped to prepare meals. She ate the mold from old bread and the rancid fat from cooking pans. Her room was in the dark stone corridors beneath the kitchen. Late at night, she would leave the castle through a forgotten servant's door and sit in the courtyard, there to stare at the moon's dead face.

One evening, she happened to notice a pale young man looking out of a window. He too was staring at the moon. His cheeks were sunken and his eyes were dark and hollow. The princess felt a strange fire in her heart. Was this love? she wondered. She had read of love in the library of the goblin palace. She regarded the human's repulsively smooth skin and his forlorn expression and knew that yes, she loved him truly.

The cook had tidings for Thousandskins in the morning. They were to work hard for many days, in preparation for three nights of revelry. "It is time for Prince Veldor to choose a bride," the cook said, "and he will be meeting all the ladies of the kingdom. All except you and I—and I would not want him, even to become queen. He is a miserable ghoul of a boy."

The cook and Thousandskins peeled potatoes and sliced onions and kneaded dough. They skinned and roasted ducks and lambs. They made exquisite desserts from fruits, brandies and rare spices. On the last day of the preparations, the cook said to Thousandskins, "You shall keep to your room during the balls. You are a frightful thing and I would not want you to be seen."

Night came, and Thousandskins took a bucket of water to her room. She removed the suit of skins and for the first time in her life, scrubbed her golden goblin fur. She put on her diamond gown, her emerald shoes, and her ruby necklace. She pinned the metal bird to her sleeve and used the forgotten door to slip into the night.

Princess Shush entered the ball through the castle's gilded gates. The people of the kingdom were amazed by this strange and beautiful maiden. Her gown, her shoes, even her skin glittered—she seemed to be covered with a fine, velvety coat of gold dust. True, her fingers were a bit overlong, and her eyes held a strange glow…but perhaps these were the markings of exotic aristocracy.

The princess pressed a small lever in the throat of the metal bird and the automaton began to sing. She waltzed with every nobleman at the ball except Prince Veldor. The shy, pale man danced with no one. He sat on his throne and stared longingly at Princess Shush. He could not bring himself to address her. He did try to catch her eye, but she only looked away. At the end of the ball, the golden woman approached the prince and handed him the singing bird. He wanted to thank her, but could not find the words. She simply smiled at the prince and walked out of the castle.

The next evening, Princess Shush entered the ball with the metal flower pinned to her sleeve. Again she danced with many noblemen. In a moment of rare bravado, Prince Veldor instructed a serving boy to deliver a note to her. In vain, in vain. She ignored the prince until the last minute, when she gave him the flower. This time the prince said, "Thank you, dear lady. And thank you for last evening's beautiful song bird." Again the princess smiled and began to walk away. "You did not tell me your name," the pale man cried. The princess stopped and gestured for him to follow her. The prince took one step, then another, and then stopped. He could go no further.

On the third night, the princess led the wee metal dancing man into the ball on a leash. The king and queen of the land watched her with interest, for their son had told them of her beauty and her fine gifts. "Dance with her, for she is cultured and graceful," the queen whispered into her son's ear. "Ask for her hand, for surely she is a princess," whispered the king into the prince's other ear.

Prince Veldor walked up to the golden woman and asked if she wished to dance. She unfastened the leash from the throat of her dolly. Then she nodded to the prince and they waltzed without speaking. The wee metal man made its way across the room and hopped onto the prince's throne. At that point, a curious thing transpired: the king and queen mistook the metal man for their son and both whispered into its tiny ears. Perhaps the princess had enchanted the metal man. Perhaps not.

At the end of the evening, the princess fastened the leash around Prince Veldor's neck—he did not resist—and led him out of the castle.

No one tried to stop them. "Where are you taking me?" the prince whispered. The golden woman said nothing. They walked through the night, over bridges and through dark valleys to the land of the goblins.

Princess Shush put a finger over the lips of her paramour as they entered the goblin palace. Thus warned, the prince kept his silence.

From that moment on, silence served them well.

The goblins considered humans unspeakably vile, and the prince was no exception. No one uttered a word about the revolting desires of the princess, and the goblin king dared not claim his tainted daughter for marriage. He wished to punish her, but did not know how: to do so would only bring attention to her transgressions. And really, wasn't the awful touch of a human punishment enough?

Princess Shush and Prince Veldor cared not what the world thought. They had each other, and that was enough.

And so the lovers lived in blissful shame for the rest of their goblin-land nights.

MR. STICKY-LIPS

If you're ever traveling by bus across the country and you see a smiling, grubby, thirtyish man in a purple baseball cap…a filthy, jaundiced weirdo who really enjoys his chocolate, bar after sticky bar.…

Don't make eye contact.

I did—and from Chicago to Cleveland, he decided I was his best friend ever, so he shared his life story with me.

He didn't know I had a tape recorder in my duffel bag, because I was going to be taping an interview at the literary convention where I was going.

He didn't hear the soft click as I hit RECORD.

I don't really know why I taped his ramblings. I suppose it was because he had such a sad look in his eyes. Ever see that painting, "The Last Supper"? He had eyes like one of those guys.

He had a big plastic bag of chocolate bars on his lap, and his lips glistened with thick brown goo as he chewed and spoke, chewed and spoke. I got off the bus about five minutes after he finished speaking. I have no idea where he is or what he's doing these days.

His whereabouts are anyone's guess.

This is what Mr. Sticky-Lips had to say:

* * * *

My dad was a mechanic and my mom was just mom. But being mom was really a full-time job because there were nine of us kids. I was the youngest. My dad didn't help out much around the house. He just sat on the swing on the back porch, drinking beer and looking at the sky. We didn't bother him none, because if we did, he'd whip off his belt and snap us with it. Mom was deaf in her right ear because he once snapped her on that side of her head and I guess he did it too hard. I always stood on her left side when I talked to her.

Mom disappeared when I was eight. She didn't take any clothes or make-up or nothing. She still had the TV on, and a pot roast in the oven. I think the aliens came and got her. I mean, what other explanation could there be? It wasn't like her to miss her favorite soap opera.

I ran away when I was fourteen. My dad probably didn't even notice. I did leave a goodbye note, though. That's just what it said. "Goodbye. Signed, Steve." That's my name. Steve.

I bummed around from city to city. I hitchhiked a lot. I was big for my age. A guy on the road can make a few bucks here and there, if he's not too picky. You know, doing people favors, stuff like that. Sometimes I even got a chocolate bar.

My mom and dad never bought us candy because they said it would rot our teeth out and we couldn't afford a dentist. I haven't been to a dentist in my whole life, but that's okay. My teeth are really strong. I always carry a toothbrush, too. I've got one on me right now, tucked in my sock.

For a few months there, I belonged to what I thought was a church. They were nice to me at first. Even gave me my own room. There were a lot of us in that house. We had to pick sweet corn in work-shifts and we weren't allowed to smoke or read newspapers or ever leave. It took me a while, but I figured it out. That was what folks call a cult.

They kept adding new rules, like, "don't call your relatives" and "don't wear anything with purple in it" and "don't eat any of the sweet corn you pick." One day they said, "don't eat anything with sugar in it." That's when I figured out they were evil.

One night I set fire to the community room and in all the confusion, I escaped. Half the cult got burned up, and some jumped out of windows to get out of there and busted some bones, but like my dad used to say, you can't make an omelet without breaking a few legs. I think maybe he meant eggs.

Eventually I found a nice mall with really crappy security and I was able to live off that place for a whole summer. One of the stores had crummy air-conditioning, and they'd wedge the employee entrance open to let in a breeze. I'd sneak in and out that way, and hide stuff under the stairs by that entrance. It was pretty slick. Sometimes I'd sleep under those stairs. It was really dark under there. Nobody could see me. I felt like some kind of movie-star cat-burglar-type secret spy.

I got my hands on some new clothes, some suitcases, and some money from a couple different cash registers. I got me a driver's license from a lost-and-found box—the guy even looked a little bit like me. So for a while I was able to travel in style. You'd be surprised by some of the jobs I've had. Of course, they weren't exactly what you'd call nine-to-five jobs. They all paid in cash. A little nude modeling, though we weren't the kind of models who just stood around. Some videos, too. Never had a desk job, though on one of those videos, they've got me strapped to a desk with duct tape.

Like I said, I never got to have any candy when I was little, so whenever I had a few extra bucks, I always bought myself some chocolate bars. Chocolate tastes so good, so yummy—so much better than anything else on this planet. Eventually I figured out that aliens must have brought it to Earth. I mean, what other explanation could there be?

So some nights, I'd stand outside and cry out to outer space, "Aliens, take me to your chocolate world so I can be with my mom you stole! You owe me that much!"

But even though aliens are usually chomping at the bit to steal humans, they never came for me. I think my advanced intellect must have scared them off.

Then! Then I figured out a way I could trick the aliens. A way to join them through the back door. A person's got to be really clever whenever they're dealing with aliens. They have those giant brains, you know. They think really big thoughts. The biggest.

I discovered that if I ate enough chocolate, I mean a lot, really a lot, I could elevate my mind to a higher plane of existence. I figured, if I got my mind high enough, I'd be able to reach the plane of the aliens. I could actually feel my mind rising up, up, up—soaring up to the chocolate door of the alien's secret dimension. Way past Mars, and that's pretty far off. A few times, I think I pushed my mind past Uranus. It helped if I drank a lot of coffee.

I wanted to see what else I could add to the mix, to get to that door faster, but the police caught me trying to break into a pharmacy, and that ended that. For a few months, anyway.

Since then I've been in and out of funny farms. They're not really very funny, though. I once got out of one by setting a fire, because really, those places are no better than cults. These days, I just cooperate with the doctors, since I've found out my meds sometimes work with the chocolate. Especially if I wash them down with coffee. And vodka. Or whiskey. Or tequila. Any old booze, really. Booze is made out of fermented plant juice, you know. They say folks should eat three or four vegetables a day, right? Same thing. In fact, they go down better if they're liquid.

Tastes better, too.

Every time some doctor sees me, he'll say my liver is going to hell and I'll probably be dead in three months. Ha! They've been saying that for five years now. What do they know? Maybe whatever I'm doing to my liver is good for me. Making me live longer. Or, maybe it's going to make me live in a *different* way. After all, once I get past the chocolate door, everything will change. Maybe I'll leave my body behind, all dead and everything, but the real soul-ghost of me will still be alive, having been prepared for any future lack of a body by my amazing liver!

I bet that's why it's called a liver. Makes sense to me.

You know what I think? I think the doctors don't want me to know the truth about how things really are. Each day, I feel myself getting a little bit closer to the chocolate door, and soon, I'll find out what's behind it. I'll be able to join the aliens and my mom. I'll even let the aliens probe my soul-ghost, since I know how much they need information on us humans.

It's the least I can do for them. They've been taking care of my mom all this time, letting her watch alien soap operas and make pot roasts out of yummy alien animals.

When we get back together again, I'll always stand on my mom's left side, just like when I was little, so she can hear everything I have to say. Unless the aliens have fixed her bad ear. Yeah, I bet they have. Why, I bet they can fix anything. Maybe they'll make a new body for my soul-ghost. Stuff like that is probably really easy for them.

Me and mom, we'll walk through fields of chocolate flowers and laugh under a chocolate sky. I know that probably doesn't sound pretty. Kind of sounds like poop, doesn't it? Like a big stinky poop world. But that chocolate won't be stinky at all, and we'll get so used to everything being chocolate, all the different shades of brown will start looking like a whole rainbow of colors, sweet magical colors. Oh, I know it will be beautiful. So beautiful.

I can hardly wait to get there.

Wow, look at me, what a big pig I am—eating all this yummy chocolate in front of you without offering to share.

Have some. It's really good.

Not hungry? Oh. Okay. Suit yourself.

I think I'm going to take a little nap now. Don't be sad or anything if I never wake up.

That's just means I'm with mom.

IT ISN'T WHAT YOU GNAW,
IT'S WHO YOU GNAW

Wilma Website: Yeah, I was a Deathquaker. I suppose I still am, but I really can't call myself one, since Dandy Voorhees isn't around anymore.

The Deathquakers without Dandy? Unthinkable! That would be like the Youthquakers from the Sixties without Andy Warhol. Everybody knows that Dandy modeled his every movement, every utterance, every moment of his existence after Andy Warhol. Andy was an artist and a genius, and so was Dandy. But Dandy gave everything a dark twist—a Goth sensibility—so he could take it one step beyond and call it his own.

Andy had a hangout called The Factory, with everything spray-painted silver. Dandy had The Funeral Parlor, with everything draped in black velvet. Andy had his paintings of Campbell Soup cans and his Brillo box sculptures. Dandy did the same thing with formaldehyde bottles and clove cigarette packs. Andy looked like a pathetic corpse—and Dandy...?

Like I said. He had to take everything one step beyond.

* * * *

Koko Fantastic: I was Dandy's first friend in his town without pity, make no mistake! I was actually at the bus station when he arrived. But I wasn't there to see Dandy. I didn't even know who he was. No one did.

No, I was arguing with my boyfriend at the time, whose name I will not even allow to cross my lips, because he was leaving town and he still owed me at least three or four thousand dollars. I was just yelling and yelling at him, telling him I was going to hunt him down like a dog, when out of the corner of my eye I saw this scrawny little white-haired man-child with sunglasses and skin three shades whiter than an onion. He was wearing some kind of tattered black-velvet suit that was falling apart at the seams.

I looked at that little piece of ghost-meat and said, "Freak, what's your story?"

He just pointed behind me and said, "Gee! That guy's getting away."

I turned around and sure enough, the bus was pulling away from the curb. I just sank to the ground and started crying, and damned if that skinny-assed albino shrimp didn't sit himself down next to me and start crying, too.

"Oh, now don't you start," I said. "You're so skinny, you'll leak out all your water and turn to dust. Why are you crying anyway? You don't know me."

"I can't help it," he said in that soft ghost-voice of this. "Gee, you're just so beautiful I can't stand to see you so sad. What's your name?"

I told him my name. My real name, that is. He shook his head. "That's all wrong for you. Your name should be Koko Fantastic. A beautiful lady should have a beautiful name."

Well now, of course I know I'm beautiful. But sadly, most folks don't appreciate that fact. They think a woman over three-hundred pounds has just gotta be—shall we say, less than pleasing to the eye. I thought little ghosty-boy was really sweet…and very observant…so I told him he could stay at my place for a few weeks. I took that name he gave me, and it turned my life around. His stay turned from weeks into years, but that was no problem, because by then, he was a force to be reckoned with, and I was high and mighty among his Chosen Ones—the Deathquakers.

* * * *

Arabella Cream: He came to town with ten bucks and a suitcase full of home-made Goth clothes and a headful of dreams about Andy Warhol. I forget where he was from, but it was some little ditchwater burg in the Midwest. Kansas? Iowa? Nebraska? One of those really flat states.

I was managing the Saunders Gallery and living in a crummy apartment building about six blocks away—a real rat's nest filled with crazy artists. But it was close to work and I hate to drive, so it was fine for me at the time. Plus, I had a little act going on at the coffeehouse across the street—performance poetry every Wednesday night—so it was a really convenient location. My neighbor across the hall was this hugely fat Southern gal—a massage therapist who had these totally impossible dreams of being a great actress. Dandy was staying with her. She'd found him at the bus station and so I guess she'd sort of adopted him. Like a stray kitten.

He started going around to all the ad agencies, trying to do freelance work for them. Andy Warhol did that back at the beginning of his career, you know. And like Warhol, he was as pale as a ghost, with patchy white hair, and so eager, so sensitive…so unearthly. I had a couple agency friends at the time, and we called him Andy Wannabe for a few weeks. Dandy was into the whole Goth thing, but I guess that made sense. If

Warhol were alive today, he'd be loving that whole lace-trimmed doom scene.

I saw Dandy pretty often, because after all, he lived right across the hall. We'd talk every now and then. He couldn't hold a real conversation: he'd either just mumble a few words or else ramble on about his latest obsession. He showed me his drawings and paintings and photos. He wanted to buy some silk-screening equipment so he could do pictures that way—just like Warhol.

Eventually I let him do a show at the Saunders Gallery—half out of pity and half because he really did have some talent. Eventually he started hanging out with a group of artist types and he became their leader. Amazing, really, when you consider how socially awkward he was. But he did have a knack for finding people who could help him reach the next stage—whatever that stage might be.

* * * *

Xavier Y. Zerba: I met Dandy at the coffee shop across the street from where he used to live. Goth men are usually so chic in their own grim, counter-culture way, but Dandy just looked ghoulish. But still, he had some definite magnetism, and I found myself spending more and more time with him, listening to him go on and on about all kinds of nonsense. He was convinced that he was the reincarnation of Andy Warhol. He said that living and dying as Warhol had given him unbelievable insights, and that this time, he was going to tilt everything at just the right angle so that his work would live forever.

Back when he was Warhol, he said, he'd touched upon the ultimate truth when he did his remakes of those old Dracula and Frankenstein movies. The truth that lurks beyond life. He just hadn't lingered long enough on those themes—not long enough to learn anything substantial.

You know, when you think about it, it really is odd that a pop-culture guru like Warhol would ever have remade a couple of creaky horror movies like that. The things Dandy said gave the whole situation a perfectly logical rationale. I found myself nodding whenever I listened to him.

His work started selling pretty well at the Saunders Gallery. I hitched him up with a few other opportunities in the city—I know everybody who's anybody. If I don't know them, they aren't worth knowing. I introduced him to politicians, newspaper columnists, club owners—even the S&M cult-freaks who run The Absinthe Martini. I was the one who introduced him to Taffy Belasco. Crazy rich girl with too much time on her hands. She had loads of old-money friends, all perfectly eager to throw cash at somebody if Taffy deigned to give that person the nod. She funded quite a lot of Dandy's projects—his silk-screening projects, his art films—she even paid the rent at The Funeral Parlor, before Dandy started making money hand over fist.

* * * *

Taffy Belasco: Dandy was simply, simply, simply divine. I wasn't attracted to him in any sort of physical way—but really, that's just as well. Sex would have ruined our relationship. We had something better than sex. We had rapport.

He was like my daddy, my brother, sometimes even my mother, all rolled up into one. People used to tell me, "Taffy, he's just using you for your money. He's sucking on you like a leech. Wake up and smell the coffee!" But I would just laugh. For a crazy little man who looked like death, he made me feel so alive! So I helped him out. I was the one who helped him set up The Funeral Parlor. He was living with Koko Fantastic, but I thought he needed some additional work-space. Her place was just so small—but then, maybe it just looked small in comparison to her. At The Funeral Parlor, Dandy finally had enough room to really launch some fantastic projects. A lot of his little movies were made there. I paid the bills early on, and in Dandy's defense, he did eventually pay me back. With interest, which is something leeches never do. Eventually I let him study the Crowley papers—though looking back, I suppose that might have been a mistake.

* * * *

Wilma Website: Dandy once told me, "I can't be around common people. They make me nauseous." So he picked his own family of uncommon folks—the Deathquakers. He was our pseduo-Daddy, and eventually Taffy became our pseudo-Mommy. And The Funeral Parlor was our spooky tree-house.

Dandy and Taffy, Taffy and Dandy—the society columns were all abuzz at the time. Who is this pale mystery man squiring everyone's favorite spoiled-little-rich-girl hither and yon? I first met Dandy through Taffy—I was designing her website, and she introduced us at a party. He took one look at me and said, "Those cheekbones! I've just got to put you in one of my movies!" He'd started making art-films. At that point, he'd only made two or three. One of those early ones was called *Fish*— they showed it at that party. It was just forty minutes of Koko Fantastic chopping up dead fish. Every now and then she'd stop to read their guts. I guess some people can read fish-guts. Sounds like pretty boring reading, though. There can't be much of a plot.

* * * *

Koko Fantastic: I was the star of Dandy's first movie, *Fish*. I didn't even have to act—I just read entrails for him, since he'd always been fascinated by the fact that I could do that—that *anyone* could do that. My mama taught me how to do it, and her mama taught her, and I suppose her mama taught her, on down the line all the way back to Eve.

That puny rich girl he used to hang out with, that Taffy, she's related to Aleister Crowley. You know who that is? Weird old black-magic guy. Born 1875, died 1947. A member of the Hermetic Order of the Golden Dawn. He was Taffy's great-uncle or something like that. He designed a set of mystic tarot cards once. Whenever Taffy couldn't make up her mind, she'd break out those cards and do a reading. One of those cards showed a golden woman holding a giant snake—or maybe she was wrestling with it, I couldn't tell. And there was this big eye shining golden light onto that snake. Yeah, I remember that one. It was the Universe card.

Taffy used to let Dandy look at Crowley's old papers—she has a bunch of them tucked away in the library at her Papa's mansion. I said to Dandy one day, "What do you want with that kind of magic? It's too evil. Too powerful. Don't look at that stuff any more."

He said, "Ask the fish guts if it's okay for me to look at Crowley's work. I'll do a film of the reading. Gee! It'll be marvelous! Just marvelous!"

Well, I've always wanted to be an actress, so I said "Sure," even though I didn't think people would be too interested in watching me read fish entrails. But I did it, and I'll tell you this: the fish-guts never lie.

The guts told me that death would come walking, and that's just what happened.

* * * *

Arabella Cream: Dandy started making those art-films of his, and before long, they were the talk of the town. Everybody wanted to be in a Dandy Voorhees movie, just like everybody wanted to buy a Dandy Voorhees painting or go to a Dandy Voorhees party. The whole city was all wrapped up in Dandy Voorhees.

After he'd been making those movies for about four or five years, I said to him one day, "Dandy, I've been good to you. Why don't you put me in one of your movies?"

He fixed his goofy stare on me and said, "Gee! What a great idea! How about this? We'll remake *Macbeth*, except we'll make it modern and interesting. You and Koko and Taffy can be the witches in the big cauldron scene. Xavier can be Macbeth. How about that?"

I had to bite my tongue to stop from laughing. Hmmm, apparently Shakespeare wasn't interesting, but Dandy was going to take care of that. Then he said, "You won't have to memorize any Shakespeare. Actors should never memorize anything—they should always put the lines in their own words. You know what might be fun? I'll see if we can work in the Chant of the All-Seeing Eye somehow."

I told him, "Never heard of it."

"No one has. But gee! It's really exciting!" he said. "It's something Crowley picked up during his travels. He found the original inscription in the tomb of the Red Pharaoh. He was going to publish a whole book about it, but he only ever got around to writing a couple chapters—Taffy has them up at her house. Crowley realized you had to combine science and religion to attain the ultimate truth of the Universe, and the Chant of the All-Seeing Eye was the way to do it. The chant reconfigures the brain so that it can see beyond good and evil. And the best part is, we'll be the first people since ancient times to use it, since Crowley never got around to publishing it."

Something seemed wrong with what Dandy was saying. "So you're saying this Crowley guy never used this chant thingy himself?"

Dandy nodded. "Yep."

"Even though he's the one who discovered it? Even though he was writing a book about it?"

He nodded again. "Yep."

"And that doesn't bother you?"

Dandy just shrugged. "Gee, why should it? Maybe he never got around to doing it. A lot of people are like that. They mean to do stuff, but then they just forget."

Dandy may have been an artistic genius, but you know, that doesn't mean he was *smart*.

* * * *

Xavier Y. Zerba: Dandy was going to make a movie called *The Legend of Macbeth and the All-Seeing Eye*, and he asked me to play the part of Macbeth. But as it turned out, I had to be out of town on the weekend he was starting production. He was disappointed that I wouldn't change my plans for him, so he said in a really bitchy voice, "Fine, I'll play Macbeth myself."

I was a little pissed off myself, since he was giving me so much attitude, so I said, "While you're at it, change the name. Your movies aren't long enough to have big titles like that."

"Well, gee! What should I change it to?" he whined.

"Use something from the show." I thought over what little I knew about *Macbeth*, and finally suggested, "Well, there's a line that says, 'boil your oil, toil and trouble'…or something like that. Call it *Toil and Trouble*. Or maybe just *Trouble*."

Dandy's face lit up like a jack-o-lantern. "Gee! That's a great title! Thanks, Xavier. I'll call it *Trouble*."

"Yeah," I said, "You do that."

* * * *

Taffy Belasco: Well, you know I simply adored Dandy. But *Trouble* certainly lived up to its name. I wasn't too happy with Dandy while he was making that picture. How was I to know it would be his last?

The problem was, Dandy got it into his head to play Macbeth himself, and he was terrible. I mean, he'd recruited some pretty far-out characters to play in some of his films, but he was about ten times worse than any of them. I tried to help. I told him: Dandy, I'm sure Macbeth never used the word "Gee!"—but of course that advice went right over his head, since he wanted all the actors to say the lines however they pleased.

The sets were just hideous. Most of his movies had funky, kitschy sets—usually rooms in The Funeral Parlor, and sometimes steam-rooms, alleys, fire escapes painted purple, you name it. But for this one, he decided to build a cemetery out of cardboard, like in the movie *Plan 9 From Outer Space*. He built it in a big, smelly warehouse—the stink was awful, a nauseating combination of burnt plastic and ammonia.

Plus, Dandy was the only person running the camera, which meant he had to rush in and out of the picture all the time, to change the angle whenever somebody moved too much. Ridiculous! He'd say, "It'll get fixed in editing." He kept talking about this chant he was going to do as part of the movie, but he said he'd be doing it last, when we weren't around. He wouldn't explain why.

He really dragged out the witch-and-cauldron scene—that probably takes up half of *Trouble*. I've never seen the whole thing, so I wouldn't know. The other parts of the movie didn't take that long to shoot, since the rest was just a super-abbreviated version of *Macbeth* with a few scenes of a homeless woman doing some sort of spastic go-go dance. He saw some weird old woman dancing outside of the warehouse, so he put her in the movie as Ophelia. I didn't have the heart to tell him that Ophelia was from *Hamlet*.

So finally, when it came time for him to do the big chant scene, he just sent all of us home. Just like that. He told Arabella and me to take the homeless woman with us. He gave us twenty bucks and asked us to buy her dinner somewhere. All the frustration I'd felt making that movie melted away as soon as Dandy asked us to do that. That was so sweet of him. So we bought that old lady a steak dinner at a nice little diner. And while she was eating she said, "That guy, he's the gate. He's gonna open the gate." She said that about five times.

Finally Arabella said, "He's the gate *and* he's gonna open the gate? What does that mean? He's gonna open himself?"

The old woman nodded and said, "Exactly." As soon as she finished eating, she got up, said "See ya!" and walked out of the restaurant. We never saw her again, which is probably just as well.

* * * *

Wilma Website: Dandy died filming the chant scene of *Trouble*. And apparently he'd made some secret arrangements with some people. The camera and sets were gone but the body was still in the warehouse. Two months later, the film premiered at a Goth art gallery called The Absinthe Martini.

The body had been discovered by some guy who'd been looking for old copper wire to sell. Dandy didn't have any ID on him—typical Dandy—but he had my business card in his pocket. I'd given it to him the day before, since my phone number had changed. So the copper-wire guy called me on a cell-phone! I told him to call the police, too. Then I drove straight down to the warehouse. It wasn't that far—only twenty minutes away from my studio. I arrived ten minutes before the police. The copper-wire guy was gone by then.

The body had turned an awful shade of sky-blue. I identified it as Dandy's, and answered a few questions about him for the police—and right in the middle of the questioning, the body scrambled to its feet in a jerky, puppet-like way, and Dandy croaked out, "Gee!" in a sad, dry, raspy voice. His eyes were shining with bright golden light. An officer stepped right up to him, and Dandy seized him by the throat and actually *shot* golden beams out of his eyes, burning two holes into the officer's face.

It was the *damned*est thing.

Another officer fired at him, so Dandy shot those golden beams at him, too—and burned two spots as big as quarters into the guy's throat. He ran over and started chewing on the second cop, who was very good-looking. We're talking Brad-Pitt-good-looking.

Then Dandy slowly turned to stare at me, and started licking his lips. Licking his pale-blue lips with a dark-blue tongue.

So of course I turned and ran. I'm no idiot.

* * * *

Koko Fantastic: The Absinthe Martini is run by a weird little clique that's into S&M, so none of us Deathquakers ever went there, even though it was Goth. Xavier knew those folks, but even he never went to their place. No sirree. But I guess Dandy went there. They were the ones who ended up with *Trouble*, so I suppose he had some kind of thing with them. An agreement. An alliance. I don't know what you'd call—what they had. I'm sure they were the ones who took away the sets for the movie after Dandy died. They left the body because they knew what it was going to become.

Eventually the police figured out a way to load him into a truck and take his zombie ass away. That's what he was, you know. A zombie. And not your garden-variety, me-want-brains, drive-in-movie-style zombie. He was some kind of freaky primal thing, cooked up out of that damned Aleister Crowley magic.

Poor Dandy. Poor man-child.

Poor thing.

* * * *

Arabella Cream: That chant, that's what did it to him. But you know, I don't think it did what it was *supposed* to do. That Dandy—he never could stick to a script.

But evidently his rendition of the chant was caught on film. I can just see him, setting up the camera, getting everything ready, then running in front of it to do his bit. Mr. Do-It-Yourself. None of us Deathquakers went to the premiere of *Trouble*—we never went to The Absinthe Martini and besides, we weren't invited. But it's just as well. The film turned everyone in the audience into zombies. Which leads me to wonder how the film was *edited*…? Maybe different people took turns editing different parts. Maybe it was edited out of sequence. Or maybe zombies edited it. I don't know.

You know, I'm really sick of art. Running the Saunders Gallery was hard enough, having to deal with whiny diva artists. But having to contend with art-film zombies—that's just too much. One of these days I'm just going to move to some small town, find me a hunky gas-station attendant and settle down to a quiet, fat, frumpy life with a few brats and a station wagon.

I'll even start using my original first name again. Darla.

* * * *

Xavier Y. Zerba: You know, I was supposed to go to the premiere of *Trouble*. The gang at The Absinthe Martini even sent me an invitation. They were a strange little group. Pale, tattooed men who always wore leather. And that was management—you should've seen the bartenders. All of them had names like Toad-Scar and Crow-Claw and Barbed-Wire Joe. They'd have been the first to admit that they loved stirring up—trouble! I guess that made the movie's title especially apropos.

I always told the other Deathquakers I never went to The Absinthe Martini, but yeah, sure I did…all the time. Just for fun. I took Dandy once, just for fun. I think he had more fun than I realized.

But I wasn't able to make it to the premiere because I was sick—stomach flu, puking and diarrhea all night. I've been pretty lucky. If I'd have played Macbeth in that movie…or gone to that premiere…I'd be a zombie now.

There were probably about a couple hundred people at that premiere—The Absinthe Martini can be standing room only on a good night. Now all those folks are zombies, roaming the streets day and night, blasting chunks out of people with their eye rays. I hear some of them have managed to turn other folks into zombies—not sure how, but I'm not sticking around to find out.

Luck only lasts for so long, so I'm getting out while the getting is good. I'll be on the first plane taking off tomorrow morning—I don't even care where it's going.

I've had a lot of fun in this city. Now I'll have fun in another city. Sans the living dead.

* * * *

Taffy Belasco: Papa has connections, so this morning, I asked him to find out what the authorities are doing to Dandy's zombie. He made a few calls, pulled a few strings—Papa's wonderful that way. He found out that Dandy is being tested at some sort of institution. They've got him locked up in a concrete room, and they're running all sorts of tests on him—which isn't easy, since he can fire those eye-beams. In fact, Papa's taking me to the institute next week. He said I can watch Dandy on a monitor. Dandy on TV, at long last! Yesterday he managed to turn one of the guards into a zombie—he recited that chant to him. So Papa said he'll have them turn down the sound on the monitor while we're watching Dandy.

The police are having a terrible time hunting down all those zombies. The horrid things don't care about bullets at all, and they can shoot that burning light out of their eyes. They're kind of like movie projectors, aren't they? They shoot out beams that make a lasting impression! It really was naughty of Dandy to use that Crowley chant to make so much mischief. So much trouble. *Trouble* begetting trouble. I wonder if he really knew what he was doing? This whole affair stinks of an experiment gone wrong.

But you know what's the funny part of this whole mess? Well, of course, the zombies attack anyone who attacks them—that's human nature, even if the human in question is one of the living dead. But if they're left to their own devices, they'll only attack and eat good-looking people. It isn't what you gnaw, it's who you gnaw! Isn't that a stitch? The media has really picked up on that—especially since some zombies have already attacked two health spas and a beauty salon. So ugly people and fatties have nothing to worry about. Ha, I guess that means Koko Fantastic is safe!

The other night, the Channel 17 Action News gal, Sharla Fontaine, was doing a report on the whole zombie scene from the street when suddenly one of those creatures rounded the corner—and marched right past her. Oh, but she was flabbergasted! She practically threw herself at it—did everything but stick her head in its mouth—but that zombie just wasn't having any of *that*, thank you very much! It was delightful! But you know, I've always thought she should do something about those teeth of hers. And those crow's-feet! A little Botox wouldn't hurt.

It seems those awful creatures have a lot of Dandy in them. Not his sweet side, which I must admit was pretty puny most of the time—but certainly his discerning nature. So maybe the meek will inherit the Earth after all, if these zombies take over and the beautiful people are turned into fodder.

Of course I still have all the Crowley papers. I've checked, and the chant is still there. Dandy didn't steal it—he must have just copied it. I bet he screwed it up. He probably left out some words when he was writing it down. And knowing him, he probably added some lines and said "Gee!" too many times while reciting it for the movie.

I'm tempted, you know. I really am. Tempted to go into the library, dig out those papers again, and recite that chant perfectly. Perfectly. Perfectly.

Just to see what happens. Or rather, what's *meant* to happen.

But not today.

I'm sure there will come a day when—horror of horrors!—my beauty will start to fade. My curves will sag. My limbs will ache and my eyes will bag.

Maybe then.

CLAWS OF THE INTERNET WITCHES

(SYSTEM MESSAGE: Internet Witch Coven No. 37 Chatroom Session 856 initiated)
(GYMALKA has entered Chatroom)
(MODERATOR: GYMALKA)
(TRANSCRIPT: initiate RECORD function)

GYMALKA: TEST

(MIZIMBA has entered Chatroom)

MIZIMBA: Greetings to you, sister. Where are the others?

GYMALKA: GREETINGS M I GOT HERE JUST A MINUTE AGO IM MODERATING TONIGHT THE CHAT DOESNT START FOR A FEW MINUTES YOURE EARLY YOUR CLOCK MUST BE OFF

MIZIMBA: You're probably right. I thought I was a little late. My clock says 12:03.

GYMALKA: HAVENT TALKED TO YOU SINCE THE LAST CHAT HOW ARE THINGS WITH YOU

MIZIMBA: I've set up seven websites since our last chat. Three turn mortals into the living dead. Two turn them into fat, delicious goats. One turns them into crows and the last gives them painful cancerous tumors.

GYMALKA: WHERE ON THE BODY

MIZIMBA: The genitals, of course.

GYMALKA: EXCELLENT

(VATHIMA has entered Chatroom)

VATHIMA: Greetings to you, sisters.

MIZIMBA: Greetings to you, Vathima.

GYMALKA: GREETINGS V

(POGMI has entered Chatroom)

POGMI: greetings to you, sisters.

(AGMELLA has entered Chatroom)

AGMELLA: Greetings to you, sisters.

GYMALKA: GREETINGS P & A

VATHIMA: Greetings, Pogmi and Agmella.

MIZIMBA: Greetings to you, sisters.

GYMALKA: I TRUST YOU ALL HAVE BEEN PRODUCTIVE MIZIMBA WAS TELLING ME ABOUT HER MOST RECENT AC-COMPLISHMENTS SHE HAS SET UP 7 WEBSITES TO TORMENT THE MORTALS WHO VISIT THEM HER SITES TURN THEM INTO ZOMBIES WE CAN USE FOR SLAVES AND GOATS WE CAN EAT AND CROWS THAT CAN SNATCH OUT HUMAN EYES AND 1 GIVES THEM TUMORS ON THEIR STINKING GENITALS SO THEY CANNOT BREED

VATHIMA: Excellent work, Mizimba. I have only had time to put up two websites. One bathes mortal visitors in radiation that cooks them to the bone, while the other turns them into monkeys with rabies. I would have set up more, but I have been having problems with my daughter Vulpa. The worry makes it difficult to concentrate on my work.

GYMALKA: WHAT IS THE PROBLEM WHY IS SHE MISSING OUR SESSION WHY IS SHE NOT HERE

VATHIMA: I do not know why Vulpa is not here. She is being very difficult. She is not sure she wants to be an internet witch. Such a ridiculous notion. Of course she must follow the way—she has no choice, it is in her blood. But still she insists she wants to be a dancer. A dancer, entertaining those putrid mortal animals!

GYMALKA: SHE IS STILL YOUNG ONLY 25 AND THE YOUNG NEVER KNOW WHAT THEY REALLY WANT THEY ONLY THINK THEY KNOW WHAT THEY WANT THEY KNOW NOTHING OF THE THREADS OF FATE THAT BIND US ALL

POGMI: she can be a witch and still dance. i dance every night.

AGMELLA: But you are very fat.

POGMI: a fat witch can dance!

VATHIMA: So what should I do about Vulpa?

MIZIMBA: She wastes time. Slap her. Someone should slap Pogmi, too.

POGMI: i will slap your head right off your body, you bitch!

AGMELLA: Do not let Vulpa stray from the path, Vathima. Pogmi strays too much. I have seen her at bars with mortals, laughing and drinking. She is a fat, stupid whore.

POGMI: how dare you spy on me!

GYMALKA: SOMEDAY THIS SHALL BE OUR WORLD BUT UNTIL THEN WE MUST BLEND IN WITH THE MORTALS WHEN WE ARE NOT AT OUR COMPUTERS TELL VULPA SHE CAN DANCE ONLY WHEN HER WORK IS DONE POGMI IS YOUR WORK DONE

POGMI: no, i have been busy

AGMELLA: Busy playing the whore!

GYMALKA: POGMI THE ONLY THING THAT SHOULD BE KEEPING YOU BUSY IS THE GREAT WORK WE MUST CONQUER THE WORLD MUST FIND NEW WAYS TO ENSLAVE THE MORTALS YOU USED TO BE SUCH A HARD WORKER POGMI YOU EVEN SET UP THIS CHATROOM FOR US SO TELL ME WHAT IS KEEPING YOU BUSY

POGMI: i have met a man and i want to have a baby with him.

GYMALKA: WE DO NEED THE MORTAL MEN FOR THEIR SEED BUT THAT IS ALL POGMI IT DOES NOT TAKE LONG FOR A MAN TO PLANT HIS SEED WHAT IS KEEPING YOU BUSY

POGMI: i love him. we are having fun. i want to have his baby and i want it to be a boy.

GYMALKA: WHAT ARE YOU SAYING YOU KNOW ANY BOYS WE MIGHT BEAR WOULD BE SLAIN AT BIRTH WE HAVE SPECIAL PILLS AND SPELLS TO MAKE SURE OUR BABIES ARE ONLY FEMALE WE DO NOT ALLOW MALE BABIES OUR

COVENS ARE ONLY FOR FEMALE WITCHES FEMALE YOU MUST BE INSANE WITH SUCH HIDEOUS TALK OF LOVE AND MALE BABIES

AGMELLA: See? She is a fat whore who wastes time on a foolish man.

GYMALKA: POGMI LET THE MAN PLANT HIS SEED AND THEN KILL HIM TAKE THE PILLS AND SAY THE SPELLS TO MAKE SURE THE BABY IS FEMALE

MIZIMBA: What is wrong with you, Pogmi? Why are you acting in such a disgusting manner?

VATHIMA: I should go to Vulpa's house and slap her to be sure she does not act as foolishly as Pogmi.

POGMI: you are all such sad, jealous bitches! i have found a fine man to love and i am going to keep him. your work means nothing to me now. i have my own work.

GYMALKA: YOUR OWN WORK WHAT DOES THAT MEAN

MIZIMBA: You had better change your ways, Pogmi, or face destruction.

AGMELLA: The fat whore has turned against us! I knew it! I shall run tracers on her sites immediately.

VATHIMA: What have you done, Pogmi?

POGMI: you can't frighten me. love has given me more power than all of you combined.

GYMALKA: I SHOULD MAKE YOUR COMPUTER EXPLODE I CAN DO IT YOU KNOW ANY TIME I WANT I AM THE MODERATOR

POGMI: go ahead! see what happens, bitch!

MIZIMBA: So you think you have found love, Pogmi? What will you do when your mortal idiot tires of you? What will you do then?

POGMI: then i will just find love again. that's how love works. love is strange. it hurts sometimes but it's still better than being nothing. better than just being a hateful machine made out of flesh.

(VULPA has entered Chatroom)

VULPA: Greetings to you, sisters. I apologize for being so late. I had to drive a neighbor to the hospital.

VATHIMA: See how she fawns upon the wretched mortals?

VULPA: Mr. Graham is very old and has always been good to me.

AGMELLA: A man! She is late because of a man! An old, sickly, useless man at that!

VATHIMA: We have a problem going on here, Vulpa. Pogmi is out of control.

VULPA: I'm sorry to hear that. I like Pogmi.

AGMELLA: I have finished running tracers on Pogmi's sites. She is giving the mortals browser updates to protect them from our websites! She has gone insane. She must be destroyed.

VULPA: Pogmi is nice! Leave her alone!

GYMALKA: GOODBYE POGMI IT IS TIME FOR US TO BE RID OF YOU

(GYMALKA has exited Chatroom)

(MODERATOR: MIZIMBA)

VATHIMA: What's going on? Where did Gymalka go?

AGMELLA: Gymalka must be having computer problems. Mizimba, you are the Moderator now, so pick up where she left off.

MIZIMBA: Will do.

(MIZIMBA has exited Chatroom)

(MODERATOR: AGMELLA)

POGMI: go ahead, agmella! You're the moderator, blow up my computer! you know you want to!

AGMELLA: With pleasure, you stupid, fat whore!

(AGMELLA has exited Chatroom)

(MODERATOR: VATHIMA)

VATHIMA: I am confused. What happened to Gymalka and Mizimba and Agmella?

POGMI: i set up this chatroom, remember? i recently changed some settings. all termination commands now redirect automatically to the sender.

VULPA: Don't try to blow up Pogmi's computer, mother.

VATHIMA: Your love of that mortal man has ruined you, Pogmi.

VULPA: Mother, I know you have always cared for father. I know you still talk to him every now and then. Maybe you love him. I hope you do. Pogmi just wants to be as happy as the mortals when they are in love, and so do I.

VATHIMA: We are too different from the mortals. We are superior to them.

POGMI: more powerful, yes. but not superior. we live like spiders, always weaving webs. but we don't have to. there's more to life than just thinking about death.

VATHIMA: I used to have such thoughts, back when I first met Vulpa's father. His name is Evan. Mortals think he is a big, strong man, but knowing how weak he really is, how vulnerable, makes me too sad. It makes no sense to love such a creature.

VULPA: Our power is our curse, mother. It only makes us hungry for more power, and so we claw and claw for more, always more. And what's the point of that? What's the point of ruling a warzone, filled with dead enemies?

VATHIMA: But what choice do we have? What else can we do?

POGMI: i have my own work to do so i must stay online. but you and vulpa can always pull the cord.

VATHIMA: Explain.

POGMI: unplug your computers. throw them in the garbage.

VATHIMA: What will I do then?

POGMI: walk in the sun. discover love.

VULPA: Turn off your computer, mother. Do as Pogmi said and throw it away. Forget about it. Just be free. Just be you. That's what I'm going to do right now.

(VULPA has exited Chatroom)

VATHIMA: Can I really do that?

POGMI: of course you can. the choice has always been yours. there's nothing to fear. the witches can't get you if you're not online.

VATHIMA: Yes. You're right.

POGMI: without the internet, you'll be just as weak as evan. or just as strong. go to him. see what happens.

VATHIMA: Very well. I shall try.

POGMI: i know you will be happy, and that is all that matters. good-bye, sister.

VATHIMA: Thank you. Goodbye, Pogmi.

(VATHIMA has exited Chatroom)

(MODERATOR: POGMI)

(TRANSCRIPT: stop RECORD function)
(TRANSCRIPT: initiate DELETE function)
(TRANSCRIPT: DELETE function completed)
(POGMI has exited Chatroom)
(End of Session 856)

SPIDERBREAD

Isn't that a horrible name for a town? Not a good name to consider for too long. Such disgusting images come to mind. Hairy tarantula legs sticking out of hot white loaves. Dark pumpernickels dotted with daddy longlegs. Or maybe plump golden buns, each with a juicy black widow baked into the center. No matter how you slice it, Spiderbread sounds absolutely nauseating.

In fact, it's a peaceful rural community, population 368, with a school (kindergarten through sixth grade), a grocery store, and a tavern (you can't really call it a bar—that's a sleazy word, a *city* word). The town is surrounded with pig and dairy farms, corn and hay fields, and it seems there are always dogs running around.

I came to Spiderbread after my ordeal. I'm not really good at talking about it, but basically, I came home late from work one day and found my wife and kids all dead around the dinner table. On the kitchen counter was an empty soup can. I remember staring at that can for about ten minutes like it was some kind of monster. And it was. I found out much later that somebody had made a horrible mistake at a canning factory.

The lawsuit made me rich. Stupid relatives and well-wishers kept telling me, loved ones aren't really dead if there's somebody to remember them, but I wasn't in the mood for pretty words. My house made me too sad, so one day I picked up the phone, tapped in some numbers at random, and asked the person at the other end, "Where do you live?"

An old woman said, "That would be Spiderbread, Iowa." She paused, then added, "Nice place" and hung up.

So I moved there. Or rather, here.

I didn't tell the Spiderbakers (that's what I think of them as) about my ordeal because I didn't want their pity. But they figured out that something was wrong. Sometimes, one of them would ask me a question, and then realize (maybe by my expression—I don't know) that he or she had crossed a line. That person would then laugh apologetically, pat my shoulder and say, "Never mind. Talk to you later," and walk off.

I didn't make any close friends, but eventually, everyone became a good acquaintance. Sometimes, that's all you want. The old lady was right: it really was a nice place. Everyone seemed to treat everyone else nicely. Even the school kids I saw hanging out in front of the grocery store all seemed nice, with just enough spirit in them to give them personality. The homemade sandwiches in the store were nice (egg salad or tender roast beef). The drinks in the tavern were nice—not too boozy, but never watered down. Even the dogs constantly running around were nice. They only barked a little, and never at night.

Nice, nice, nice. Nice was what I needed, and what I got.

I didn't have to, or want to, work. So I watched a lot of TV. Sometimes I made stuffed animals out of my old business clothes and gave them to the kindergartners. Sometimes I just cried from dawn to dusk.

One day, in addition to crying, I also threw dishes around, and tore up curtains. I really made a mess of things.

I remember that day well. It was a Tuesday. I woke up around 7:30 and started crying at about 8. Fifteen minutes later, I started breaking things. Then Alva from next door stopped by. It didn't help, seeing Alva. She's plump and blonde, like my wife Valerie was, and she talks with a cute lisp. Like Valerie did.

"I was hanging up some wash out back," Alva said, "and I heard you. Thought you might like some rice pudding." She handed me some Tupperware, gave me a worried smile and left.

The pudding was delicious. Lots of cinnamon. I cried, ate pudding, cried some more, broke more stuff, ate more pudding.

Around 10, Alva's sister Lisa from down the street came by. "Sis told me you needed some cheering up, so I thought I'd give you this video to watch. It's called *Muy Bueno* and it's so funny, it's about this divorced guy who goes to Mexico, and—Oh, you're not divorced, are you? Hope that's not what's bothering you, because if it is, don't watch the tape. Anyway, it's pretty funny."

I watched about ten minutes of the movie. It didn't help. Sure, the guy in the movie was divorced, but at least his wife and kids were still alive. They even lived in the same town. He could drop by or call them to see how they were doing.

At noon, somebody's little girl dropped off a teddy bear. She told me her name but I've forgotten it. She reminded me of my youngest, Judith. Red hair in a ponytail and a gap between her two front teeth. It broke my heart to look at her. After she left I kicked in the TV screen.

Twenty minutes later, a kid in his late teens brought me some beers. He told me they were from the fridge in his dad's workshop. He gave me a big lopsided grin and said, "Maybe these'd help ya chill out, ya know?" He didn't look at all like my son, but still, I couldn't help thinking: This stupid boy is alive and my smart boy, my straight-A boy, my Sean is dead.

The townspeople were really going out of their way to make me feel better. But it just wasn't helping.

My mailman came by at 1:15 and made me some tea. I always have a half-dozen varieties on hand, and he made me a combination of chamomile and green tea. He said chamomile was just what I needed for my nerves. Valerie used to say that.

I kept on crying, and more people kept stopping by. Finally, at about 4, three old women arrived and led me to the town's nice little park, and there everybody was, the entire population of Spiderbread. They'd all stopped whatever they were doing to come and see me. Chubby housewives with bright neon curlers in their thin hair. Redfaced farmers in coveralls spattered with mud and cow poop. Teenage boys with greasy bangs and forehead zits. Teenage girls who smelled like bubble gum. Some old guy with dark teeth and two fingers missing on his left hand. A skinny, mildly retarded middle-aged man carrying a puppy. In each of the townspeople, I saw some sad, quirky detail that reminded me of Valerie, of Judith, of Sean.

But of course, they had no way of knowing this.

They meant well. They really did. They all took turns comforting me, stroking my face, saying good things, right things, nice things, over and over and over.

"It'll be okay. We're here for you."

"We all love you. Whatever it is, we can help."

"Don't be afraid. Don't be sad. Just tell us what we can do."

"We all want to help. Really. No trouble at all."

"What can we do?"

"We love you. What do you need?"

"Say the word. We can help."

"There's nothing we wouldn't do for you."

That went on for about three hours. People kept bringing me tissues, and I had a huge pile of them crumpled around my feet. I felt like an awful mess, a complete baby.

I couldn't stop crying. And they kept trying and trying to help, help, help.

It was more than I could handle. Finally I just screamed, "Stop it! Get away from me! *I just want to be alone!*"

My outburst suddenly cleared my mind and I looked around at all the surprised Spiderbakers. They all had the same look in their eyes—a sad, sad look that whispered *sorry.*

Then I passed out. From exhaustion, I suppose.

* * * *

I woke up around noon the next day, on the couch in my own house.

I soon discovered that I couldn't open the front or back doors. And, the windows were all boarded-up from the other side. They'd brought in dozens of boxes of books and clothes, as well as a couple more refrigerators, filled with food. The phone didn't work. They'd hauled out the broken TV but didn't bring in a new one. My hammer was gone—I guess they didn't want me to pound my way out. Or, maybe they thought I'd hit myself over the head with it. I banged my fists on the front door, but no one came to open it. So I decided to wait. And—

I'm still here.

I think they somehow soundproofed the house, because I can never hear any noises from the outside—no barking dogs, no car horns. They enter the house while I'm sleeping to replenish the refrigerators. I haven't been able to find any surveillance cameras or peepholes, but I'm sure they look in on me. How else would they know when I'm asleep? I have no idea how long they are going to keep me like this. They wouldn't have been able to gain access to my money, so I guess they are paying for my food and the utilities.

I used to worry about this situation. What if a tornado swept through town? What if the furnace broke down in the middle of winter? What if I became sick and needed medicine, or an operation? I had to keep reminding myself: they wouldn't let anything bad happen to me. They are good. They are caring. They are nice.

And, perhaps they know best. The first three or four decades by myself were pretty tough, but in the past few years, I've begun to feel a real sense of peace creep over me. The quiet has a therapeutic quality, I think. It would be hard to go back to a life of noise and bluster. By now the world's probably filled with spaceships and jetpacks and noisy junk like that. I suppose Spiderbread looks like some sort of future-world nightmare, with robots and bug-eyed aliens wandering all over the place.

Well, as far as I'm concerned, they can take their time opening that door. I'm far from lonely. Folks used to tell me that loved one's aren't really dead if there's somebody to remember them, and at last, I've come to realize—they were right.

Valerie and Judith and Sean are here with me, here in the loving, healing silence, and I've never been happier.

ASCLOSEASTHIS

From "Cinephilia," a review column by Cameron Raske, Associate Editor, in *MetroShock Magazine* (Fall 1991 issue):

Oh, But You Will, the last work of independent filmmaker Erik Hofman, defies classification. The themes/icons of horror, avant-garde, film noir, and even pornography blend to create an intensely personal vision of pain and dark sensuality.

The grotesque imagery of Hofman's first work, *Candy Box* (1965), drew international critical attention. *Positive* attention, which is surprising, considering the blatantly misogynistic content of the wedding/nightmare sequence. How else could one interpret thirteen minutes of a wolf-headed bride tearing her groom and the priest to shreds? The theme of lover-as-predator appears in most of Hofman's works—*Skeleton Sun* (1967), *Three Scars* (1972), *Tears of Flame* (1977), and *The Poison Flowers* (1980). Hofman completed *Oh, But You Will* in October of last year. Two months later, he was found dead in the meeting hall of a controversial private society in Stockholm—a scenario seemingly lifted straight from one of his films.

In *Oh, But You Will,* Hofman explored the mythical aspects of the lover/predator theme. The image of Morla (played by newcomer Ingrid Thel), the harelipped art collector, is juxtaposed with statues of the Sphinx and the Medusa. Morla shapes her nails with a variety of implements: emery boards, small scissors, a tiny hooked blade, even her own teeth. Many critics have made much, much, entirely too much of the fact that Hofman died the victim of violent crime (true, his belly was slashed to ribbons, but he made the film before he died, n'est-ce pas?). Still, it is intriguing to note that Ms. Thel, Hofman's lover off-camera, is currently being sought for questioning.

Oh, But You Will is not for the faint of heart, but then, so little of today's quality cinema is. Morla's romance with the blind poet Zendo is a celebration of parasitism, the truest form of love. The scene in which Morla feasts on Zendo's useless eyes is poetry in itself, and a startling new manifestation of the Oedipal theme. And what of Morla's constant references to Azu, Lord of Fleshy Appetites? A delicious metaphor: Morla is a disciple of desire, a priestess of dark lust incarnate.

In the dream sequence (what is a Hofman film without a dream sequence?), Morla eviscerates a department store mannequin with her wicked nails. Instead of entrails, the mannequin pours forth endless coils of film. Here Hofman effectively explored new territory in the eroticism of textures: the velvet skin of the mannequin, the oily sheen of the film. Again, critics have made laughable attempts to contrast this scene with the director's actual death. Surely Hofman was providing sly commentary on his own industry: most filmmakers have no guts!

I imagine Ms. Thel is the prime suspect in Hofman's death. Granted, I'm no criminologist, but I doubt that this slim reed of a girl could have gutted the barrel-chested Hofman. I only hope this singularly beautiful actress will be able to return to the screen. Her compelling presence in *Oh, But You Will* brought feverish life to Erik Hofman's savage obsessions.

* * * *

A letter received by Cameron Raske on Feb. 14, 1992 (the next morning, a package wrapped in pages from *MetroShock Magazine* was left on his fire escape):

Darling Boy,

Your latest column took my breath away. "Singularly beautiful"! What a precious dear you are! Of course, you are lovely too. Whenever I pass this way, I drop by some of the finer clubs. And so often I have seen you, dancing, laughing, just being delicious.

I've read every issue of *MetroShock*. Only recently, when they ran your picture with your column, did I realize that the so-clever columnist was also the so-lovely dancing boy!

Your praise has shown me that you are truly discerning. Certainly we should get to know each other better. You have no idea how hard it is to find lovely playmates who know how to have fun.

No return address, I'm afraid. Moveable feast and all that. You'll be receiving a little art film, made just for you. You can give me your review when we meet.

With love,
Ingrid

* * * *

From the journal of Cameron Raske:

2/15/92—Went uptown, dropped by Alexis's (cab $8). I wanted to show her the video Ingrid Thel sent me. The hare-lipped fugitive, in love with me! Can it be? She missed the irony in my use of the word "singular"—but then, so did Alexis when I explained it all to her. So I'm oblique. That's what they pay me for.

And the video! Ingrid and three masked studs! Alexis is such a size queen. She kept going on and on about the mega-hung stud with red hair. And she used the word "PECKER"! I couldn't believe my ears! Delicate little Alexis, She of the Pencil-thin Heels, talking like chainsmoking white trash! I laughed so hard I fell off the couch.

And for the record: I've seen bigger. *Done* bigger.

Alexis told me about this new club she went to a few nights ago. Some drunken fish kept calling her "Sir" just to be funny. The place sounds like a pit. These days, every tacky fool is tossing up streamers in some old warehouse and calling it a club.

Alexis goes in for the snipjob in two weeks—everyone's thinking she'll get pre-op jitters and back out, but really, the sooner she unloads that baggage (that *pecker!*) the better. Ah, well. Boys will be girls.

Alexis said I should give the tape to the police. I'll think about it.

Later we went for drinks with some of Alexis's friends (cab $12). A Japanese student (bleach-blonde—a hot look for him) bought all my drinks. His parents own a VCR factory. He wanted to take me home but I didn't like his teeth. Too pointy and way too many.

I keep looking up at the spots where I used the "p"-word (I'm not going to write it down again!). I'm tempted to cross them out—I hate bowling alley lingo—but that would be self-editing, that would be wrong, why keep a journal if you're just going to censor yourself?, blah blah blah. I read too many self-help books. Still, it's the kind of word Mom used to say.

Memo: answer letter from that Australian mag.

* * * *

2/16/92—Received two hang-up calls. Ingrid?

Had lunch with Alexis (cabs $14, lunch $35). She did her nails right at the table. I found myself trying to imagine her with fur.

I watched Ingrid's tape again today. I think one of her toy-boys has pointed ears. It's hard to be sure. I try pausing the picture, but that only made everything fuzzier. It's funny, though: when the show is in action, none of them are looking into the camera. And yet when I hit pause, they are all staring straight at me.

I'm not going to give the tape to the police. They'd never give it back.

* * * *

2/17/92—Four hang-up calls today. I walked to the drug-store for some magazines ($12) and twice I saw someone pale dressed in solid black. Out of the corner of my eye.

Alexis must have given the Japanese student my address because he stopped by around noon with a sack of pastries. I was a little embarrassed since I'd forgotten his name, but he just laughed and told me to call him Sam. He stayed for about an hour. We're going to see *Lobster Salad* later this afternoon. I'll be meeting him at the Cineplex. Perhaps I should dress like a slob, or not comb my hair or something. I don't want him think-ing it's a big date. But who knows? I never really like anyone the first time I meet them. Six months from now I'll probably be aching for him, and he'll have moved on to someone else, and I'll be whipping myself. Same sad story, every time.

Sam is utterly into clubs—pish-poshing the old ones, alter-nately fawning over/trashing the new ones—but for me, that's all getting old hat. But what else is there? Poetry readings? Oh, I'm sorry: *spoken word* readings, rantings, whatever. And could I *possibly* see *more movies?* Maybe I'm just getting old (The "o" word! Almost as bad as the "p" word!). I need something new, but I don't know what.

*

Later. Just got back from *Lobster Salad* (admission $8, snacks $14, cabs $19) and I don't know what to think. I really don't. It's this insipid big-studio monstrosity about a struggling actress/waitress (Leela Holly) and a rich playboy (Rex Dennis) who for some stupid reason wants people to think he's a busboy. The lighting was bizarre—in one shot, a thin shadow bisected

Holly's lip and she looked just awful. And I kept seeing long crawling shadows in the background, even during scenes when everyone in the audience was laughing! The sound was poor, too. There was this constant rumbling, like a little engine, or a dog growling. For a while I thought the director must have been a Hofman wannabe—so many lingering shots of long-nailed hands. But when I was talking in the lobby to that culture vulture who writes for *The Paperboy,* I mentioned the hands and she said, "What movie were *you* watching?"

During the movie, Sam reached over to stroke my hand with his fingertips. I'm looking at my hand now and it's covered with scratches.

* * * *

2/18/92—Last night, I dreamed of a wolf that filled the night sky. But it wasn't a wolf per se—it had pale hands and stylish eyebrows. I kept watching the right eyebrow move up and down as the wolf talked. I can't remember what it said. I watched Ingrid's tape over and over all morning. Every now and then I'd hit *pause*—they'd stare at me—then *play,* and they'd look away. Pause. Play. Paws at play.

More hang-up calls.

Mom would never leave a message, but at least she'd grace me with a little sigh before she hung up. I know I should have called her more. But it's not my fault she killed herself. And it's not Dad's fault, even though he wasn't there ("But then, he was *never* there," blah blah blah). She did it all by her widdle self.

* * * *

2/19/92—It's late. I just got back from the new club Alexis had been going on about. I went with Sam, and he paid for everything. I'm finding out that he can be a real pain when he doesn't get his way. He'll fiddle you 'round and 'round— "But why...? How about... But why...? How about..."—until you just give in. You have to, because he's being nice the whole time. Nice, nice, nice.

So Nice Sam and I went down to the Funk Hole (what kind of a name is that?) and it was this huge, horrible garage, with mannequins in '70s clothes scattered everywhere. From out of nowhere, Sam handed me a shot of tequila. We'd only been there thirty seconds and already he was oiling my gears.

We started talking to some slim Gothic critters, who kept blowing their clove-cigarette smoke in our faces. They gave us little black cigarettes that had more than cloves in them—more than drugs, too. As I smoked mine down, little bright pebbles fell out of the ashes. I picked one off the floor—a tiny chunk of crystal. We had some more tequila, too, and soon Sam was out on the dance floor, shaking his wiry little body to some unbearable techno-crap.

By then the Gothic wisps had drifted away. I turned to a cute guy next to me and said, "What is this shit?" and he handed me another shot of tequila and said, "It's dog shit!" and another cute guy said, "Coyote shit!" and yet *another* guy said, "Wolf shit!" and when I looked at the third guy, I saw he had red hair, and I had to stop myself from looking down for the bulge of that much-vaunted PECKER. All three studs started laughing and putting their big hot hands on me. I might have enjoyed it if their laughter hadn't sounded so much like howling.

I cut through the crowd, trying to get away from them, though I don't suppose they wanted to hurt me. I kept knocking over mannequins (and apologizing!). At one point, I fell down and Sam, who by now was reeking-drunk, grabbed me by the foot and dragged me out on the dance floor.

Now everybody was laughing. I was on my back, bone-tired, looking up at all the laughing people. Then I saw something up among the rafters. There she was, naked as sin, sitting crosslegged on a beam, and even from so-very-far-away, I could tell she was applying lipstick.

Before I passed out, I found myself wondering how one would apply lipstick to a harelip.

I woke up on a ratty old couch in a back room. I still had my wallet, so someone must have been watching over me.

* * * *

2/23/92—Lost a few days there, O journal mine. Not that I've been busy. On the contrary. I've been watching TV. The idiot box has never been more fascinating.

The networks are filled with harelipped announcers. And the coffee in the commercials is filled with hallucinogenic crystals. And the soap opera studs all have red hair, and the cameras dare not shoot below their waists.

More calls but no hang-ups. Just sexy grrrrowling.

I suppose one of these days, I should zip down to my wee cell down at *MetroShock*. Check in. See if I have any messages. And my other projects—I still haven't figured out if I want to do a column for *Queenslander,* that Australian magazine. Actually, I don't give a fuck.

*

Later. Loud music.

I was about to pound on the bedroom wall when I realized the noise was coming from my own apartment. I found the slim little Gothics sitting in the living room, smoking their slim little ciggies. They'd turn the stereo all the way up. One turned its head in my direction (was it a boy or a girl?) and said, "It's Mr. Tequila."

I turned down the stereo and stared at them. Their pasty faces looked—brittle. Unreal. I noticed that one had a shiny bit of something dangling from out of its shirt. I reached over and pulled at this odd little bit and before I could blink, shiny film came spooling out of the Goth's belly, spooling and drooling out in coils that gathered at my feet. One of the others shouted, "Now you've done it!" and another stage-whispered, "No, you've *un*done it."

And finally I said, "This is all a dream, isn't it?"

The disemboweled Goth looked into my eyes with a sad look and suddenly I thought: *I know that look! Mom used to have that look all the time! Whenever some guy dumped her! Whenever some damn PECKER dumped her!*

"A dream?" the gutless Goth said with a dead little smile. "You wish."

That's when I started laughing. Laughing so hard that tears came to my eyes. Laughing at the absurdo-tragedy of the little Goth, my little Mommy, and this crusty little clump of cosmic shit known as the planet Earth. I dried my eyes just in time to watch all the little Goths fade away.

* * * *

2/24/92—I hardly recognized myself in the mirror this morning. The same face, but a new expression. Not guilt. Not sadness. For the first time in a long time: anticipation.

Alexis came by with Nice Sam. Both now have golden eyes, split lips, pale hands. They took me to bed and took me. Nicely. And my flesh is covered with their too-toothy love-bites. They are lounging in the bedroom right now, smoking black cigarettes laced with crystals.

I'm ready for you, Ingrid. I never thought I could feel this way about a woman. I saw you in the park across the street, three huge wolves prowling and weaving around your feet. How I long for your singular beauty. You were right, I do know how to have fun—but for far too long, I was only partying to keep my half-assed little woes and worries at bay. What do I care if everyone and everything gets fucked up, down, all around? At least I'm being provided with quality entertainment!

* * * *

2/25/92—The air is filled with clove smoke, feral musk and the sweet reek of freshly applied nail polish. Alexis and Sam haven't left yet. They were going to take off for the Funk Hole late last night but then Ingrid and her pets arrived.

Someone rang the bell, but there was no need for me to open the door. A roiling black mist seethed through the woodwork. The mist condensed into four wolf-headed serpents with fur instead of scales. Alexis and Sam howled their salutations. The largest serpent—a red-furred, grinning thing—writhed round and round my body.

Ingrid changed her form many times for me. She became a jungle beast—a deliciously shapeless velvet mass—a cluster of adroit tentacles—a swirling vortex of hot wetness. She can make others change, too. Alexis won't be needing her sex-change now. Ingrid rearranged everything to everyone's satisfaction. Sam now has a pelt of long, luxuriant white fur.

Ingrid told me of Hofman's transgressions. For years, he had prayed to Azu with admirable zeal, and Azu had rewarded him well. But eventually Hofman had taken up with an S & M society in Stockholm. He turned away from the Lord of Fleshy Appetites and began to worship Pain ("How bourgeois!" Ingrid hooted, raising a deftly plucked eyebrow).

But Azu is wise and magnanimous. In the end, He instructed His Priestess to lavish Hofman with all the pain he desired.

My new lover is now stroking my legs with her painted claws. She has told me of the delights to come once I learn to change my shape, my gender, my species, all by myself. I could let her do it, but I want to make her proud. I want to think up new and surprising ways to pleasure her. I want to be sly and inventive and reckless and infinitely desirable. I want to play in the clever shadows long after the rest of the world has died whimpering in the stark, stupid daylight. And I will, I will—Oh, but I will.

* * * *

From "Around Town," the gossip column of *The Paperboy* (April 1992 issue):

MetroShock recently waved bye-bye to associate editor Cameron Raske, who, after one too many weeks AWOL, turned in a column that weighed in a bit light realitywise (he referred to freaky filmmaker Erik Hofman as "the late documentarist"). Cameron seems to be taking the news well. The once-legendary club fixture has returned to his old stomping grounds with a vengeance, partying like some kind of wild animal. Also, he's been seen ascloseasthis with a trendy waif in a veiled hat. Hope the mystery lady can give him a few career tips. His life's gone to the dogs and he simply couldn't be happier.

THE VOICE OF THE PANGYRICON

I was onboard the Pangyricon when Velasko's Crane scooped up and deposited its most hideous prize. Perhaps you've seen the movie based on the incident—*Attack of the Space Zombies.* That studio paid me big bucks to act as a consultant for that project, but they didn't stick with the facts. They had the zombies talking, shooting guns—the creatures didn't do any of that. The movie didn't even mention Daniel, which really surprised me.

Let me tell you what really happened.

My name is Leon Sybek, and I was one of two-hundred Care Technicians on space station Pangyricon. Care Technician—a great title, but it only meant that I helped take care of the animals. A glamorized farmhand.

Before that, I was loading dishes in the washers at SpaceTech Industries. A kitchen goon. So when I found out that Project Hermes needed folks with agricultural experience, I signed up. I grew up on a dairy farm, milking cows and feeding calves. As a child, I'd hated the work because it was so lonely and boring. But I figured, maybe farming would be more interesting in space.

And it was.

Sure, the tasks never changed from day to day. But it was thrilling to be up in space as part of a big mission—that made me feel pretty important, even though I was only tending to livestock. Plus, the other Care Technicians were friendly and liked to talk about all sorts of things, like books and current events and of course, Project Hermes.

Hermes was the messenger of the gods in Greek mythology, but I don't know why the project was named after him. Basically, the goal was to prepare Mars for colonization by Earth. That meant building enclosed work communities on the planet surface, changing the atmosphere, integrating flora and fauna, and thousands of other related objectives. I suppose they chose the name Hermes because we were delivering a message to Mars: Hey, we're moving in.

Of course, Mars was the Roman name of the Greek war god Ares, so they should've called it Project Mercury, since that was the Roman name for Hermes. Maybe they named it Hermes because there was already a planet Mercury—and Earth wasn't about to colonize that sun-scorched chunk of real estate.

Mars was a dead planet, but a clean one, too. Clean and dry. No lava, no sloppy oceans of liquified poisonous gases. Mars was *workable.*

The Pangyricon is a revolving space station in orbit around Mars. It's shaped like a giant wagon-wheel, with a huge spherical hub and five spokes that serve as hallways to the circular outer frame. Us workers lived in the hub and carried out our duties in the frame, where the supplies and animals were housed.

The hub contained a machine known as Velasko's Crane. I'm not a scientist, so I don't completely understand how it works. Here's what I know about the machine and the man who invented it:

There used to be a brilliant man named Daniel Velasko who was like a space-age version of Thomas Edison—always working, rarely sleeping, and coming up with incredible ideas on a regular basis. His greatest invention was the Crane, which made it possible to transport matter across great distances instantaneously. He'd named it after a carnival game he'd enjoyed as a child. The game featured a glass booth with a toy crane surrounded by prizes. The player used a crank and maneuvered the crane's scoop to grab at the little trinkets.

I once got to play that game at a retro outdoor festival that tried to recreate the old carnival experience. The glass prizes were always the hardest to grab because they were so slippery.

Velasko's Crane had three parts: a chamber that housed the control panel and power unit, and two rectangular platforms, each as big as a full-size mattress. One platform was set by the chamber and the other was taken to the final transport destination. When something needed to be transported, the item was placed on the platform by the chamber. The operator would make the appropriate calibrations, hit the right buttons and in a flash, the item would disappear and then show up instantly on the other platform, wherever that had been placed. Any platform could send or receive, but it needed a nearby chamber to send. Without the chamber, it could only receive.

I know all that because Daniel told me the details. Or rather, Daniel's electronic persona. Velasko had been one of the designers of the Pangyricon, and he'd loaded his memories, personality and intellect into its main computer decades ago. These elements had been integrated into the computer's behavioral programming to create a logical but friendly thinking machine. The space station didn't have a captain—it had a board of directors back on Earth, but no one person at the helm, symbolic or otherwise. It didn't need one, with Daniel looking after things.

Daniel was the voice of the Pangyricon, and he used to chat with me while I did my chores. A person could talk to the computer from any point on the station. Unlike a real person, he could talk with hundreds of different people at the same time. He always came across a smart, helpful friend who was both interesting and interested in what you had to say.

I remember the day he told me about the early days of Velasko's Crane. I was feeding the calves, which hopefully would spend their adult years grazing on the surface of a greener Mars.

"Attention, Daniel," I said. You had to start any conversation with those words to get the computer's attention. "How long did it take to come up with the Crane?"

"It only took me a few seconds to 'come up with' the idea," he said in its low, firm voice, which had a very slight metallic buzz. I liked that he acted like he was his own inventor. "It took much longer to actually make it work. Thirty years. With a few mistakes along the way, too. But that's to be expected."

"Yeah? What kind of mistakes?"

He laughed. "Where do I begin? Hmmm. Let me put it this way. Some substances transport better than others."

"You mean like glass?" I then told it about my own experience with the carnival crane game.

"That's the right idea," he said. "But it's easy to transport glass with my Crane. Glass sits still."

"I suppose any crane works better when the cargo isn't moving around," I said.

"Yes! Exactly!" His voice rose a couple notes when he was pleased or excited. "Right now the process of transportation is practically instantaneous. But in the early days, it used to take a few seconds. After if the cargo item was not absolutely still…it would either show up damaged or just not appear at all. Living things usually died—even if they weren't moving on the outside, their organs were still active on the inside. Like their beating hearts."

At that point, a few other Care Technicians came by to ask if I wanted to join them for lunch. One of them was Quinn, a young woman who liked me quite a lot. I enjoyed talking with her, but I wasn't attracted to her because she was very skinny and nervous. She reminded me of a hungry hummingbird in need of a nectar fix. "Gotta run," I said. "Talk to ya later, Daniel."

"See ya later, alligator," he replied. The computer ended most conversations that way. Just like the real Daniel Velasko, I suppose.

Later that week, we were scheduled to receive two new calves—holsteins, which are black and white and grow to be quite large. The calves already onboard were smaller, yellowish-brown jerseys.

Most of our coworkers were in the main leisure area, watching a broadcast of a baseball game. Quinn and I weren't big sports fans, so we'd agreed to take care of the livestock transport at that time. The platforms were phenomenally expensive, which was why we only had one onboard. Two or three would have been more convenient—especially in the livestock quarters—but that sort of expense just wasn't in the budget.

"Why holsteins?" Quinn asked as we stood by the platform. "Holsteins get too big! And they're not as manageable as jerseys. They're just big and stupid."

"They're only sending two," I said. "And they're just calves. It's probably part of a feasibility study. They do need to consider holsteins—they give more milk, and its low-fat, too. If they don't work out, they probably won't send any more. Don't get all upset about it."

"I have a right to be upset," Quinn said. "I grew up on a farm with holsteins on it. That information is in my personal file—I'm well-informed on the matter. I wish somebody had thought to ask me."

I ruffled her hair. "Well, if I was ran this banana boat, I'd run every major livestock decision your way."

She gave me a very sweet smile.

"Okay," said Remson, the Transport Technician. He was in the chamber, speaking over the room's audio system. "Here they come, fresh from the dewy fields of Earth. Ready?"

"Sure," I replied. The calves would arrive harnessed within a metal stall, so it wasn't like we'd have to catch them.

We stood by the platform—but nothing happened.

"What's wrong?" Quinn said.

Through the glass of the control chamber, I could see that Remson was talking on a communicator. Apparently he'd turned off the audio system so we couldn't hear what was being said.

Remson finished his call and then stepped out of the chamber. He walked up to us and said, "I don't think the calves are going to make it."

"Hooray!" Quinn shouted.

Remson gave her an angry look. "This is serious. I'll tell you what happened, but you didn't hear it from me, okay?"

"Maybe you shouldn't tell us at all," I said. "Daniel will hear you telling us." I looked up at a small black box in the far corner of the ceiling. That box housed Daniel's eyes, ears and other sensors for that room, as well as his voice.

Remson smiled. "Daniel sees and hears everything. But so long as no person or property is being injured, and nobody says…" He then mouthed the words 'Attention, Daniel,' "…it doesn't become part of the permanent log. So don't say—you know what."

"Okay already," Quinn said. "What's up with the calves?"

"One wasn't harnessed right," Remson said, "and it broke out of the stall just before transport and ran—bang!—right into the side of the chamber in mid-transmission."

Quinn laughed. "See? Holsteins are nothing but trouble."

The Transport Technician continued. "The other calf and the stall were sent, but—well, they're lost. Who knows where. Just like Valesko."

"Whoa!" I said. "What does that mean—'just like Velasko'?"

Remson shrugged. "That's how he disappeared. No body ever showed up. Didn't you know that? There was a big court case long ago. Somebody even made a movie out of it—*Murder By Crane*."

"I saw that," Quinn said. "Velasko's wife used to help him in the lab, and she had a boyfriend on the side. She wired a chamber so it would switch off in mid-transmission the next time hubby traveled by Crane, leaving him out in…" She gestured vaguely into the air. "Wherever."

"Yeah," Remson said, "and that's where that calf is right now. Wherever."

Suddenly a sequence of beeps issued from the transport chamber. Remson ran back inside and picked up the communicator. He listened for a minute and then said to us over the audio system. "They've managed to lock onto the transport coordinates again. They're going to try and finish the transmission. You two ready?"

"I don't like this," Quinn said.

I ruffled her hair again. "Oh, give it up, holstein-hater. Yeah, we're ready!"

I once read that a long time ago, a fire devastated the city of Chicago after a cow knocked over a lantern. Who'd have thought another rambunctious bovine could kick-start a catastrophe in space? I was there to see the first step.

And it literally was a step. The metal stall appeared, its pipework structure drenched with blood. But there was no calf to be seen. And something horrible stepped off the platform.

It was a corpse. A walking corpse with blue skin, streaked with dust and what looked like thick strands of yellowish-green cobwebs. Its eyes were tightly squinted shut. Its face was smeared with blood and strings of meat still hung from its broken teeth.

"Attention, Daniel!" I screamed. "Daniel, help us! Activate security systems!" None of us had any weapons. There had never been any need for them.

"Interesting!" the computer said in its higher voice of excitement. "I've completed a brain-scan on this being and though the organ is profoundly altered, I can detect familiar patterns. That is my original body."

"Don't just scan that thing!" Remson said as he came out of the chamber. "Activate security systems!"

"Yes! Look what it did to the calf!" Quinn cried.

"I detect animal blood, but no animal," the computer said. "I cannot activate security systems based on an external occurrence."

The creature's eyes slowly opened, revealing twin milky-white orbs. Apparently it had needed some time to get used to the light. It rushed to the door, which slid open, like all work area doors when somebody stepped up to them. The thing then raced down the hall.

Remson ran into the transport chamber and got on the communicator. Quinn went to the emergency intercom by the fire control equipment and tried to summon a Security Technician.

I looked around the room for something that might be used as a weapon. I noticed the wall-mounted fire extinguisher—a long metal cylinder. Good enough.

"Attention, Daniel!" I screamed as I ran out of the chamber, holding the cylinder over my head. I was ready to bring it down on that dead thing's skull. "Where did the creature go?"

"Creature?" Daniel said.

"Your body. Where did it go?"

"My body is simply moving through the station. It has not injured any person or property." The computer's voice was low and steady, as always. "You, however, appear to be acting in an aggressive manner. You are holding that extinguisher in a position that suggests attack."

I lowered the extinguisher and cradled it in my arms. "Sorry, Daniel. I just wanted to see if I could lift it over my head." I hated having to lie, but this was a desperate situation. "Can you tell me where your body went? I want to welcome it onboard and show it how this fire extinguisher works."

"It is now leaving elevator 7 on level 3," Daniel said.

"Quinn! Remson!" I shouted into the transport chamber. "That thing just got off the elevator by the laundry area. Let Security know!"

I then hurried to elevator 6, which opened onto the third level near the medical area. I wanted to warn those folks before going to the laundry area, which was probably empty, since most workers were watching the baseball game. The Security Technicians were probably enjoying the game, too. They had communicators, but of course, those only do the job if their users are carrying them. We only had two people in Security, and they also had other duties onboard, since Daniel was fully equipped to take care of most defense issues. They really just served as a backup in case of a computer failure or malfunction.

Once I was on the third level, I ran to the medical area, where a young male nurse named Duane was looking at a magazine centerfold. He blushed when he saw me.

"Take your porn and get out of here," I said. "There's an—an intruder onboard." I had been about to say "monster," but I'd figured he wouldn't believe that.

"An intruder?" he said. "Attention, Daniel!"

"Yes?" the computer replied.

"Is there an intruder onboard?" the nurse asked.

"No," Daniel said. "I am familiar with every person currently onboard."

The nurse stared curiously at me.

"Attention, Daniel!" I said. "Is there a person with white eyes, blue skin and blood on his face wandering around on this level?"

"Yes, there is," the computer said. "He is now in the laundry area."

A scream echoed from down the hall.

The nurse grabbed his magazine and ran out of the room.

"Find a Security Technician!" I called after him. Then I ran toward the laundry area. When I got there, I found, slumped in a corner, the body of Kitchen Technician Barnes, a middle-aged, heavyset woman. A strand of that strangely colored cobweb was stuck to one of her legs. Her left hand had turned blue and even as I watched, the color began to creep slowly up her wrist.

"Attention, Daniel!" I screamed. "Your body has killed Barnes! Activate security systems!"

"My body took Barnes by the hand." Daniel's voice was in the higher, excited mode. "It was interesting! He did not appear to be hurting her, and yet she made a noise of alarm. She then moved to the floor."

"She's dead!" I screamed. "Your body took a living person and made her dead. That is personal harm, Daniel! Activate security systems!"

"I have scanned Barnes." The computer's voice rose yet another note. "I can still detect brain-wave patterns. The organ has been altered, but it is still functional. Also, I can still detect cellular activity. Barnes is becoming more like my body."

"But that's bad!" I said.

"Define 'bad' in this instance," the computer prompted.

"I give up!" I said. "It's no use talking to you."

"Very well," he said, back in his lower voice. "See you later, alligator."

"No, wait! Attention, Daniel!" I looked down at Barnes. Her arm was now blue from the fingertips to the elbow. "I have a funny question for you. What would you do if I manually activated the lock on the laundry area door?"

"The manual locks are only for fire or security emergencies during times of computer failure," Daniel replied. "I'm fully functional, so there'd be no reason to do that. We are not experiencing any emergencies. I would unlock the door."

"Can I ask another funny question?"

"I don't understand your sense of humor, but sure. Ask."

I watched the blue creep slowly up Barnes' arm, toward the shoulder. "Actually it's a three-part question. Part one: if you saw anybody hurt someone else, what would you do?"

"Well, I have defense mechanisms in place throughout the Pangyricon," he said. "If I detected somebody acting in a violent, aggressive manner, I would incapacitate them."

"Part two: what would you do if I bashed in her head with this fire extinguisher?"

"I would incapacitate you, using one or more of several methods, such as electric shock or sedative gas."

"Now for part three: what would you do if your body tried to touch me while I was unconscious?"

"Nothing. That would not be a problem."

"But don't you see? Your body is carrying some kind of energy force, or plague or pestilence, or...or..."

"I cannot detect any such radiation or microorganisms," Daniel said.

"But it's something you've never encountered before!" I shouted. "Damn you, Daniel! I can't tell you what's wrong with your body because I don't know. But something is very, very wrong! Why can't you believe me?"

"I am sorry you're upset," the machine said. "But if I believed every single thing any person told me—without the subsequent presentation of supporting data—I would be of no use to the Pangyricon. I require some form of documented verification."

I ran out of the laundry room. I didn't want to be in there when Barnes got up. I had the horrible feeling that she'd want to take me by the hand. "Attention, Daniel. Where is your body now?"

"In the dining area." That was at the other end of level 3.

"Has it touched anybody else?"

"Yes. It has touched thirty-five crew members. All are currently resting. Now thirty-six. Thirty-seven. Thirty-eight."

"That's enough."

"See you later, alligator."

I decided the only thing to do was escape—to get back to Earth and tell the authorities what was going on. So I took the elevator back down to level 2 and the transport room.

Remson and Quinn were both in the chamber with its door closed. When they saw me, they came out. "Leon, you're okay!" Quinn said, rushing up to hug me.

"What's happened since I left?" I said.

"Security isn't responding and Daniel refuses to acknowledge that anything is wrong," Remson said. "He won't even let us lock the door of this area because there isn't a fire. And to make matters worse, the entire Crane system is shut down. Earth has it turned off on their end. Same with the colonies on Mars. So we're here stuck in the middle. The folks at SpaceTech want to talk to Daniel before they do anything else, but he sees no reason to involve them."

"Why is the Crane shut down?" I said.

"Velasko wasn't the only one to get lost in the Crane over the years," he said. "There have been about nine or ten others. We should never have told them what happened. Now they're afraid those other zombies will escape from whatever void they're been in all this time."

"Zombies?" The term, at that time, didn't mean much to me. I thought it meant somebody who was extremely stupid, or just walking around in a daze. "Who's calling them that?"

Remson nodded toward Quinn.

"I collect old horror films," she said. "Some of those movies had zombies in them."

"Well, I don't watch scary movies," I said. "What are zombies?"

"Zombies are dead bodies that have come back to life," she said. "They eat the flesh of the living, and if they bite somebody, that person turns into a zombie, too."

I looked at the dried blood on pipes of the metal stall. "Why didn't the zombie go after any of us when it got here?"

"It wanted to get the Hell out of here," Remson said. "Away from this equipment." He nodded toward the transport platform. "That's the only thing that can send it back to the void. Not that the machine can do us any good now."

"Maybe those movie zombies eat people, but this one hasn't bitten anybody." I then told them about Barnes and my frustrating conversation with Daniel.

"Perhaps it doesn't eat humans," Quinn said. "I think it just wants to convert them. Maybe they hunt down their food in packs. I wonder what kind of animals live in that void of theirs…?" She picked up a length of cobweb draped over the edge of the platform. "Look how fat this strand is. If this is from some kind of spider, it must be as big as a horse." She flicked the sticky thing off her fingers. "That zombie wouldn't need much help to hunt here on the station. All the animals are in pens. Completely helpless. I hope it hasn't found the livestock yet."

"Attention, Daniel!" I said. "Is your body still in the station's central hub?"

"Yes. In the main leisure area."

Quinn's eyes went wide with horror. "Oh my God!"

I dreaded asking the next question. "How many people has it touched?"

"Three-hundred and thirty-six."

Remson rushed to the transport chamber. Quinn and I followed him. "Attention, Daniel," he said. "Bring up the leisure area on my main monitor."

"Sure thing," the computer said.

The image sprang into view on the screen, along with a chorus of echoing screams. The zombie simply wandered through the auditorium, which was filled with people running and shouting. Every now and then it would place its hand on someone. That person would instantly stop moving and slowly sink to the floor, as though suddenly very tired. There was nothing violent or aggressive in anything the creature did.

"Are any of the people who have been touched by your body moving around now?" Remson asked. "And if so, how many?"

"Yes," Daniel said. "Seventy-three. Now seventy-four. Seventy-five."

"Shut up," the Transport Technician said.

"See you later, alligator," the computer replied.

"Well, isn't that great," Remson said. "While we're having ourselves a nice cozy chat, that monster is turning this space station into zombieland. People are probably wondering why the Hell nobody's helping them. And Daniel's just sitting back, watching the whole damned freak show. He won't even let us fight back."

"Because he hasn't got a clue," Quinn said. "Follow me!" So saying, she left the chamber and ran out of the room.

Remson and I ran after her. "Wait up!" I called to her. "What's going on?"

"I know what I'm doing," she yelled. "Just follow me!"

So we did. What else could we do?

As we ran, we passed an empty meeting room that had recently been used for a retirement dinner. I noticed a pile of soiled tablecloths on one of the chairs. "Wait a second!" I shouted. I ran in and grabbed the whole stack.

"Put one of these around you," I said, handing out tablecloths. "That way a zombie can't touch your bare skin."

"Great idea," Quinn said. "Now let's get going."

There were two left over, so I decided to carry them in case one of us lost our covering. We followed her down the hall, and I soon realized we were heading toward the workers' living quarters. Just as we reached an intersection with another hallway, a group appeared directly in front of us.

A group of zombies, with the Velasko creature leading the pack.

Daniel Velasko's ghastly head tilted slightly to one side. The corners of his mouth drew back in what might have been a smile. The rest turned their staring white eyes toward us, and reached out with writhing hands. The group included several Care Technicians and both Security Technicians. Barnes was there, too, her face as blue as a summer sky.

I ran ahead of Quinn and flung a tablecloth over them. One of the creatures reached out for my shoulder, but it only grabbed a handful of linen.

We went around them and continued down the hall. The creatures simply followed us, and the only sound they made was the brisk shuffle of their feet moving down the hall.

At another hall intersection I saw another group coming our way. "I hope you know where we're going, Quinn," I said.

"Through here." She gestured toward a small game room. After we entered, she closed the door behind us. Then we cut across the room to a door leading into another hallway, which was clear.

She pointed two doors down. "There. My room."

"Your room?" Now I was completely confused. "What's in there?"

"Please, don't ask questions," Quinn said with a tight, almost grim smile. She opened her door and we followed her in. Then she locked up behind us. We piled the tablecloths by the wall.

She opened the door of a closet and pulled out a wheeled cart with an old-fashioned movie projector on top. She plugged it into an outlet with a special adapter.

Quinn grabbed a reel of film off a lower platform of the cart. She installed the movie on the projector and spent a few minutes rolling the reel around, looking closely at the frames until it had reached a particular spot. Finally she set up a screen on the other side of the room.

"All set," she said, picking up a pen from her coffee table. She turned down the lights and switched on the projector.

The scene that popped up before us depicted decayed, blood-spattered corpses chasing a screaming couple through a field. She'd mentioned that she collected old movies—this had to be one of them. An old horror movie with zombies in it.

"Attention, Daniel!" Quinn called toward the black box in the corner of her living room.

"Yes?" the computer said, helpful as always.

"Look at the screen," she said. "Evidence of the living dead going after humans. That's just what's happening here. That's what those creatures are—walking corpses. Zombies. Look, damn you! Documented evidence! *Just look!*"

The couple on the screen raced down a country road—only to find themselves stumbling into a cemetery filled with the glassy-eyed horrors.

"I am unfamiliar with this data source," Daniel asked in his high, excited voice. "What is this I am watching?"

"Archived news footage," she lied. Quite convincingly, too. "The information was suppressed by the government so that people wouldn't go into a panic. I have the last remaining bit of evidence. Look, Daniel! That woman is crawling out of a grave. The dead aren't supposed to come back to life. You know that!"

"You'd better do something about all this right now," Remson said. He'd obviously picked up on Quinn's plan and was proving himself to be a fine actor. "Do something right now before more people are turned into zombies."

"Zombies," the computer repeated. "I have no data files regarding that subject."

Quinn stood directly between Daniel's box and the projector, and I saw her quickly jab the pen into the workings of the projector. The image on the screen froze as the film began to bunch up inside the machine. She turned it off. "Damn!" she said. "This stupid old clunker isn't working right." Quinn had thought through her plan well. It wouldn't do for Daniel to see too much of the movie. One bad special effect and he'd realize that the evidence was questionable.

Quinn turned toward Daniel's box. "I think you've seen enough. You saw them, right? The zombies? You saw how scared the living people were, right? They were scared for their lives—just like us!"

For a moment, Daniel was silent.

At last he said, "This situation requires further investigation. In the meantime, I will seal off all rooms and hallways containing the zombies." He paused, as if to give the matter more thought, and then added,

"I will vent liquid nitrogen into those sectors to cryogenically freeze them. If there are any unaffected humans in with them, they can be sorted out and revived later. I will contact my board of directors on Earth and tell them that we need additional assistance."

"Great idea, Daniel," I said. "You do that."

"See ya later, alligator," he said.

Now you know the real story behind *Attack of the Space Zombies*.

At the end of the movie, I was named the captain of the Pangyricon. Sorry, but that didn't happen. The writers did get one fact right: Quinn and Remson fell in love, got married and moved to a Martian colony.

I went back to Earth and made some big bucks with that movie studio, like I mentioned. Eventually I opened a pet store with the money.

The Daniel persona was removed from the Pangyricon and according to Remson, is now being used on a hydroponics farm on Mars. Daniel now makes daily recommendations regarding the nurturing of okra, asparagus and tomato plants.

Some of my old coworkers drop by my pet store when they vacation on Earth. They tell me that the big decisions on the space station are now being made by actual human beings.

Imagine that.

THE LAST POETRY NIGHT AT THE SATURNALIA COFFEE HOUSE

I used to go down to the Saturnalia Coffee House every Friday night. To listen to poetry. Occasionally, to read my own poetry. To watch the pretty young things and the not-so-pretty old things mill about, guzzling wine coolers and flavored bottled water. Men and women alike flirted with me. On a scale of 1 to 10, my looks alone would rank me at 6, maybe 7 (I have dark hair and eyes and have been called "ruggedly hand-some"). Fortunately, I'm somewhat glib, so my conversation brought my rating up to a firm **8**.

The Saturnalia was actually the living room of a run-down mansion, or perhaps I should say mansionette, on top of a wooded hill. The exterior was decked out with fancy trim, but the place was fairly small: two floors (one with four rooms, the other with five) and, enclosed within the gambrel roof, an attic.

The place was owned by Nose: he had a real name (Ambrose, I think) but we all called him Nose because, well, he had a large, thick, ruddy nose with huge pores and little hairs all over it. It looked like a fuzzy baby sponge. He smelled like ointment, too…a hospital sort of smell. We were all so rude—we actually called him Nose to his face. He didn't seem to mind. He only smiled and asked if we wanted more raspberry spritzer.

I do miss the poetry readings. Now Nose is dead and the Saturnalia is now nothing more than a weed-choked patch of charred boards and bricks.

But I'm getting ahead of myself.

The poetry nights at the Saturnalia were started by my friend Meg, a petite, frizzy-haired bird of a woman who just loved to read her short stories and long, long poems aloud. Her writings usually concerned such topics as her various lovers; her pet snakes, cats, and tarantulas; and her love of the moon and all things nocturnal. Some of Meg's poetry had been published as a chapbook, *Lullabies for Snake Babies*. She had started the readings to promote her chapbook and to give would-be bohemians a fun place to hang out. Every Friday there were two guest poets (friends of

Meg, usually) and an open reading. Halfway through the night's festivities, Nose passed a floppy red beret around for donations. "To help pay for the beer," he would say, even though the big, ice-packed tin tub of beverages by the fireplace never included beer.

One night, a newcomer at the Saturnalia caught my eye. He looked to be in his early twenties. He was the palest man I had ever seen. His skin was as white as milk—so white that it was almost blue. His eyes were light green and his eyebrows were practically translucent. His buzz-cut hair glowed with the faintest tinge of cornsilk yellow. His teeth were very small and white and square. His nose was small and flat, like a cat's. His height was about average and he was very muscular. I forget what he was wearing that night, but in the weeks to come, I came to realize that he always wore subdued earth tones.

I watched Pale-Boy out of the corner of my eye. When he laughed, his light-pink tongue touched the tips of his front teeth. He squinted when he smiled, too. At one point, he lit up a cigarette. Several of the poetry night regulars informed him he should smoke outside, so out he went, and I followed.

When we were outside, I tapped him on the shoulder. "Can I borrow a cigarette?" I said.

"You gonna give it back?" he said as he handed one to me.

"Well, no…"

"Then you're not borrowing it." He flicked his beige plastic lighter and lit me up. "Sorry. I'm not usually such a smart-ass."

He maintained almost constant eye contact with me as he talked. A good sign.

"How do you like the poetry?" I asked, trying not to cough. He smoked unfiltered cigarettes.

He shrugged and shook his head simultaneously. "I can't really judge. I'm like most writers: I think my stuff's great and everyone else is pumping out shit."

We talked for about half an hour. In that time, I found out that his name was Chad and he worked in a record store. He lived alone in a three-room apartment above a Chinese restaurant. He wrote poetry about vampires, the end of the world, death, loneliness, etc., etc. I was a little disappointed that he didn't ask anything about me.

While we were talking, Chad noticed a little path going off into the trees behind the mansionette. "Let's see where that goes," he said.

I followed Pale-Boy into the woods. I liked the back of his neck: the short hair there formed a light-yellow V pointing down his muscular back. Soon the woods grew too dark for me to see the golden V. Chad was only a light glow of a silhouette, a human aura. He stopped and turned around.

"Here we are," he said, placing his hand on my crotch. "Yep. Here we are." He said that over and over as he opened my pants, as he knelt before me, as he massaged my erection. "Here we are. Here we are." Then he took me into his mouth and could say no more for five, ten, fifteen utterly perfect minutes.

Of course, I returned the favor. I'd had sex with four other men before Chad, and I'd considered all of them generously endowed. But compared to Chad, they were all baby carrot farmers. His erection seemed too huge to be human. For a moment, I was a bit taken aback. But only a moment.

When we returned to the reading, Meg was giving the last poem of the night, as was her way. Chad crossed the room to get a spritzer from the tin tub. I stood by the door. Nose walked up to me and gave me a wink.

"I see you've met my boy," he said.

Panic-striken, I said nothing.

"Yep, he finally decided to pay the old man's funny farm a visit." He squinted as he smiled. "Oh, I know it seems impossible, an old dogface like me having a little Greek god Apollo for a boy, but it's true." He leaned closer. "You two were gone a pretty long time. Just wanted you to know I don't mind. Nope, not at all. Young people are supposed to have fun."

He winked again, then turned and wandered off. His ointmenty, chemical reek hung in the air.

Chad returned to my side and handed me a wine cooler. "I saw you talking to my dad. What did he say?"

"Nothing, really. He guessed what we'd been doing, but he didn't mind."

"I didn't think that he would." He sighed with obvious irritation, which surprised me.

"What's wrong with that?"

"Oh, it's just that now he's going to be really, really nice to you. Like you're his new kid or something. And that'll probably scare you off." He had a sad, puppyish look in his eyes. "Right?"

"Don't worry. Nose is okay," I said. I studied his Chad's fine pale features. "I guess you take after your mother."

Chad nodded. "Yep. I like men."

* * * *

During the next few weeks, Chad and I met at movies, restaurants, our apartments, and the poetry readings, where we'd sit next to each other. Everyone knew we were a couple, and it was fun: nobody minded, and since Chad was so very handsome, it made me seem that much more attractive for having snagged him. Nose always made a point of handing me a wine-cooler and chatting with me. When the night grew boring, Chad and I would slip out for a cigarette and a walk in the woods.

Chad started bringing his poems for the open reading segment of the evening. He once gave me a copy of one of his poems, printed in dark red pencil:

HUNGRY FOR YOU

I want to chew on you eat you with
whispering teeth and make you my own
I want to envelop you like a venus
flytrap folding its cold elegant flesh
in upon your tasty smoothness
and so I shall you are mine all mine
you are my delight my love my
sweet surprise my sustenance and
now you are a part of
me

The audience didn't care for his morbid tidbits, and really, neither did I. His poetry did have a certain darkly erotic quality, but frankly, it didn't reflect upon our relationship. I've always had a bit of an ego. I wanted him to write poems about my subtle charms…my wit! my broodingly handsome good looks! my finesse as a lover! But then, one doesn't always get what one wants.

Once, while Chad was talking with some poet friends, Meg took his place by my side. "He's gorgeous," she said. "No offense to Nose, but it's hard to believe they share any chromosomes."

"What do you think of his poetry?" I asked.

"Oh, it's all right," she said, rolling her eyes. "I'm not really big on weird scary stuff. What's going on over there?" She nodded toward the other side of the room. Nose had joined the group of poets and even though I couldn't hear what was being said above the noise of the room, I could tell that Nose and Chad were arguing. Chad rushed out of the room and his father followed, shouting and waving his arms.

Meg beckoned to one of the poets—a sandy-haired haiku enthusiast in his late teens named Richard—and he rushed over to us.

"What was that all about?" Meg said.

"Nose doesn't want Chad reading his poetry here any more." The boy said, grinning. It was obvious he enjoyed being in-the-know.

"But why?" I said.

"I don't know!" Richard's eyes grew round. "He just kept saying, 'You know better,' and giving Chad this really poisonous look. I can't believe Chad is being censored by his own Dad."

"It doesn't make sense," Meg said. "I mean, people read about all kinds of stuff here. Acid trips, menstruation, kinky sex…you name it. Just last week Daniel read that really long thing about elephants fucking."

"Dads are so lame." Richard nodded knowingly. "My own dad thinks that haiku isn't really poetry because it doesn't rhyme."

He blathered on and on, but I was no longer listening. Somewhere in the house, I could hear, faintly, Nose shouting.

Eventually Chad returned to his seat. His eyes were red and puffy from crying.

"Is everything okay?" I whispered to him.

He shrugged. "I can't talk about it. It's a family thing."

It occurred to me then that I'd never seen Mrs. Nose. "Can I help?" I said.

Chad took me by the hand. Without a word, he led me out of the house and into the woods.

* * * *

During the next few weeks, I brought up the topic of Chad's mother several times.

His responses to all of my questions were maddening. He always replied in vague sentence fragments: for example, when I asked what she was like, he shrugged and said, "A loner." I couldn't even tell from his responses whether or not his mother was still alive. At his apartment, I asked if I could meet his mother someday and he simply said, "I doubt it." He then began to undo my pants…his rather affectionate (and certainly effective) way of saying, *let us please change the subject.*

* * * *

One Friday night, I showed up at the Saturnalia Coffee House before Chad and everyone else. I found Nose setting out the tin bin of beverages.

"How's the missus?" I said.

He turned and looked sadly at me. His ointment smelled seemed especially strong that day.

"I don't talk about that—" He paused for a split second. "—woman. Don't get on my bad side. You're a nice guy, Brent. I don't mind Chad liking boys and all that. That's fine with me. And it's just as well."

"Just as well?" I could only echo his words, since I had no idea what he meant.

"Well, yeah. Chad ought not to start any families." He began to say something else, then paused, as though rethinking what to say next. "Me and Chad, our relationship is all screwed-up. It wasn't easy raising him. All by myself."

I decided to be persistent. "What about his mom?"

As soon as the words were of my mouth, Nose looked up. Almost involuntarily. Then he looked back at me and said, "His mother is dead. We don't like talking about her."

I thought about what was above us. The second floor? Nose lived up there. Every now and then, he would ask one of the poetry night regulars to fetch something—a corkscrew, or extra glasses—from his upstairs kitchen. The place had piles of newspapers and old clothes scattered everywhere. The third floor? That was the attic. I'd never been up there.

I left Nose to his chores and walked out of the mansionette. Once outside, I looked up at the attic. A dim, slightly bluish light shone through the curtains in the windows.

As I stood there, staring up at the Saturnalia Coffee House, I began to wonder…to formulate theories. I *knew* she was up there. Had Nose chopped her up and stuffed her in an old trunk? Was she hanging from a noose, all withered and moldy? Maybe she was still alive but as scary as hell--drooly and white-haired and insane…

The poetry folks began to show up. I walked around to the other side of the house, thinking. Was there some way I could slip up to the attic?

A catalpa tree, a bit taller than the house, grew next to the back porch. Several of the branches extended over the roof. A gable window jutted from the side of the roof. Of course, I had no intention of shimmying up that tree…

I then noticed that the tree had a makeshift ladder of old boards nailed up along the trunk, leading to the remnants of a treehouse.

I walked into the woods and waited for an hour. By that time, I knew, the poetry reading would be in full swing. There was a full moon out, so I had enough light to see where I was climbing. I ran to the tree and began to climb up the board ladder.

The boards were fairly close together, to accommodate a small child. I pictured an eight-year-old Chad climbing up to the treehouse, and the image saddened me. I felt that the treehouse would have been a place for Chad to hide. From Nose…from other mean kids…or perhaps, from his mother.

I glanced down and even though I wasn't afraid of heights, I had a brief attack of vertigo. I had no idea what I was going to do once I reached the window. Would I be able to get inside? If not, would I be able to get back down the tree? What would I do if I found myself stuck on the roof? Suddenly my mission seemed incredibly foolish. I was risking my neck just to satisfy my curiosity.

"Who's up there?"

The voice came from the base of the tree. I looked down through the branches and saw Richard standing there. He was holding hands with someone, but there were leaves in the way and I couldn't see who it was.

"It's me, Brent," I said.

"You're going to break your neck." This was a girl's voice.

"Yeah. What are you doing up there?" Richard was now talking in a loud stage whisper.

"It's a secret," I said. I leaned out to see who Richard was with (a girl with a partially shaved head...very retro-punk) and as I did, my foot slipped and I slid a bit down the tree. My foot caught the next board down, but I still cried out in surprise.

"Oh my God, I think he's going to fall!" the girl cried.

"You wait here," Richard shouted, "I'm going to get Chad." So saying, he ran off to get help, even though I was in no danger whatsoever. I called out for him to come back, but he didn't hear me.

"Are you trying to rip off Nose?" The girl was stage-whispering like Richard. "Can I help?"

I began to climb back down the tree—I didn't want Chad to see me breaking into his father's house. But on the way down, my pants leg caught on something. I looked down, and could dimly make out what was snagging me—it looked like a bent nail.

"He's up there," I heard Richard say.

"Brent! Are you okay?" Fortunately, Chad sounded more concerned than angry.

"Yes, but I'm stuck. I'll be down in a minute."

Chad said, "Thanks, you two. I'll take care of this," and I heard footsteps walking away.

"Are we alone?" I said.

"Yes," Chad replied. "Why were you up in my treehouse?"

"I didn't get that far," I said. I realized then that I could have used the treehouse as a perfectly good excuse for climbing the tree...but I had no real desire to lie to Chad. "I was trying to reach the roof. I wanted to look in your Dad's attic."

"Why would you want to do that?" Now Chad sounded frantic. Actually frantic. The tone of his voice answered my curiosity.

"Your mother's in there, isn't she, Chad?"

I heard Chad sigh. Then I heard a rustling in the leaves. The rustling grew closer, closer—and Chad appeared before my eyes. Floating. Floating up through the wide, flapping leaves of the catalpa tree.

"Chad! You're flying!" Now I was the one stage-whispering. He reached over and unsnagged my pants. Then he grabbed me around the chest and pulled me away from the tree. We floated slowly back down to the ground.

"How did you do that?" I looked at Chad's face in the moonlight. He was handsome. Boyish. A little too handsome and boyish. There was something a little…artificial? no, but perhaps *surreal*…about him.

"If you want to see the attic, I'll take you there," he said. "But we'll use the stairs."

I waited for him to take my hand, but he didn't. He simply began walking. And so I followed him into the Saturnalia Coffee House.

Nose watched us as we walked past the poetry reading. I could feel him watching us as we climbed the stairs to the second floor. Inside Nose's kitchen, Chad opened the bread box and removed a key from between the slices of a moldy loaf of bread.

"Chad? What's going on up there?" Nose was calling from the bottom of the stairs.

"Go back to the poetry reading, Dad," Chad called back. Chad used the key to open a door next to Nose's refrigerator. A smell of dead flies and ointment hit my nose as I looked into the attic stairwell.

Chad flipped on a light switch. The stairs were covered with a thick, shining layer of dried-up dead flies and moths.

Up the stairs we went, insect bodies crunching beneath our feet. The first thing I saw when we reached the top was the couch. It was huge and purple and turned away from the stairs. I looked around and realized that the far corners of the attic were filled with appliances and gadgets. Toasters. Microwave ovens. Food processors. Word processors. A dehumidifier. An old air conditioner. VCRs. Stereos. All of these things were, to some degree, disassembled. At the far end of the attic, I saw a work table loaded with bits and pieces of machines.

Chad took my hand and led me to the front of the couch. "I'd like you to meet my mother," he said.

I looked down at the couch and stared in silence for about ten seconds. And then I screamed.

Chad's mother glowed with a pale blue light. She had an enormous, too-smooth bald head, dominated by the hugest eyes in the world. They were light green, like Chad's. Her mouth was a tiny, red-rimmed slit. She had a small bonelike jut of a nose. Her fingers were probably about seven inches long. Her breasts looked like swirled white rosebuds. Her belly was enormous and her hips were utterly gargantuan. White, slime-streaked slug-tails flapped and twisted where legs should have been. Inset into the folds of her neck and into her armpits and tail-pits were… machines. Strange little machines that flashed and whispered and purred. They looked cobbled-together, like pathetic science-fair engines.

That red slit of a mouth opened and a dry whisper wheezed out. "Chad. The friend makes a bad noise. Chad. Make the bad noise stop. Chad."

Chad squeezed my hand hard. So hard that I felt as though I would pass out from the pain. "You're upsetting Mom, Brent," he said. "Cut it out."

Suddenly footsteps thundered on the attic stairs. "Chad," whispered the white couch-thing. "The Love is coming. Chad. The Love is angry. Chad. Make no bad happen. Chad."

Nose came running up to the couch. "What have you done, you idiot, you stupid moron idiot?"

The couch-thing began to float a few inches off of the couch in Nose's direction. "Love. No anger. Love. Make no bad happen. Love." Her dry whisper of a voice was incredibly sad.

She turned and looked at me. I looked back into those huge, moist eyes and felt sorry for screaming. I smiled at her because I could see that she liked me. Her eyes told me everything. These were kind, soft eyes. Loving eyes. She wanted to be my friend. My mother. Perhaps my lover. She wanted to be my everything. I could feel my soul begin to swirl down into the hungry vortex of her eyes. The sensation was indescribably delicious.

"You whore!" Nose's scream startled me, breaking the spell. The white slug-tails were crawling over my lower body. Chad and Nose were pulling the now squealing couch-thing away from me.

"Bad. Me want yummy boy. Bad Chad. Bad Love. Me want. Me want. Bad." The voice of the creature had risen to a shrill squeal. It seized Nose's collar and popped most of his shirt buttons, revealing a hairy chest covered with open sores. The sores appeared to be coated with some sort of brownish grease.

"He's mine, Mom," Chad said with an angry and incredibly odd rumble to his voice. "I just wanted you to look at him. Get your twisties off him. You've already got Love."

"You crummy whore!" Nose slapped the couch-thing across the face. "How many men do you want?"

"Many. Many yummy boys. Bad Love. Many many yummy boys." The couch-thing grabbed Nose by the throat. Nose responded by slapping at one of the many machines scattered on her body.

"Stop it!" Chad screamed. "You're going to hurt her!"

"She's hurting me!" Nose cried. "She started it!" He pounded and pounded at the whirring, flashing engine. Then he reached down and punched at some of the other machines until they shot forth smoke and sparks.

"Bad. Bad. Bad Love. Malfunction." The couch-thing's eyes did the impossible: they bulged even larger.

Sometimes, when I'm having an especially bad time, I'll find myself thinking about the humorous aspects of my situation. It's a sort of kinky reaction to stress, I think. For example: if I'm at a funeral, I'll ponder whether or not the corpse has stiff nipples. At that moment, I thought that the couch-thing's cries seemed to resemble a badly written avant garde poem. As the creature continued to scream, I mentally reformed the words:

> "Bad.
> Bad Chad.
> Bad Love.
> Malfunction.
> Bad.
> Need repairs.
> *Malfunction.*
> Need.
> Need.
> Bad.
> Bad Love.
> *Malfunction.*
> *Malfunction.*
> *Malfunc—*"

To this day, I think of the couch-thing's final words as the last poem read within the walls of the Saturnalia Coffee House. It could say no more: pale bile spewed from its lips, choking it. The creature was in a sorry state. Flames billowed from its machines and milky ichor poured from the folds and crevices of its pale bulk. The couch-thing pulled Nose to its breast just as its little engines began to explode, one by one.

I heard sirens outside of the house. No doubt someone downstairs had called the police when I'd started screaming.

Chad threw open the nearest window. Tears streaked down his cheeks as he wrapped his arms around me. We floated out of the window and up into the night sky. We drifted for hours and hours. I didn't try to console Chad. I simply couldn't find the right words. Eventually I fell asleep.

* * * *

That was ten years ago.

I once asked Chad what his Mom *was* (of course, I phrased my question with a bit more tact than that) and he told me that she was a Saturnian who'd crashlanded on our world, and that Nose had found her and nursed her back to health. When I told him there's no life on Saturn, he said, "Oh? Have you looked?"

Chad and I now live in a farmhouse in the middle of nowhere. We're living off of the insurance money Chad collected after Nose died and the Saturnalia burned down.

The locals don't know about Chad. He started changing a few years back, so I keep him in the attic. I bring him appliances so he can build himself little life-support machines. He seems to know instinctually how to put them together. I let him suck my blood every now and then, and I have to rub a special ointment on the wounds. Chad makes the ointment out of a brownish secretion from a gland on his back of his neck. We joke about that every now and then. He'll hand me a cup of the goo and say, "Just like Mom used to make."

Since he's part Earthling, Chad doesn't look a whole lot like his Mom. His cock is far too big for conventional sex now, but that's okay, because he has grown a few other appendages—and some orifices, too—for my amusement.

What can I say? I adore Chad, and I'll stay with him forever, no matter how he changes.

He is my best friend. My lover. My terror and my delight. You cannot imagine the pleasure he gives me. He is my god. My cosmos. And I understand his poetry now.

Only too well.

THE REVELATIONS OF McDETH

I. WHO AM I?

I am not like other men.

I look, sound, smell, feel and probably taste like other men. But there is something different about me.

My name is McDeth: M-C-D-E-T-H. I am the last remaining descendant of a very old and powerful family. In fact, Shakespeare named his character Macbeth after one of my ancestors. Shakespeare changed the name a little and switched the ethnic prefix from an Irish M-C to a Scottish M-A-C. Still, he pissed off my family. They didn't mind that he named a character after a McDeth, but they *did* mind that he spelled the family name wrong. So they killed Shakespeare.

You didn't know that, did you? Shakespeare was murdered. By my ancestors. My studies of old family diaries reveal that Shakespeare was one tough son-of-a-bitch. Small but scrappy. It took five whole hours to kill him. But my ancestors applied themselves to the task and eventually Shakespeare joined the ghost of Hamlet's father in the Land of Eternal Beddy-Bye.

Yes, I am the last McDeth. But that's not what makes me so different. Under certain conditions, when I put my mind to it, I can absorb knowledge straight out of the Universe.

Don't ask me how I do it. I just can. I just do. I just did a few minutes ago. And I will a few minutes from now.

I suppose the reason or reasons I can may be because:

a.) I am the Chosen One of a religion that hasn't started yet;
b.) Both of my grandmothers were witches;
c.) I have an extra male chromosome; and/or
d.) Self-confidence.

Why I am sharing my knowledge with you? Because I have something to say. When I wait in line at the grocery store, I look at the tabloids on the racks there, and the headlines all scream and rave about four things: glamorous celebrities, weight-loss plans, the internet, and baffling ancient mysteries. Apparently those are the concerns du jour. So I'll stick to those topics. They're all equally esoteric. They seem to go so well together, like kittens and yarn, junkies and hypodermic needles.

The usual disclaimers: celebrity names have been changed to protect blah-blah-blah, and I will not be held responsible in any way, shape, time-zone or dimension if people misuse or misinterpret my revelations and as a result, somebody loses a finger, unleashes a killer mummy, dies screaming, blah-blah-blah. You get the picture.

Okay?

Then let us begin.

II. THE ORIGINS OF THE LOCH NESS MONSTER

A lot of idiots think the Loch Ness Monster is some kind of alien. But the thing is, the Monster is a water-dweller. Plenty of aliens visit the Earth, but none of them are aquatic. I mean, *Duh!* Aquatic life-forms and space travel don't mix. That would be like a carp trying to build an airplane. Besides, the construction of space vehicles requires welding, and sea-things are completely ignorant when it comes to advanced thermal technology.

The Loch Ness Monster is a dinosaur sorcerer—I call them dino-sorcerers, though nobody else does. He put a longevity spell on himself back during dinosaur primetime, and it's never worn off. Sometimes he uses an invisibility spell when news cameras start nosing around.

I've talked with him in dreams. He's a nice guy, though he talks really *slooowww*. Takes him forever to answer a question. But patience has its rewards. I have learned much in my dream-conversations with him.

Little known fact about the Loch Ness Monster: one eye is blue and the other is black. Also, people think all dinosaurs had small, walnut-sized brains, but the Monster has a very large brain—as big as a watermelon. He is incredibly intelligent, a genius of global proportions—but he is also slimy and hideous, so of course the human race would never be able to accept him. Which is truly a pity. People could learn so much from him. Oh sure, he may eat the occasional sheep or tourist, but hey, it's his loch. Finders keepers.

III. HOW HEATHER ST. LORRAINE
LOST 45 POUNDS

Heather St. Lorraine. Her friends called her H.S.L.

Her enemies called her "that fat-assed rich bitch who thinks she owns the world."

Well, it's rude to call anyone a bitch, but she was rich, she did have an ample rear end, and she really did think she owned the world. Probably because she was so incredibly wealthy.

Her daddy was the third richest man in the world, and her first husband was the ninth richest. And she owned plenty of her own businesses, investments, stocks, bonds, all kinds of green. Her personal fortune placed her at No. 5 among extremely rich women.

But despite all her money, all the astounding resources at her fingertips…she just couldn't lose weight.

Oh, occasionally she'd drop five pounds, maybe six, but the next week she'd pick up seven or eight. Diets, exercise and personal trainers couldn't even scratch the surface. She was allergic to anesthetics, so liposuction was out of the question. Maddening.

One day, while vacationing in Monaco, she met a slender, elegant, elderly man named Dr. Sakarna in the hotel lounge. He was quite charming in a grandfatherly sort of way, and they chatted about everything and everything else for several hours.

Heather asked what he was a doctor of, and when he purred "Endocrinology" and mentioned that weight-loss research was his greatest interest these days, her eyes went quite wide and a smile curved its way across her pudgy face.

Within two days, Heather began receiving regular injections from Dr. Sakarna. This new compound, he told her, was truly miraculous and totally natural, made from a hormone extracted from the female reproductive organs of a rare Brazilian tree-frog. The compound, he added, would speed up her metabolism in no time.

Heather was so taken with the new doctor, she hadn't even bothered to arrange a background check. That information would have revealed that he was not allowed to practice medicine in the United States. And if he ever returned to the U.S.A., he would be arrested on the spot.

The compound did indeed speed up her metabolism.

And her pulse-rate.

And her mind.

And the aging process—an unforeseen side effect.

Heather St. Lorraine shrivelled into a gaunt, frantic, shivering old woman, screaming and screaming and screaming for the duration of the transformation.

Eventually she stopped aging and shriveling and shivering and screaming. Her husband divorced her within the week. Oddly enough, she didn't press charges against Dr. Sakarna. She really wanted to, but she also knew that she liked talking to him about everything and everything else.

Two months later, they were married.

They tell people they've been a couple for fifty years. They do look charming together.

IV. THE TRUTH ABOUT THE PYRAMIDS

For centuries, people have wondered how those ancient Egyptians built those enormous pyramids. The general consensus seems to be some clever combination of slaves and pulleys and rolling big stone slabs around on tree trunks. Yeah, right.

The ancient Egyptians were 24-7 party people. They had slaves, but they were sex-slaves, and so they really didn't mind, because everybody was so damned good-looking back then. All tan and fit and really into eye make-up.

The royal families actually did all the construction work, and it wasn't that hard, because they were telekinetic. In fact, they were specially bred for the task. Those big gold headpieces they wore back then amplified their psychic powers by three-thousand percent. So yeah, Pharaoh and the missus did all the work while the people had fun. Even the slaves.

The ancient Egyptians used to hang out with a race of animal-headed aliens who also liked to party, but that's more of a late-night story, if you know what I mean. I do have something to tell you about a descendant of those aliens…I'll get to that later.

V. HOW BRIANNA STYLES LOST 22 POUNDS

Brianna Styles, pretty auburn-haired songbird, was every teen boys' dream. All the teen girls wanted to look like her and especially dance like her. Her top-ten singles and music videos made her the queen of the world for a golden season.

But seasons end. One day, the vast majority of people realized they were sick of Brianna Styles. Sick and tired and bored to tears.

Brianna was only nineteen at the time.

Fast forward eight years and three husbands later. Poor Brianna: two kids, two drug habits, twenty-two pounds overweight, and two-hundred bucks in her checking account.

The kids were staying with Grandma one weekend. On Saturday afternoon, Brianna got drunk, took a few pills, snorted a few lines, got out the vacuum cleaner and a kitchen knife…and did a little home lipo-suction. Eventually she passed out, and woke up screaming twelve hours later.

She survived, and a sympathetic surgeon did try to even out the hideous results. She still looks a little asymmetrical, and she can't feel her left thigh or buttcheek. But at least she's back on top with a new book and a movie, both based on her ordeal, and plenty of talk-show spots. Plus, a private collector bought that vacuum cleaner from her for a quarter of a million dollars.

VI. SECRETS OF THE INTERNET WITCHES

They are all pale with dark red hair and they laugh like dogs barking. Even the baby ones.

You can see them any time you like on their unholy websites. You can read their rants, some of their spells, or perhaps a few of their recipes, always for desserts. Learn how to make vulture's egg cupcakes, hell muffins, cheesecake made from the milk of black goats.

But whatever you do, do not click on the green glowing eye in the corner of each webpage. Nothing will happen if there are other people around, but if you are alone, green lightning will spring forth from the screen, split in mid-air, and strike you in both eyes.

You will fall to the floor dead and then a crow will appear, even if there's no window, and pluck out one of your eyes and fly off, the same way it arrived. A moment later, your glowing, one-eyed corpse will walk the earth as a radioactive zombie, as that crow carries your eye far, far away, to the main computer of the internet witches. It will stick your eye on a wire and download everything you have ever seen.

So please, surf only friendly webpages, the puppy and rainbow sites, the silly, harmless, happy spots. Fill your cyber-shopping carts with toys and books and CDs. Such fun!

Who knows, maybe you'll meet a pretty young thing in a chatroom.

Maybe you'll exchange e-mail addresses.

Maybe she'll send you a link to her webpage—

—and then you'll forget my warnings and click on the glowing green eye in the corner.

Before long, the main computer of the internet witches will know everywhere you've ever been…everyone who've ever loved…everything you've ever done.

Maybe.

Maybe not. Who can say?

It's a big world, with so many possibilities.

And they all begin and end in the dark.

VII. HOW REGINALD FARTHINGTON LOST WEIGHT IN JUST ONE DAY

Reginald Farthington was never really what anyone would call a celebrity. He didn't have tons of groupies or a breakfast cereal named after him. But he was a pretty good writer—not great, but pretty good.

He wrote gentle, cultured, mannered little stories, in a world that wanted big-city car chases and trashy alien chicks doing it with robots. Ooooh yeah.

Reginald could have, should have settled for pretty good. Pretty good ain't bad. But the problem is, he reeeally wanted to be great. And the need to be great burned within him.

So he tried to extinguish that inner fire with lots and lots of drinks. Stupid man. Pouring alcohol on a fire is the worst thing you can do.

He had diabetes, his boozing led to health problems, and one day, he couldn't feel his feet.

They were dead. No circulation. His doctors only had one answer for him.

Chop, chop.

Poor sad Reginald lost some weight—and a little height, too.

VIII. WHAT'S THE DEAL WITH VAMPIRES?

So many people have had so many theories about vampires over the years. Are they part-demon? Undead spirits? Aliens? Another species? Or just folks who really like drinking blood?

The truth is really quite simple.

Vampires are time-traveling slave-clones from the far, far future, when it will be possible—quite easy, really—to manufacture slave-clones and blood in mass quantities. Slave-clones emerge from their synthetic wombs fully grown, but not really altogether alive. They need a shot of some fancy futuristic glowing green goo to get them started. That's the stuff that makes them vampires. It also makes them allergic to natural sunlight. Those slave-clones run off of blood, like cars run off of gasoline. Just give them a big can of blood and they'll bite two holes in the top—one to suck, one to let air in the can.

The future-clones aren't sex-slaves like those ancient Egyptian folks. The clones are built strong to work in the time-machine factories. Security is tight in those places, but vampires can be tricky customers. Occasionally a small group of them will steal a time machine right off the production line, so they can go back in time and be free.

Some of them do go to ancient Egypt to become sex-slaves. Still, that's not really what you'd call work.

Unfortunately, those escaped slave-clones must resort to sucking blood out of folks, since the past isn't stocked with big yummy blood-cans, like the far future.

Somewhere along the line, folks got it into their heads that vampirism was contagious, like rabies or mono. That's not exactly true. Here's the deal about that. Once a vampire sucks all the blood out of you, you're dead—unless the vampire takes pity on you and injects you with the glowing green goo used to bring slave-clones to life. When a dead human is injected with that stuff, they come back to life, but they need blood and hate sunlight. Plus, it reacts badly with the calcium in real humans, so it makes their teeth grow into fangs and their fingernails into talons.

So when you see an ugly, pointy-toothed vampire in a movie, that not really an accurate depiction of a real vampire. Real vampires look great, like lifeguards and fashion models. What you're seeing on the big screen—or the little screen, if it's on TV—actually looks more like a vampire's human victim, reanimated with the glowing goo.

But of course, you'd never know that from watching movies. Those movie people just make up stuff as they go along. They don't go digging for the real facts, like me.

Whatever you do, don't ever tell one of those time-traveling clones, "Gee, it must suck, being a vampire."

They've heard that joke a million times.

IX. THE UNHOLY COMPUTER VIRUSES OF THE OMEGA COVEN

Of all things living and dead, internet witches enjoy eating tripe most of all.

Tripe, in case you didn't know, is the stomach tissue of a hooved animal, like a cow or an ox or a sheep. At least, that's the kind of tripe you can buy in a butcher shop. Internet witches don't always limited themselves to tripe from hooved critters. In their opinion, the tastiest tripe of all comes from humans. But how to get it...?

The internet witches formed a committee to handle that problem: the Omega Coven.

Using their magic and technology, the members of the Omega Coven created a subspecies of tiny invisible monkeys. Then they converted the monkeys into digital energy and packed them into evil computer files. These files are known to the general public as e-mail viruses.

Once a virus gets into a person's computer, their hard drive is automatically infected with the evil monkeys. The monkeys radiate out of the computer monitor as light energy and enter the person through their eyes. They can travel in that fashion to and fro, from the monitor to the person and back, quite easily. Once inside someone, they rob the person of chunks of their stomach tissue—little chunks, not enough to kill a human. They convert the chunks into digital energy and carry it out of the person, through the eyes into the monitor. From there, the monkeys transport the digitized flesh via the internet back to the witches. The witches then convert the digital chunks into tasty human tripe for their dinners.

That is why so many people who operate computers have ulcers. The virus-monkeys are stealing little stomach chunks, creating painful sores.

The virus-monkeys also steal vital information out of the computers, and they usually screw up the workings, too, just for the Hell of it.

Perhaps you are saying, "Oh, I have nothing to worry about. My computer has all the latest anti-virus software on it. My hard drive is fine. I'm fine."

That may be true. Still, for the sake of your stomach and perhaps your soul, don't spent every waking minute in front of a computer screen. Go outside. Get some sunshine. Take a walk with a loved one. If you don't have a loved one—find one. There are plenty of lonely, good-hearted people out there. They don't have to be lonely. And neither do you.

X. HOW MICHELANGELO DELGADO LOST 17 POUNDS

Michelangelo Delgado was a real Hollywood heart-throb, and he knew it. What a prima donald.

He had to have everything his way on the set of each of his movies—champagne and fresh strawberries in his huge dressing room, a new purple silk robe every day, eleven different types of sushi, salads made with hand-picked gourmet wild greens, double-mocha macadamia nut cookies, the list went on and on.

Michelangelo was unbearable on the set of *Gauguin!*, a movie about the famous French painter who lived a tropical island. Perhaps it was the lavish tropical setting that brought out the snitty, snotty man-diva in him. He bitched and moaned about everyone and everything, when in fact he was lucky that he had it so good. Michelangelo wasn't what anyone would call the sharpest knife in the drawer. Nor would he be called the brightest bulb in the marquee. In fact, most people would just call him a moron and leave it at that. He spelled "cookie" with a "y" and a "u," and his interpretation of "macadamia" had a "k" and an "h" in it.

The only reason he was so rich and popular was because he had a great Hollywood agent—who was also his mother. She'd spoiled her special boy rotten, so of course she thought the world had to follow suit.

That is why he drove everybody nucking futs during the on-location filming of *Gauguin!* They were working on a perfectly lovely little South Pacific island. Paradise on Earth. But did that matter to Michelangelo? No. He screamed for prettier island girls. Greener thatched huts. Whiter sand. Less clouds in the sky. The director assured him that most of those things would be enhanced or added in during post-production, but that didn't stop Michelangelo from having a screaming tantrum every four hours on the first day—and every three hours on the second day—and every two hours on the third day. And so on.

At the end of the eighth day of production, the cast and crew got in their boats and left while Michelangelo was taking a nap. It was really just a practical joke, but they also hoped it would teach him a lesson about cooperation. They were going to leave him alone overnight on the island—with no champagne, no cookies, no soft and silky robes, not even a roll of toilet paper.

At that point, it wouldn't even have mattered if Michelangelo had thrown a fit and walked out on the filming. They'd finished shooting all his scenes that afternoon. There were a few beach scenes left, but they were going to use a body double for those, since Michelangelo had a little bit of a potbelly on him, from all those double-mocha macadamia nut cookies.

At first Michelangelo was confused, when he woke up and found that everyone had left him. Confusion soon gave way to sadness, but that stage didn't last long. The sadness turned into a little bud of anger, which soon blossomed into a huge, gaudy jungle orchid of livid rage. But only the crabs on the beach and the monkeys in the palm trees heard the brittle clatter of his gnashing capped teeth.

And speaking of teeth…do you remember those time-traveling vampires I mentioned earlier? That night, a whole time machine full of them appeared on the island. They were very surprised to find Michelangelo there. Surprised and delighted, for they were all very hungry. They tied him up with tikuuni vines and then proceeded to suck all the blood out of him. Some of those vampires even took a few bites out of his belly, since it was a little on the big side anyway. Altogether, they sucked and bit seventeen pounds of Michelangelo out of, or off of, him. After he was dead, the vampires felt sorry for what they'd done, so they injected Michelangelo with that glowing green goo, to bring him back to life.

Pretty-boy Michelangelo wasn't so pretty after that.

Mama Delgado was distressed to learn that her special boy had become a gaunt, blood-thirsty freak with fangs. But she was an agent, and so with a sad maternal sigh, she shifted her mind into agent-gear and considered all the money-making possibilities.

In the years that followed, Michelangelo became one of the world's greatest horror actors, starring in such fright-flick classics as *Starship Bloodsuckers*, *I Saw Who You Bit Last Winter* and *Dracula's Deadly Hug*. His mother made a secret deal with a Hollywood blood bank, so she always made sure he had plenty of bags of juice to take with him on long trips to foreign locales.

On the plus side, that high-protein diet made it easy for him to keep slim and trim. No more champagne. No more double-mocha macadamia nut cookies.

XI. INTERNET SCHMINTERNET

Lex Crayton, CEO of CyberKitty Industries, wasn't always mega-rich. No indeed. He used to be a regular Joe Schmoe. On weekends, Lex worked at a coffeehouse with internet terminals. On weekdays, he created digital graphics for a video production house. Evenings, he built webpages, freelance. He was a busy boy with a peachfuzz haircut and a watch on each wrist.

Each day, he would get up, drink some cappuccino, read his e-mail (it ain't gonna answer itself, ya know), feed the cat, go to the job du jour, drink more cappuccino, work work work, come home, make more cappuccino, build some webpages, and then ride, cruise, surf, whatever one does to or with the internet until it was time for bed. And his kitty would curl up and lull him to sleep with her purrs.

But then he started taking on extra hours at the production house. A few more hours at the coffeehouse. A few more webpages. He made his cappuccino stronger, and wore more watches to create the illusion of extra time. He bought some pills, too, to help him concentrate. When friends tried to stop him on the street for a quick chat, he would rush on by, shouting, *"Send me an e-mail!"* Sometimes Mother would stop by his apartment and he would have to waste an entire half-hour talking to her. She had no use for computers and would counter any talk of that sort with a cry of *"Internet Schminternet!"*—swinging her lime-green purse like a tacky Luddite.

Our busy boy ordered little wristwatches for his kitty and starting carrying her around with him in a bookbag. Even now and then he would slip her a piece of raw beef or fish. Lex was a hard worker, so his coworkers overlooked his eccentricities. He had a cappuccino machine installed in his cubicle at the production house. He had video equipment moved into the spare room of the coffeehouse. He loaded webpage software on all these computers. He bought more pills, and more and more and more coffee beans.

Months passed, and he gradually weaned himself down to three hours of sleep a night. He hired a consultant to invest his earnings in software, hard drives, and coffee, always coffee. His investments blossomed like velvety red roses, so he was able to buy out the coffeehouse and eventually, the production house. His consultant became his right-hand man, and this trusty fellow was allotted the task of dealing with folks when a time-consuming face-to-face meeting was required. Still, our busy boy could not bypass Mother so easily—she insisted on stopping by his big new house, wasting his time with the same old boring anecdotes and crying out "*Internet Schminternet!*" at the slightest provocation.

To save manhours (because that e-mail ain't gonna answer itself, ya know), Lex strapped on more wristwatches and started work in his basement workshop on a mega-machine that was part computer, part coffeemaker, and part microwave oven—after all, he still had to eat. To this magnificent work-in-progress he soon added a variety of other appliances and even an internal habitat for his kitty to wander around in, complete with a self-cleaning litter-box and an automatic feeder filled with raw meat.

By this time, he was quite wealthy: he owned a nationwide network of coffeehouses and production houses, and a few pet shops, too. He only communicated with his right-hand man by modem. The mega-machine continued to grow, up the basement stairs, through the kitchen and into the dining room. He even built himself a habitat within the machine, since there was so much to do in there. He had to change its filters and oil its gears and calibrate its electronic components and every now and then he took a catnap, lulled to sleep by the velvety purr of its workings.

But Mother did not like the mega-machine. It took up too much room and it smelled, too, she announced during one of her visits, clutching her lime-green purse as she stared up at the purring, whirring, buzzing behemoth. Surely no woman would ever marry a man, no matter how rich, with such a godawful machine hogging up space. Lex just laughed and whispered, "*With a machine like this, who needs a woman?*"

Then a panel flew open and a thick flexing cable, topped with a pointy-eared head about the size of a ripe lemon, popped out of the machine. Some parts of the head were metal, while others were furry and still others glistened with either oil or kittyspit. From between its velvety cleft lips rumbled these words: "YOUR CAPPUCCINO IS READY YOUR DINNER IS HEATING UP I'VE SELECTED A VIDEO FOR THIS EVENING YOU HAVE MAIL WOULD YOU CARE FOR A PEDICURE AN ENEMA A FULL-BODY MASSAGE ALLOW ME TO LANCE THAT BOIL YOU HAVE MAIL THE REQUESTED INFORMATION HAS BEEN DOWNLOADED EVALUATION OF GLOBAL

DEFENSE SYSTEMS COMPLETED CAN INITIATE NUCLEAR ANNIHILATION AT YOUR COMMAND YOU HAVE MAIL."

Lex smiled, scratched behind cyberkitty's ears, and said, *"Don't worry, Mother, I won't blow up the world—it's just nice to know that I can. Now please, get up off the floor."*

But Mother did not get up, did not even cry out, *"Internet Schminternet!"* She simply stared and stared. Her stiff white hands clutched her chest, not her tacky lime-green purse. Our busy boy began to cry. A silvery thread of drool spooled down from cyberkitty's raspy pink tongue as the rumbling voice intoned: "THAT MEAT AIN'T GONNA EAT ITSELF, YA KNOW."

XII. THE LOATHSOME CHARMS OF THE MEDUSA

The Medusa. What a gal.

She was a descendant of the race of the animal-headed aliens who used to hang out with the ancient Egyptians. Ancestrywise, she was about two-thirds animal-headed alien, one-third human. She lived in ancient Greece, and looked like something that had been fried up in some ancient grease.

She thought human males were the sexiest things on two legs, but they all thought she looked like the ultimate bad hair day in Hades. The poor love-sick thing had lime-green snake-locks, owl eyes, piranha teeth and alligator skin—and those were her good qualities.

The Medusa had once spent a carefree summer with the Loch Ness Monster, back before he'd realized he was gay. He'd shown her a few magic spells, since he was a great dinosorceror, and from him she'd learned a spell for a visual aphrodisiac: you just put on a few drops, and anybody who looks at you will want to get it on. It only had an effect on males, but as it turned out, that was okay for the Loch Ness Monster.

When the Medusa returned to Greece, she brewed up a batch of the visual aphrodisiac, but unfortunately, she made the same boo-boo that Dr. Sakarna would make many centuries later—attempting to cross the freaky bio-chemical border between humans and cold-blooded critters. The reptilian oils and musks on her bumpy hide combined with the formula, changing the chemical compound and amplifying its effects.

You know what they say: be careful what you wish for. She wanted to make men hard, and by Zeus, that's just what she got.

She ended up alone, refusing to see any more male visitors. She already had more than enough statues in the garden.

XIII. WHO ARE YOU?

And there you have it. I have given you forbidden knowledge from the past, present and the future. Do what you will with the information. Just don't hold me responsible.

One day, while I was in line at the grocery store, I overheard a bit of conversation between the clerk at the cash register and the customer she was helping. The customer, a sloppy, heavyset man with a bad complexion, had bought a tabloid because he was worried about the young starlet on the cover. Apparently the starlet was having relationship difficulties with her boyfriend, a handsome, lanky rock star with an expensive drug problem.

Do you know what I wanted to tell that man? I wanted to tell him, "Hey, mister. I think you have more important things to worry about. You obviously have health problems. So why are you buying those two tubs of ice cream? That bottle of vodka? That big package of sausages with cheddar cheese in them? Don't waste your time thinking about celebrities who don't give a crap about you. That pretty young starlet will get along just fine without your help. But you! You need all the self-help that you can get. So think about yourself for a change. Think about improving your health…your appearance…your job, your house, your relationships…your life!"

So you out there…yes, you, the one drinking in my words. I have one more bit of wisdom for you. It's not forbidden knowledge. It's just a suggestion, really. And here it is:

Be good to yourself.

That way, you'll always have one person on your side, no matter what happens to you. No matter who opposes you. No matter how many fresh dog turds are plopped in your path on the treacherous sidewalk of life.

True, that one person—that one steadfast supporter—will be yourself. But still, that's more than some people have.

Have a nice day.

ABOUT THE AUTHOR

MARK MCLAUGHLIN's fiction, nonfiction, and poetry have appeared in almost one-thousand magazines, newspapers, websites, and anthologies, including *Living Dead 2*, *Dark Fusions: Where Monsters Lurk!*, *Black Gate*, *Galaxy*, *Fangoria*, *Writer's Digest*, *Cemetery Dance*, *Midnight Premiere*, *Dark Arts*, and two volumes each of *The Best of the Rest*, *The Best of HorrorFind*, and *The Year's Best Horror Stories* (DAW Books).

Collections of McLaughlin's fiction include *Best Little Witch-House in Arkham* and *Beach Blanket Zombie* (Wildside Press); *Motivational Shrieker*, *Slime After Slime*, and *Pickman's Motel* (Delirium Books); *At the Foothills of Frenzy*, with coauthors Shane Ryan Staley and Brian Knight (Solitude Publications); and *Raising Demons for Fun and Profit* (Sam's Dot Publishing).

McLaughlin is the coauthor, with Rain Graves and David Niall Wilson, of *The Gossamer Eye*, which won the 2002 Bram Stoker Award for Superior Achievement in Poetry.

With regular collaborator Michael McCarty, he has written *Monster Behind the Wheel* (hardcover from Corrosion Press, ebook edition from Medallion Press); *Partners in Slime* (Damnation Books); *All Things Dark & Hideous* (Rainfall Books, England); *Professor LaGungo's Delirious Download of Digital Deviltry & Doom* (Darkside Digital); and *Professor LaGungo's Classroom of Horrors* (Bucket o' Guts Press).

He is also a successful marketing and public relations executive who regularly writes articles for business journals, newspapers, trade publications and websites.

To find out more about his work, visit:

www.Facebook.com/MarkMcLaughlinMedia

and his blog,

www.BMovieMonster.com

www.ingramcontent.com/pod-product-compliance
Lightning Source LLC
Chambersburg PA
CBHW031417250626

47155CB00004B/1520